About the author

The author was born in Leicester in 1965. His fondest childhood memories are of strikes, glam-rock and power-cuts. He studied philosophy and politics at Warwick University, a degree that teaches very little other than how to question the unquestionable to annoying effect. After a long career questioning the unquestionable to annoying effect in the financial services industry, he applied an abrupt handbrake turn in 2020 to become an author. He writes because it is the only thing he is really any good at. He currently lives between Lancashire and South West France with his wife and two Jack Russell terriers. When not writing, he enjoys testing the patience of his friends and family and arching a sardonic eyebrow at the world. *Purge* is his debut novel.

PURGE

Neil K. Wootton

PURGE

Vanguard Press

VANGUARD PAPERBACK

© Copyright 2021
Neil K. Wootton

A CIP catalogue record for this title is
available from the British Library.

ISBN 978-1-80016-157-3

Vanguard Press is an imprint of
Pegasus Elliot MacKenzie Publishers Ltd.
www.pegasuspublishers.com

First Published in 2021

Vanguard Press
Sheraton House Castle Park
Cambridge England

Printed & Bound in Great Britain

Dedication

This book is dedicated in its entirety to my wife Helen, without whose love and encouragement it would not exist at all beyond the first few chapters.

Acknowledgements

For somebody who is not a professional historian, writing a historical novel can be a daunting task. In addition to more traditional academic sources, of which there were many, I would like to acknowledge the work of Wikipedia and its army of volunteer editors. Without their efforts, creating the illusion of truth would have been very much harder.

Proverbs 25:5

Take away the wicked from the king's presence, and his throne will be established in righteousness.

Malachi 3:5

"I will come to you in judgment; and I will be a swift witness against the sorcerers, and against the adulterers, and against the perjurers, and against those who oppress the hireling in his wages, the widow, and the fatherless, and who deprive the foreigner of justice, and don't fear me," says Yahweh of Armies.

Exodus 22:18

You shall not allow a sorceress to live.

Letter To The Gentle Reader
(London: October 1675)

Gentle Reader,

It is thirty years since the passing of the strange events to which this narrative relates, and I was not a young man even then. Nor have the years been kind. My body is fragile, and my memory often plays tricks on me. I suppose this is the price the old pay for exceeding their expected time on Earth. I am blessed, or cursed, to have outlived my friends, my comrades, my lovers, my enemies and the youthful health of my faculties.

I am sanguine about these things and ask only that the reader show patience should my mind begin to wander, or should the narrative appear to hesitate or stall in places. I promise only that I will endeavour to be faithful to the tale to the very best of my ability. I trust to the forbearance of you, gentle reader, when these failings manifest, as surely, they will. I am an old man and that is all that I can offer in my defence. Have patience! The old fool is trying his best.

Already I realise that I have been remiss in failing to introduce myself, as is the proper custom on these occasions. In many ways, it may be of no relevance to you who your guide through this tale might be, yet still it seems to me a failing of common courtesy for which I ought to apologise.

The name given to me by my beloved father and mother is Nathaniel. My family name is of even less importance, but for the sake of completeness, and to allay any curiosity you may yet entertain, I can tell you that it is Wright; a common enough name for a common enough servant of man and God.

My own part in the passing of the events about to be related to you, dear reader, is of no significance whatsoever. I am nothing more than a humble observer of the works of greater men. Suffice it to say that it was my privilege during a span of some twenty-five years to have been an acquaintance, confidant and clerk to Sir Richard Easeby, a man of no mean intellect, obstinacy, kindness or humanity.

It is Sir Richard's lot to be the principal protagonist of this tale, a role that he always wore with humility and grace. There are few men whose deeds touch and enrich all those of honest intent whose paths cross with theirs, or equally enrage and vex those of a more malicious humour. Sir Richard was one such man.

I will leave it to the unravelling of this tale to persuade the reader of the veracity of this opinion. Suffice to say for now that no man has yet dissuaded me from my view, though God in his infinite wisdom will know that many have tried.

It is often the lot of the old to suffer a failing of their eyesight, and the narrator of this tale, gentle reader, is no exception. I have grown myopic and find that distant objects are now a curious blur to me. It is as though I see the world through a thick pane of leaded glass, made opaque with age.

Worse still, as the years have come and gone, most colours have diminished in their vibrancy and distinctiveness to the point where there are now only two that I can clearly discern.

The first of these is red, the longevity of which in my mind's eye I attribute to the blood so freely spilled in those days, and to the striking scarlet of the sashes of the parliamentarians as they cut down the old king's men on the battlefields of England. The impact of that badge and all that it represented on the mind of my younger self was one of no small consequence. I am not, and never have been, a man of radical politics or fundamental religion; yet a modest man of principle I hope always to have been. Whether it is enough, I know not and will not discover until my final hour of judgement.

The second colour I see, in all its myriad shades, is brown, and to whatever that can be attributed, I know not. It is indeed a source of much chagrin to me that of all the colours on God's Earth, it is this most commonplace and unremarkable of shades that I see most clearly.

So, this is the world now as I see it; an opaque blur of sepia and red, and these are the colours in my mind as I narrate this tale. To beg further the indulgence of the reader, if you were to imagine this tale as through a filter of those shades, then you would best see it as it is in the mind of its teller. I will leave that choice to you, gentle reader. It is, after all, nothing more than a frivolous conceit of the writer.

One thing I must entreat of you, however, is to suspend your incredulity regarding the events I am about to relate. As God is my witness, my narration contains nothing but the truth, or the closest approximation to the truth that my memory and understanding will allow.

I know not in what times you may happen upon these words, or whether the nature of your times will make them easier or more difficult to comprehend. I am a rational man in a world where the irrational oft holds sway. Do not allow the strangeness of these events persuade you they cannot be true, or if they are true, that they must be the result of something that cannot be explained. Trust to the example of Sir Richard himself. Even where mystical elements appear to be at play, there is almost always a rational alternative.

Alas, in a world where superstition and prejudice hold sway, the opposite is more often held to be true. In the events of this tale and the times of their manifestation, the difficult to explain was most commonly attributed to the work of the devil, assisted in part by witches and acts of 'maleficia'. This is perhaps the principal fault of my age and it has, in truth, been an age of many faults.

I beg the patience of the reader should the style of writing appear tortured in parts or, in others, somewhat arcane. These faults in style derive perhaps from my work as a clerk in law and business affairs. It is beyond the wit of this humble servant to amend them now, in the winter months of his life.

To test still further the fraying strands of your patience, dear reader, I narrate this tale as though I am an observer of my part in it. I do this for two reasons: firstly, in many ways I am a different man to the one involved in these events. Time has a way of making our younger selves appear as strangers to us; the past is indeed a foreign country.

The second is that there are many elements of the tale that I did not observe with my own eyes, but rather rely upon hearsay and the words of others. It seems to me that for the coherence of the whole, it is better that all things be told as though viewed through the same pair of eyes, even if they be eyes other than my own.

But enough! Already I have dallied too long. At this rate of progress, I will be dead and complaining in my grave before the tale is told, and I sense your patience already wears thin. And so, to business!

Nathaniel Wright: Clerk and Executor of the Estates of Sir Richard Easeby (In the year of our Lord, 1675)

**Part One
The Arrest
Autumn 1645**

1
Fog

A man needs to be wary on days like this. The fens are dangerous enough on a bright, godly day, but when there is fog, only the desperate or the foolhardy venture abroad.

On this occasion, the mist that descended late the previous evening had, by dawn, thickened to a dense fog. It was the kind of fog that is particular to the eastern counties of England: a cloying, unhealthy pall, sometimes hovering for long hours or even days at a time; the kind of fog that may easily devour the soul of a man, veiling any charms the featureless landscape can be said to hold, and God knows, there are few enough of those.

Jonah Salt was no fool. There was business to be done this day and, fog or no fog, he rose early and against his better judgement, took to the Great North Road by foot.

He made slow progress. It was just six miles from his home near the village of Wood Walton to the town of Huntingdon — a distance he would normally expect to cover in little more than two hours — but with no features to mark his way, and the road itself hardly visible beneath his feet, he was forced to walk with extreme caution.

Salt had travelled the route more times during his fifty-nine years than he cared to remember, but today he found himself frequently veering off course. On more than one occasion, he lost the road completely, his feet sinking into the soft fenland earth; a mistake that could so quickly lead to the unknown places from which no return would be possible.

Cursing his ill judgement, he retraced his steps, walking backwards and placing his feet into his own footmarks to avoid turning and becoming even more disorientated. Finding the rutted tracks of the road beneath his feet once more, he then adjusted his direction by a matter of degrees and proceeded on his way.

In this manner, it was perhaps two hours or more before he reached the wayfarers' post marking the halfway point of his journey.

If there had been a sun to be seen, it would have been rising above the horizon as Salt sat with his back to the post. Deciding to rest, he breakfasted on a meagre meal of bread and cheese. Instead of sun, there was a barely perceptible lightening of the gloom.

Nothing more.

There is one other quality characteristic of an eastern fog. It has the effect of deadening sound; muffling and throttling it so that it hardly reaches the ear of the attender until the source is upon him.

So it was that Salt failed to hear the sound of the approaching horse until it appeared suddenly out of the enveloping gloom directly beside him. As startled as Salt by the sudden and unexpected encounter, the beast reared on its hind legs and at first appeared in danger of bolting. Its nostrils flared and its eyes grew wide in panic as the rider struggled to regain control and retain his place in the saddle.

"Whoa, whoa! Easy now, easy!"

The voice was that of a youngish man, yet the unflustered level of control seemed incongruous to his age. There was something both commanding and unsettling in his tone that affected Jonah Salt and the horse in equal measure. Each became now instantly calmed, the horse bowing its head and digging at the road with its front hooves, whilst Salt stood and watched, observing the man with an appraising eye.

"What road is this?" asked the rider finally, now fully in control of his mount. "I have ridden through the night and I am tired. These are truly godforsaken lands!"

Salt followed the young man's gaze as it sought to penetrate the gloom ahead. A puritan clearly by his manner of dress, but that was not the principal source of Salt's curiosity. Puritans were common enough in these parts, but a puritan alone, in the fenlands at dawn; and in a dawn shrouded in fog?

"The road to Huntingdon, sir, as well you must know. No man would be on this road without knowing where it led on a foul morning like this. Why do you ask? What business do you have there?"

The rider appeared to relax, bowing his head for a moment. "Puritan enough," thought Salt. "A preacher?"

"My business is my own, sir. I share it with no one but the Lord my God and the ordained executors of His will. Tell me, how far from Huntingdon are we?"

"That is no secret, sir. Look at the sign if your eyes can but see through the fog. It is three miles from where we stand; but I ask you again, what business do you have there? These are troubled times for a rider to be abroad, especially in weather like this. A stranger who says he has ridden through the night? We live in times of war, sir. Forgive me, but normal courtesy is by necessity a forgotten companion in such times. It is my duty as a citizen of this shire to ask questions of such a man and I do only what I must. I ask you again, what is your business, sir?"

The rider hesitated, bowing his head and fixing his eyes on what little of the road he could see ahead. There was a sudden tiredness in his demeanour; it lasted just a moment before, with a click of his heels, he urged the horse forward. The fog quickly enveloped the beast and its rider once more as they continued on their journey.

Disembodied now, but clear and distinct, a reply finally came from the fog ahead, drifting back towards Jonah Salt in the same level tone.

"Witches, sir. My business is witches."

2
Rufford

Sir Richard Easeby lifted his head from his work as the young man entered his study. It was a cold November day in West Lancashire and a fire burned fiercely in the hearth. The season had recently turned, and after a long-extended summer, which seemed to last well into October, autumn had finally announced itself.

Easeby knew the boy well. He had been a servant at Rufford Hall since becoming orphaned at the age of ten, when Easeby took him in. That must have been some six years ago now. He had repaid the kindness well, proving himself to be both loyal and useful. This was the first occasion Easeby had ever had cause to admonish the lad.

"What is the girl's name?" he asked by way of introduction.

The boy stood in front of the desk, scrunching a shapeless felt hat between his hands, throttling it like the throat of a stricken game bird. He reddened noticeably at this abrupt cutting to the chase.

"Rebecca Standish, sir."

"And she is just fourteen, I understand."

Again, the boy blushed. "She is fifteen in January, sir."

"Then she is fourteen as of today, is that not so?"

"Yes, sir."

Easeby stood and approached the hearth, staring at the tongues of flame as they danced and cavorted in the grate. He had often wondered to himself how it would feel to be burned alive and how long the pain would last. Whether it was the heat or the smoke that would kill a man first and whether such a death would be preferable to drowning or the other way round. Burning was the Church's prescribed punishment for heresy, but heresy against what? It had always appeared to Easeby that a man's conscience was entirely his own affair and none of the Church's damn business.

"Do the girl's parents know she is with child?" he asked, addressing his question to the flames rather than directly to the boy.

The question caught the boy completely off-guard. "How did you know that, sir? We have told nobody that!"

Despite the gravity of the situation, Easeby smiled to himself. Of course, he had not known that: not for certain anyway, and not until the boy had just confirmed it. He had always found that the way to the truth lies as much in the manner a question is asked as in the way it is answered. That is the art of cross-examination.

"And what do you intend to do now? The girl's reputation will be lost as soon as the knowledge becomes public. Her parents will likely disown her."

The boy stammered, tears welling in his eyes. "I do not know, sir. Becky tells me she knows of someone; a woman, who might be able to help us…"

Easeby cut him short, anger suddenly coming to the fore. "No, not that! I forbid you to meddle with those things, do you understand? The woman is likely a charlatan. She will take every last penny you have earned and leave the girl bleeding to death in return. If you follow that route, Master Cooper, you will leave my employment immediately without reference or pension from this household. Am I entirely clear?"

The boy bowed his head, staring at the worn oak floorboards beneath his feet. "Yes, sir, I understand."

"Do you love the girl?" Easeby's tone was now softer. He regretted his sudden loss of temper.

"I do not know, sir. We have known each other for so short a time. I think so, but I do not know, sir, and that is the honest truth."

Easeby smiled, and turning, placed his hand on Cooper's shoulder. "Good, at last you start to make sense."

"Why good, sir? Surely it would be better if I knew for sure? That way I would know what to do. I would visit her father and ask him for her hand."

"It is good because by admitting to your doubt, I know that you are speaking the truth. Had you said yes without hesitation and married a girl you barely know, I would know that you were lying. To lie in those circumstances would only compound the pain you have already inflicted. You would risk condemning her to a life of misery."

Not for the first time in his short life, Joshua Cooper realised he did not fully understand Sir Richard's words, and yet the way he said them could lead to no other conclusion than that he was right.

"But what should we do then, sir? Becky is already two months into her term and though it does not show yet, that moment cannot be too far away. She is a slender girl, and it will be impossible to disguise it for long."

Easeby returned his gaze to the flames in the hearth. How could something so fascinatingly beautiful also be so dangerous? At last, he spoke.

"Then this is what we will do. The girl will come to live in this house, where she will work as a maid for as long as she is able. During that time, you will court her under strict observance of proper etiquette. You will never be with her alone and without chaperone, although God knows, it is a little late for that to make any difference now!

"If, after the full completion of her term, the two of you discover there is love between you, then you will marry and stay together in this house as husband and wife. You will have my complete blessing and patronage. But should either of you find there is no such love, the girl will return to her parents' household. If she so wishes, her infant may stay here and remain a secret from her family. Under those circumstances, the child will become my ward. Now, what say you, Master Cooper?"

"I do not know what to say, sir. Your kindness leaves me struggling for my words."

"Then let me help you, Master Cooper. The answer is yes."

Just then, there was an urgent knock at the study door.

"Yes, yes, come in," said Easeby, dismissing the boy with a nod of his head as Nathaniel Wright, his clerk and secretary, entered the room.

"Richard, there is a messenger at the gates. He has a letter that he says he must deliver to your own hands. He will not be parted with it other than directly to you."

"Letter? What letter? Did he say who it was from?"

Nathaniel Wright hesitated for a short moment. "Yes, Richard. The messenger says it is from an old acquaintance of yours. It is from Oliver Cromwell."

3
Widow

Sarah Wenham retired later these days than had previously been her custom.

It was in bed during the small hours that she found she missed him the most, and it was often not until three or four in the morning that she would finally succumb to sleep, finding there a couple of hours' respite, from the pain of her loss before the day began again.

This damned war!

She had not wanted him to go, of course; that made her no different from any wife of this or any other parish throughout England. Many, like her, were now widows, but mostly they at least had the support and sympathy of their neighbours to help ease the pain and deal with the practical matters that come with death and bereavement.

Sarah Wenham was different. Firstly, she was a rich woman now, the not inconsiderable estates of her late husband falling solely to her on his death. He had left to fight in the war with the wedding vows they made still echoing in the nave of the parish church. There were consequently no offspring to consider. That at least was a blessing of sorts.

One effect of wealth is to create an instant barrier between those who hold it and those who do not. Sarah found herself now barred from the society of those neighbours who might otherwise have comforted her. It was that curious combination of deference and envy, which only the truly wealthy experience and can therefore fully understand.

The second reason was even more divisive and perhaps insurmountable. In a county where the vast majority of the population had embraced the entwined causes of parliament and unorthodox religion, her husband, a royalist to the last, had taken up arms in the name of the king. He was a man of principle and would not be swayed by those around him.

Sarah was proud of him for that and though holding no strong allegiance to either side in this ridiculous dispute herself, she realised her duty lay in a wife's wholehearted and unquestioning loyalty to her husband. She had never wavered from that once his decision had been made.

The effect of that decision was that Thomas Wenham died on the wrong side of the war and his widow now found herself a figure of suspicion bordering upon open hostility.

Each Sunday, she would dress herself in her widow's weeds and walk the short distance from her home at Wood Walton Manor to the very same village church where she had wed. From the moment she left the bounds of the parkland fronting her estate, she became aware of the glances cast in her direction. Half-finished conversations were left hanging in the air as she walked past.

Then there were the murmurs and the whispers from the pews on either side of the church as she walked the full length of the aisle to her seat on the front-most row; the privilege reserved for her on account of her status.

It was always the women who were the worst, and that somehow made it all the more difficult for Sarah to understand and bear. Surely, there ought to be some sort of solidarity and empathy between the members of her own sex? She would do her best to hold her head high as she passed. She fixed her eyes ahead and did not let her emotions show, but it was never easy.

And then, when the service had concluded, she made the self-same journey in reverse.

On one occasion, a young lad of maybe ten or eleven had even dared to spit on the track in front of her feet as she was making the homeward journey. His friends had clearly been urging him to do it and they now stood smirking expectantly, waiting to see what she would do.

Sarah had stopped and half considered scolding the impertinent wretch, before thinking the better of it. What was the point? Surprised at her own restraint, she simply stepped over the foul mess and continued on her way.

A minor victory perhaps, but a victory nonetheless, she felt.

There was something else troubling Sarah that autumnal night, however. The fire had long since begun to die in the hearth as she pulled her shawl more closely about her shoulders and considered once again her predicament.

The estate would not take care of itself. Her staff was now seriously depleted, the war and the effects of her husband's decision having both taken their toll. One by one, the men had left to fight, and she knew with certainty that many would never return. Many of the women had stayed at first, but most had now tendered their notices, unwilling to stay and become tainted by association. Only three young girls and a lad of similar age remained.

There were few people who Sarah could think to turn to for support. Most of her associates were in a similar position to her own. The king's cause was looking increasingly hopeless, and many of her peers had already begun to vacate their lands, taking what they could of their possessions with them.

A new age was dawning, it seemed: an age of the self-made man. These were men of ability and guile who had gambled and won on the likely outcome of the war. Men such as Isaiah Felt.

Sarah Wenham shuddered at the name. She had always been aware that her widowed status and the wealth she had inherited would make her a target of some unwanted attention, but there were limits.

Isaiah Felt was an obnoxious man. Sixty if a day, it was scarcely a week since learning of her husband's death that he first called to pay his respects, if "respects" could be considered the right word.

He repeated his visits every day for a week before offering a proposal of marriage. Even for a sixty-year-old, increasingly mindful of the passing of time and opportunity, it could not be considered anything other than presumptive, insensitive and impertinent.

Nor was it even a valiant or romantic attempt. He had presented her not with a heartfelt declaration of affection, but rather with a statement of assets and liabilities — fully audited — and a business proposition based upon the aggregated sum of their combined capital.

Sarah had interrupted him before he even reached the column marked "debtors". She laughed at him, though she knew she was being rude; she could not help herself. It had been so long since she had laughed; then, recovering her composure:

"I thank you, sir, for your kind and considerate offer, but I wish it to be known by you and others who harbour similar designs that I have no intention of ever remarrying. My heart remains wed to just one man and it will remain so for the rest of my life, even though he is now lying in his grave. Please leave me now, sir. I bid you good day and ask you to do me the courtesy of never returning to this matter."

When Felt had gone, Sarah allowed herself another smile and considered once more how she had not smiled since her husband had left for war, yet the smile proved ephemeral and fickle.

There had been something in Isaiah Felt's eyes as he left that unsettled her. She thought long and hard on how she would describe that look and eventually realised she could think of no other word.

It was a look of hatred.

4
The Magistrate

Jacob Smog held the small mirror at arm's length to get the best view he possibly could of his own reflected magnificence. The glass itself had come from London and had been extortionately expensive, but Smog would happily have paid twice the price for a larger example. As it was, he would have to make do.

The tailor cooed and purred with admiration. "The cut so accentuates your finest attributes, sir. The shorter length is very much the fashion these days. It fully complements the manliness of your physique."

"And you are quite sure this is what the finest gentlemen are wearing in Flanders and the Netherlands?"

Jacob Smog had to admit that even by his own high sartorial standards, he looked very fine indeed.

"Oh, absolutely, sir; in Amsterdam, Antwerp and London, too. The military cut is *de rigueur* in all the capitals of Protestant Europe. It is dashingly handsome, but under-stated in a way that exudes gravitas; just like your good self, sir. It is the perfect look for a serious magistrate of law and civic affairs."

"Yes, yes, that is just so," Jacob Smog replied, addressing the comment to his own reflection rather than to the tailor. He was holding the mirror as far away from his person as he could, and the tightness of the fastenings heaved with strain against his not inconsiderable paunch.

"I can have two of the garments made for you if you wish, sir; the leather version you are wearing now and a near identical twin in cut, but made from fine wool for more formal occasions." The tailor was never a man to miss a cross-selling opportunity.

"Oh, yes, I think that would be a splendid idea. Quite splendid! Please do attend to it immediately."

"And the matter of your account, sir?"

Smog coughed. "Tender it to the court's exchequer as usual if you would be so kind. I will authorise the remittance immediately."

"Very good, sir."

As the tailor left, Smog sat at his desk and wondered once again what could have detained that irritating man, Jonah Salt. It was now two hours past the time of his appointment and Salt was never late. That was practically the only thing that Smog liked about the man: his punctuality.

But then this had been a strange year all round in the town of Huntingdon. After all, it was not every year that the town could claim to have entertained the King of England, if only for a matter of days.

Of course, Smog had been the very first local dignitary to welcome him to the town, just as he was the first to congratulate the dragoons who turned up three days later to send the king and his contingent packing.

Smog had long held the view that it really did not matter what side you took in a dispute, as long as it turned out to be the winning side. There was nothing to be gained by being on the losing side, and if by some misfortune you found you had chosen injudiciously, there was simply nothing to be done but to switch before it was too late.

Then there was the curious business of the failed harvest. Indeed, this was the very subject that Salt had wished to speak to Smog about. It was curious because the weather had been fine, all year. The conditions were good and there appeared to be absolutely no reason why the crop yield should be so bad, yet bad it was; disastrously bad in fact, and there was a growing sense of panic amongst the farmers and landowners of the town and surrounding villages as the threat of a long, hard winter loomed.

Where was that damned man, Salt?

In response to the unspoken question, there was a sudden, loud rap at the door, startling Smog from his reverie and almost causing him to spill the large glass of port he had just poured himself from a decanter.

"Come in, Salt, you damned fool! What is the meaning of this? How dare you keep me waiting for two hours? Oh!"

The figure entering Smog's office was dressed in the plain manner of a puritan. Smog noticed with some disapprobation that the man had not even removed his hat as he crossed the threshold. Even worse, his riding boots and the cloak he wore over his plain jacket and breeches were both splattered with mud.

He was tall, but with a slight stoop as though he had spent too long in the saddle. His eyes were a piercing, cold grey and his nose aquiline and long. Smog estimated his age to be about twenty-five and the overall impression was of a carefully controlled intelligence, which the magistrate found instantly unsettling. In short, the man most assuredly was not Jonah Salt.

"What is the meaning of this intrusion, sir?" asked Smog. "And who in the name of damnation are you?"

"Do not use that word so lightly, sir! Damnation is precisely why I am here, though not yours or mine, I trust. And in answer to your second question, Mr Smog, my name is Malachai Harkiss. I am originally from the town of Manningtree in Essex, though that is of no relevance whatsoever. I am a friend and I have ridden a long journey through the night to come to your aid."

"Aid? What aid, sir? I have not summoned you here to avail me of your assistance."

"Perhaps not, Mr Smog, but others have, and even had they not, I would have come anyway. You have an infestation in this town, and I have come to help rid you of it."

"Infestation? What in the blazes are you talking about?"

"Acts of maleficia, Mr Smog! I speak of unnatural acts committed by members of these parishes; alliances with demons and Lucifer himself; terrible, terrible things."

"What price the soundness of your mind, Mr Harkiss? I say you are quite mad!"

"Price, Mr Smog? That part at least is easy. It is five shillings a neck plus my expenses."

"A neck? Whose neck?"

"A witch's neck, sir."

5
An Appeal

Nathaniel Wright showed the man into Sir Richard's study. He was dressed in the military uniform of a dragoon and had clearly ridden many miles that day. Sir Richard's keen eye quickly identified the man's rank.

"Good day, Corporal! My secretary here tells me that you have a message for me from Master Cromwell. Have you come directly from him? Where is he currently?"

"That I am not at liberty to tell you, sir, as I am sure you will understand; but the answer to your first question is yes, I have come directly from him, a journey of four days by horse. Commander Cromwell bids you greetings and has instructed me to hand you this note. He requests you to read it and compose your response, which I will return to him immediately. He asks me to impress upon you, sir, that the matter is one of extreme importance."

"Four days, you say? That is quite a feat of endurance, Corporal! You must be exhausted and your horse even more so, I'll wager. Urgent or not, there are limits to what is humane.

"Nathaniel, please ask Joshua to take the corporal's horse around to the stables and ensure that it is well fed and catered for. The poor beast must rest!"

"Yes, Richard."

"And then, please show the corporal here to the kitchens and ask cook to feed him and find him a corner to doze in for a while. You will avail yourself of some Lancashire hospitality for a few hours, Corporal? Even ironsides have need of sleep and sustenance, I imagine."

The corporal started at the jibe, but thought better of making an ungracious response. After all, it was entirely true that he was starved, both of food and warmth, and in much need of rest.

"I thank you, sir. I will, but for a few hours only."

Only when he was alone, did Easeby allow himself a glimmer of curiosity. He and Cromwell had been good friends during their student days in Cambridge, but that must have been twenty-five years ago now.

Since those times, he had followed his old friend's career with some interest, but they had met only on three or four occasions during the intervening period. On each occasion, Easeby had been struck by how serious and earnest Cromwell had become. He was a political animal through and through, and the final occasion, some five years ago, had ended in harsh words and great bitterness. He had not heard from him since; until this day, that is.

Sitting at his desk, he quickly cut the seal with a knife and began to read the still familiar hand:

Richard,

I trust to God you are well. I have little time to indulge in small talk, so please forgive me if this letter appears abrupt in style, especially after an estrangement of so long. I do not mean it to appear thus.

Matters are coming to a head, Richard, and I believe this war is now approaching its final act. I pray that I am right. The king's position is hopeless and I hope only that he comes to his senses and ends it now.

It saddens me every day that our last meeting ended with bitterness. I did not wish it so. I know that your commitment to the cause was never any less than my own, though we differed always on the means of achieving it. Who knows whether it was you or I who was right? I suppose that is no longer of any consequence. The die is cast, as they say.

Richard, there is now a great necessity in ensuring that with our victory, we do not cede the moral high-ground and make a martyr of the king's cause. There have been many terrible things executed on either side of this conflict. We must remain mindful of that and trust only to the judgement of God, which brings me in a circuitous manner to the purpose of this letter.

There have been many strange things come to pass in the eastern shires of this realm in recent times, Richard. Men who call themselves "witch-finders" roam abroad, moving from village-to-village and town-to-town searching for those they claim to be in league with the devil. They say they have the means to identify these "witches" and bring them to justice.

I know not what truth there is in such claims. If they are genuine, then surely, they do God's work and are to be commended. Already, sixty women and several men, too, have been found guilty and hanged as a result of the witch-finders' work, and their enthusiasm for the task shows no sign of abating.

For the most part, the accused are poor peasant folk. There is much fear and suspicion generated, as you might imagine, but nothing of any political consequence. There is, however, one exception: a woman called Sarah Wenham has recently been accused and is soon to be examined and interrogated by a man — a puritan like myself — called Malachai Harkiss. It is in my birth-town and former constituency of Huntingdon. The associations with me are sensitive and potentially embarrassing, as I am sure you will recognise.

The woman has connections, Richard. Her husband fought and died valiantly in service to the king. To our enemies, Thomas Wenham is a hero, and with good reason. I witnessed his bravery on the battlefield myself and can vouch for it.

The widow Wenham is a gentlewoman of wealth, and we cannot sit by and see her persecuted and hanged if she is innocent of the deeds of which she is accused. We cannot afford a martyr to be made of her. The political stakes are too high.

Richard, you have the finest analytical mind of any man I have met. You are also a man of conscience. I trust to your intellect and instincts in this.

Go to Huntingdon, Richard. Discover the truth in the matter. If she is a witch, then she must hang. If she is innocent, then her life and the good name of our cause must be spared. You must defend her against the charges.

If ever our friendship meant anything to you, please do this for me, Richard. I have many other concerns to attend to. Respond immediately so I have at least one less thing to vex me.

Oliver

The November light was fading as Easeby finished reading the message for the fourth time. He stared once again into the flames of the fire as they danced in the grate. Then, picking up his quill and dipping it into ink, he penned a short response:

Oliver,

I will come, but I come for the woman's sake, not for yours. Do what you can to delay the trial until I arrive.

Richard

6
Voices

Jonah Salt waited until the sound of the horse bearing the mysterious rider had faded into the distance. He then gathered up the remains of his breakfast into the small, leather sack he carried with him and followed in the same direction.

The weather showed no signs of lifting; indeed, the fog appeared to be thickening still further and he could scarcely see the road beneath his feet. On more than one occasion, he considered turning and returning home, but that was senseless, having already passed the halfway mark. Better to reach Huntingdon, keep his appointment with Smog and then wait it out there until the weather had lifted a little.

The meeting had been his wife's idea. A superstitious woman, Elizabeth Salt read more into the failing crops than mere bad luck. It was true that there was no apparent explanation. It had been a good summer — not too warm or too wet — and there had been every expectation that the harvest would be a good one; but as the weeks passed, the crops showed no sign of growth. It was not just Salt's smallholding; the entire village appeared to be affected.

Everybody, that is, except Sarah Wenham.

Her estate flourished despite losing most of her staff to the war. Her wheat grew tall and strong, whilst her neighbours watched theirs wither and die. Acre upon acre of fertile soil yielded nothing but stunted grass and the promise of a winter of privation looming on the horizon.

The rumours about Sarah Wenham began quietly enough: half-whispered conversations between village goodwives across hedgerows and wooden fences. But soon they became louder, more pervasive and bolder. It was well known, of course, that her husband had taken up arms with the king. It was also widely believed that the king leaned heavily towards popish ways under the influence of the queen, and everybody knew that the Pope was the devil's emissary on Earth.

When the war started, most God-fearing folk in the neighbourhood had joined cause with Parliament, but not Thomas Wenham. When news of his death reached the village, the tears shed in sympathy for his widow were few and rarely sincere.

Perhaps it is a short step from being the widow of a king's man to the suspicion of something more sinister, and it is a step that Sarah Wenham had unknowingly taken.

And then there were the other rumours. They filtered back to this small corner of the shire slowly but persistently. Across the whole of the eastern counties, witches were being flushed out, tried and hanged.

Legion upon legion of demented souls, in league with the devil, had been exposed. Certain men had made it their life's work to rid the land of the infestation. It was a time of the witch-finders.

Elizabeth had first used the word "witch" as she sat eating with Salt one evening. Her voice became suddenly hushed, her shadow on the wall leaning towards his as the fire flickered morosely in the grate.

It was she who suggested the meeting with the magistrate, to raise the matter with him and to seek his counsel. Salt had refused at first. He could not abide the god-awful man and would have done anything to leave the matter to someone else, but the threat of her nagging became too much for him and eventually he acceded to her demand. The time and date were soon arranged.

Jonah Salt's mind snapped back to his recent encounter on the road. Had others gone a step further and approached another kind of authority entirely? He would know soon enough when he reached Huntingdon, he supposed. Even so, the idea sent a chill through his veins; a chill not helped by the cloying damp of the fog that seemed to swirl and envelop him even as he trudged warily and wearily onwards.

"Where are you going, Jonah Salt?"

When it came, the voice seemed faint and far away; a female voice, but barely audible, like a whisper.

Salt stopped in his tracks and craned his neck in the direction whence the voice had come, cupping his ear with his hand and listening.

There was nothing. He took a few steps forward.

"Jonah Salt! Where are you going?"

The voice now seemed to be very close, almost directly behind him. He started, and turning on his heels, peered into the mist again. Silence.

"Who is it? Who is there?"

Salt shouted the words into the dank, grey wall of fog. In response, there was a moment's silence and then a giggle, like that of a small girl-child and very different from the voice that had first called his name.

"Be careful, Jonah Salt; be careful not to lose your way."

Once again, the voice confused Salt. Each time, the words seemed to come from a different direction.

Turning again, he felt his heartbeat begin to quicken. There was something strange about the voice: distant and yet close by. It was at once both young and old.

"Who is it? Who is there? Are you lost? Show yourself to me!" Salt struggled to make his voice carry through the fog; he felt suddenly weak and disorientated.

"Not lost, Jonah Salt. We are not lost, but are you?"

This time, the voice seemed far away once more and to come from a different direction entirely. Salt turned full circle, desperately searching out the source.

There was another brief silence and then he heard what sounded like a child again. This time it seemed more like mocking laughter than an innocent giggle, and was followed by the unmistakable sound of youthful singing. Straining his ears, he could just make out the words. They were sung in sing-song, nursery rhyme fashion:

"Poor, poor Jonah Salt
What will the old fool do?
Lost he is, poor Jonah Salt
Alone here in the gloom!
Poor, poor Jonah Salt
Should we tell him when
He left the road, poor Jonah Salt,
And stepped out on the fen?"

Salt suddenly became aware of the cloying, thick ooze of mud around his knees. In his confusion and disorientation, he must have wandered away from the road and out onto the nearest boggy reaches of the fen; worse still, he no longer had any idea in which direction the road lay.

Breathing deeply to regain his composure, he began to think quickly and urgently. He could not have wandered far. It was only a few seconds since he had first heard the woman's voice, and a man could not travel far in that time.

He resolved to take five steps in the direction he best guessed the road to lay. If he did not find it, or if the ooze and mud became deeper, he would simply retrace his steps back to this spot and try once more in a different direction.

"Poor, poor Jonah Salt
Which way should he go?
He's lost his way, poor Jonah Salt
And now he doesn't know!"

Ignoring the childish taunts, Salt attempted to take the first step, but even in the short time he had been thinking, his feet had sunk deeper into the mud. Trying to lift his foot, he stumbled and fell backwards, sinking to the level of his chest. Cursing, he reached down with his hands to try to lever himself upright, but they sank deep into the soft mud-bed beneath him. He felt himself begin to sink.

"Take care, Jonah Salt!" the woman's voice returned, now seeming very, very close to him. "Do not struggle. The fen will only drag you down the quicker."

"Help me, damn you! Help lift me to my feet!"

Salt began to panic. He knew very well what people said: once a man had sunk to his waist, there was no extracting him. Even with the help of an ox and a rope, the resistance is simply too great and his body will be torn in two.

The filth had now risen above Salt's chest, all the way to his chin. Struggling violently and uselessly, his contortions only caused him to sink deeper and deeper, the mud dragging him further down.

Spluttering and kicking, the foulness began to enter his mouth and nostrils. He opened his eyes wide in panic and tried to emit a plea for help, but no sound would come. With all the strength he could muster, he lifted his head, taking one final, deep breath of fog-thickened air before sinking back down beneath the surface.

"Fare thee well, Jonah Salt
The end must be the end
Be at peace now, Jonah Salt,
Alone here in the fen!"

The words drifted lifelessly through the air and then they were gone.

7
Hue and Cry

Malachai Harkiss refused the magistrate's offer of a seat. Instead, he remained standing near the door, his tall presence dominating the room and imbuing it with silent malevolence.

Jacob Smog shuffled uneasily in his seat. Never in his fifteen years as magistrate had he felt so unnerved by the presence of a stranger.

"Tell me, Mr Harkiss, who asked you to come to this town?"

"I have received several reports, Mr Smog. They concern separate matters, but the subject is common and shared by each of them. What do you know of Sarah Wenham?"

Smog was unaccustomed to being questioned; it was usually he that was the inquisitor, and he didn't care for the reversal of roles one bit. He also felt his feathers more than a little ruffled by the news that his jurisdiction had been circumvented like this. It was all highly irregular.

Feeling the need to reassert his authority, he, too, now stood, but the discrepancy in stature between himself and the stranger caused him instantly to regret the decision. Harkiss continued to tower over him.

"I know of the woman. She is a widow, as are many in these parts. A minor gentlewoman would be the best way to describe her. She keeps herself to herself since her husband's death. Of what relevance is Sarah Wenham?"

Harkiss ignored the question. "When did the husband die and what was the manner of his death?"

"War, Mr Harkiss. He was killed on the battlefield earlier this year at Naseby. There is nothing unusual about that in these times."

"Nothing? Perhaps you are right, Mr Smog. On what side of the war did Wenham fight?"

Smog felt himself instantly on his guard. Politics were a complicated matter these days. It was very difficult to keep on the right side of events as fortunes ebbed and flowed.

"He was a royalist I believe, Mr Harkiss. That is unusual in this shire perhaps, but not entirely unheard of. He was certainly not alone in harbouring those sympathies."

"Indeed not, Mr Smog, but it may yet be of some relevance. Where there is grievance, the devil finds succour, and those who flirt with the king flirt also with the incubus in Rome, it is said. The widow keeps herself to herself, you say?"

"Yes, she has retained a small staff on her estate; mainly women. The male retinue are mostly dead or at war. She hires in help where she can to farm and maintain the estate, I believe."

"Mostly women, you say?" The gaze now became more intense and intimidating. The witch-finder latched onto his words and Smog sensed himself becoming flustered.

"Yes, maids, housekeepers and such; they are mostly young girls."

"Young and impressionable; that is often the way." The words were muttered to himself rather than to Smog, who could make no sense of them.

The magistrate turned away and looked out of the large mullioned window of his office. He noticed with surprise that the dense fog had lifted, seemingly as quickly as it had come. A weak, watery autumn sun was now clearly visible, slowly sinking in the afternoon sky. In the cobbled street below, people were going about their business, catching up with deferred errands and making the most of the unexpected change of weather.

A small, white terrier could be seen, snarling and barking fiercely at a cornered rat. The stand-off continued for a few moments until, lunging, the dog appeared to grab the thing in its jaws, and with a powerful, frenzied shake of its neck, killed it cleanly. Smog shuddered and turned his back on the scene. He was no longer watching as the dog began to disembowel its prey.

"Let us speak for a moment on another matter, Mr Smog. I am led to believe that the harvest has failed in the parishes to the north of this town. Is that so?"

"Your information is correct, sir. In fact, I was due to meet someone to discuss the matter just as you arrived."

Smog wondered again what could have happened to Jonah Salt. Perhaps he had simply decided not to keep the appointment, the fog being as it was. He would be sure to have stern words with the man when next he saw him. A magistrate's time was a valuable commodity.

"Mrs Wenham has land in those parishes, I believe."

"Again, your information is correct."

"And are her crops similarly affected? I imagine that must certainly be the case."

Smog did not trust this man for one moment. It was clear he already knew the answer to the question. Was he trying to catch him out? Even so, the matter was indeed puzzling.

"No, Mr Harkiss. Mrs Wenham has been fortunate in the matter. Her harvest was a good one and gathered in time and good order. I think the men were grateful for the wages she paid them. Very few had anything of their own worth gathering."

"You call it fortunate, Mr Smog. Others might deem it strange, is that not so? I imagine the prices she now commands are significantly inflated, given the circumstances. In your tenure as an officer of this town, have you ever before known a year when a blight has destroyed all the crops bar those of a single landowner?"

"No, sir, I have not. I have been magistrate here for fifteen years and have never known such a thing. It is unusual, as you suggest."

"Not just unusual, Mr Smog; it is unique. It might even be called unnatural."

Malachai Harkiss emphasised the last word, savouring and delivering it with an actor's flourish. He allowed it to hang heavily in the silence that followed. Any good angler knows the importance of holding perfectly still when the fish has bitten before making the strike.

"Mr Smog, I will come to the point. Sarah Wenham is accused of witchcraft. The charges against her are four-fold:

"She is accused of bedevilling the son of her neighbour, Catherine Monk. The lad is recently returned from the war and is now demented and tormented out of his wits by demons.

"She is also accused of bewitching the men of her village, enticing them with adulterous lust and licentious designs. Her motive, it is alleged, is simple carnal gratification, envy and spite.

"She is further, and most grievously, accused of profiting from her husband's death; a profit she now jealously guards, using witchcraft to cause the failure of all crops in the parish but her own.

"From what you have told me, I also believe it highly probable that she has enlisted the help of others in these deeds. She has created a coven, Mr Smog; a group of impressionable young women to assist in the execution of her acts of maleficia. When you find a rat, it is wise to be wary; there are bound to be others nearby. We must root them out, every last, stinking one of them!"

"These are grievous charges indeed, Mr Harkiss! What further evidence do you have? This is all circumstantial, surely?"

"The collection of evidence is my job, Mr Smog, and incontrovertible evidence I will collect. All witches have a demon-familiar, and no witch is separated from her demon for long; it is usually just a case of watching and waiting. When the demon returns to suckle, we will identify her as a witch. All this we will do, Mr Smog. We will purge these parishes of the disease once and for all and return the place to godly peace. Mobilise yourself, sir, there is not a moment to lose!"

Jacob Smog hesitated. This was all far beyond the reach of his experience and reason. Could such fantastical things really be true?

Sensing the hesitation, Malachai Harkiss recast his line, this time with a more heavily baited hook:

"This could be a great moment for the magistrate of Huntingdon, Mr Smog. The deliverer of this town is likely to become the stuff of legend. You will be spoken about with reverence for the rest of your days and even beyond your grave. I have seen much lesser men profit this way."

Jacob Smog straightened himself to his full height. The image would have been a compelling one, even to a man less vain than he.

***

Within two hours, the hue and cry had been raised, and as darkness began to fall, a hundred or so men and boys had gathered in the town square. From there, they began to march to Wood Walton and the house of Sarah Wenham.

At the head of the procession strode the unlikely pairing of Jacob Smog and Malachai Harkiss.

8
Torches

Sarah Wenham lay in her bed. The time must have been shortly after midnight, because the candle by the side of her bed had not yet fully burned down.

Unusually, she must have drifted early to sleep as she found herself awoken with a start. There was a sound, but in her state of drowsiness, it took her a few seconds to identify the source as the latch of her chamber door being lifted.

Sarah froze. Her heart was beating quickly as the door began to open and into the space appeared the figure of a man. Sarah recognised him instantly as Abel Carter. Even in the dim light cast by the dying candle, she recognised his features.

Sarah had employed Abel Carter on two separate occasions, as a joiner and a carpenter to undertake repairs to the barn and the stables. There was something about the man that had always made her feel uncomfortable. He was taciturn to the point of sullenness, but there was something else. It was the way she often caught him looking at her out of the corner of his eye. It was a look that any woman living alone comes to recognise and quickly learns never to return.

"Abel Carter, how dare you! What are you doing here? Leave this house immediately and go home to your wife!"

The strength of her voice surprised even Sarah, and for a moment she thought the man had come to his senses. He turned as if to go, but then, to her horror, she saw that it was only to close the door behind him.

"Nay, Mistress Wenham. I know that's not what you want: not really. How long has he been dead now? Six months? Seven? And more than two years since he went off to fight with that papist bastard! That's a long time for a woman like you to go without."

Carter was approaching the bed, pulling his white linen shirt from his breeches and loosening his large leather belt.

Sarah struggled to jump out of bed, but he was too quick. Her strength was no match for his and he easily pinned her down, one hand clasped tightly around her neck and stifling the scream she was about to let loose.

"You've bewitched me, Sarah Wenham! Aye, you've bewitched me with those eyes and those lips of yours! You know exactly what you're doing, don't you?"

"Leave now, Abel Carter! You are deranged!"

"Aye, perhaps I am deranged, Sarah Wenham! Where'd you learn to sway your hips like that, eh? Walking to church? I think not!

"My wife says you're a whore and a witch, and I reckon she's right. Where'd you learn those things, eh, Sarah Wenham? In some Southwark whorehouse?"

Sarah struggled frantically, kicking out violently as he dragged her out of bed, throwing her onto her knees in front of him.

"We all know what a good whore wants, eh? Well, here you are, Sarah Wenham. Have a taste of what you've been missing!"

Grabbing her hair, the man let his breeches fall to the floor and forced himself into her mouth. The taste of it almost made her gag. It was a taste of stale sweat and semen.

Regaining her composure and with only one option open to her, Sarah relaxed and began to suck him.

"Like this, Abel Carter?" she said, removing him for a moment and looking up into his eyes. Her voice now feigned a seductive tone and Abel Carter closed his eyes.

"Aye, Sarah Wenham, just like that!"

Closing her own eyes, she returned him to her mouth, sucked him twice again and then bit down on him, as hard as she could.

***

The screams brought the whole household racing to their mistress's chamber. Once there, they were greeted by the sight of Abel Carter, writhing around on the floor in a state of agony. His white linen shirt and woollen breeches were heavily stained with blood, which was still flowing freely.

Sarah was seated on her bed, watching him as though transfixed. She looked up as her maid, the first on the scene, entered.

"Jane, find Luke and tell him to ride to the village and fetch the physician. Tell him to be quick or this man will bleed to death."

"Yes, mistress." The girl continued to stare at the writhing figure on the floor, unable to tear her eyes away.

"DO IT NOW, JANE!"

"Yes, mistress!" With that, the girl was gone.

"Annabel, Anne, quickly now! Take the sheets from the bed and tear them into long strips. We need to stem the bleeding until the physician arrives."

Nobody dared to ask their mistress what had happened as they began to go about their business.

It was Sarah herself who applied the first bandage. The man had not been completely severed, for which she felt thankful. The idea of spitting the thing out made her stomach retch; but still, the injury was significant. She could still taste his blood in her mouth, but the little she had swallowed was nothing compared to the pool that was still gathering where he lay on the floor, doubled up and now in a silent swoon.

Sarah applied the bandage as tenderly as she could and then added a second. Once satisfied, that there was nothing else she could do until the physician arrived, she sat on the floor next to him and lifted his head into her lap. There she wet his lips with a few drops of the brandy one of the servants had retrieved from the library room.

It was only another five minutes before Luke appeared at the door. There was no way he could have saddled a horse in that time, never mind ridden into Wood Walton.

"Forgive me, mistress, but I think you had better come. There is something you should see."

"What's the meaning of this, Luke? You were given instructions to fetch the physician."

"I know, mistress. I am sorry, but I think you had better come now."

Sarah followed Luke as he led her to the great window fronting the house. She noted that the moon had fully risen, casting a silvery glow across the parklands; but it was not the moonlight that arrested her attention.

Along the drive, all the way to the gates, she saw a procession of figures approaching the house, carrying torches. There must have been a hundred people, maybe more, like a river of flame flowing towards the main entrance.

And at the front of the procession were two figures. The first she recognised instantly as the absurd magistrate, Jacob Smog.

The second figure she did not recognise. He was a tall, youngish man, plainly dressed and with a slight stoop.

"So, they have come already," whispered Sarah Wenham, more to herself than to anyone else.

9
A Spy

Nathaniel Wright was charged with making the preparations for the journey to Huntingdon. The party was to be a small one. Haste was needed above all else, and a small travelling group would be far easier to organise and would travel at greater speed than a larger one, Sir Richard reasoned.

After great deliberation, it was determined that the company would comprise Sir Richard Easeby, Nathaniel Wright (to act as clerk and recorder) and Joshua Cooper (to serve as man-servant, scout and to undertake chores).

For the first stage of the journey, three stable hands — Ned Jones, Timothy Wellens and Benjamin Farrier — were selected to accompany them. Their task was to tend the horses, carry the provisions, and lead spare mounts for when the beasts bearing the riders tired.

The party would ride many miles eastwards, across country as far as Doncaster in the county of Yorkshire. It was a journey of at least three days, but more likely four. From there, they would commission, or if needs be, purchase a stage wagon to take them south along the Great North Road. The alternative route, southwards and eastwards from Lancashire, was shorter but would take them closer to areas of conflict and through lands still loyal to the king. They could ill afford to be delayed by war or, worse still, apprehended and held as enemy spies.

A rider was dispatched immediately, a day ahead of the main party, to ride at speed to the inn known as The White Hart near Doncaster; there to make the preparations for their onward journey.

All in all, Nathaniel calculated that the journey to Huntingdon could be completed in no fewer than eight days, even assuming everything worked to plan. In all likelihood, it would be nearer ten days before they arrived.

Was that soon enough to intervene before Sarah Wenham hanged? Would Cromwell send word for the trial to be delayed as Easeby had requested, and would the authorities in Huntingdon pay heed even if he did? From what Cromwell had written, a state of frenzy held sway in the eastern counties, and men in such mood could not be trusted to act rationally.

Easeby was greatly troubled when Nathaniel relayed the news to him, and even more so when another matter arose.

Rebecca Standish had recently arrived at the house and had gone into such a state of temper when she learned that Joshua would be leaving her, that Easeby very nearly sent her packing straight back to her parents. Her tantrum exceeded anything he had ever witnessed before. Crockery and profanities were thrown in turn; tears were shed and pitiful pleas made for her to be allowed to accompany them. That, of course, was totally out of the question given her condition, still early in her term though she was.

It was more the effect on Joshua, though, that most troubled him. The boy was in a state of such abject misery that he half-considered excusing him from the journey. The boy would be needed, however, and Easeby was in no mind to leave the two together in the house other than under his direct supervision.

There was also the question of his authority over the new-arrival. To his surprise, he had taken an instant liking to the girl. There was a determined intelligence about her that he recognised instantly, but with it came a petulance and wilfulness that would need to be tamed.

There was nothing to be done. Perhaps the separation might even do them good, testing their commitment to each other. Even so, Easeby felt greatly vexed by it and could not sleep. He paced about his chamber long into the night.

The next day — the third since the arrival of Cromwell's messenger — dawned clear and bright; a good omen, thought Nathaniel Wright, as the small party gathered in the cobbled courtyard. Only a few of the household had congregated to see them on their way, and there was no sign of Rebecca Standish amongst them. Joshua pulled the hood of his cloak above his head to ward off the crisp chill of the November morning and to hide the disappointment on his face.

The first day's riding was uneventful and they made good progress over a landscape that was largely flat and easy-going. Stopping only twice to eat and to change horses, they arrived before dark at a small tavern just outside Manchester. There, they billeted for the night, enjoying a hearty enough meal of potage, mutton and cheese. By Nathaniel's calculation, they had travelled perhaps thirty miles or so and he felt satisfied with the progress.

The second day was another matter entirely. As soon as they left the outskirts of Manchester behind them, the path began to incline steeply. The trees became fewer and further between, until they eventually gave way fully to a landscape of forlorn gorse and barren moorland. This was Saddleworth Moor, an area of dangerous reputation, especially amongst travellers. The moors held many traps and obstacles for the unwary.

Progress became achingly slow and their stops more frequent. As they picked their way through the difficult landscape, Nathaniel noticed Sir Richard glancing behind him on more than one occasion, and eventually asked him to explain the reason.

"I do not know, Nathaniel. I have a feeling we are being followed. Have you not heard the sound of another horse at some distance behind us? Every time we stop, whoever it is seems to stop also. When we resume the journey, I catch the sound of the horse again. It is as though someone is keeping us in his sights but does not wish to gain on us. It is hard to be sure, but it is worrying me. I wonder if there is a spy on our trail."

Nathaniel could hear nothing above the sound of his own horse and admitted as much to Sir Richard. The ground was soft, even on the path, and it would require a sense of hearing far better than his own to discern another animal at such a distance. Sir Richard, it seemed, possessed senses far more acute than his own.

"What do you propose we do, Richard? If we are indeed being followed, it is hard to imagine it is with benign intent. Perhaps someone knows of our errand and has been instructed to observe and report on us. Or maybe it is a common highway thief waiting for an opportunity to rob us. Either way, we would be ill-advised to ignore the matter until something happens."

"I agree, Nathaniel. Your reasoning is sound."

Looking around, Easeby noticed a small area of gorse set well away from the side of the path behind them. The bushes were fully-grown, perhaps five to six feet tall, and though not at all large enough to hide a horse fully from sight, they were perhaps sufficient to break its outline on the featureless landscape and thereby disguise its presence from a man until he was at very close quarters.

"I am going to make some enquiries of our friend, Nathaniel," said Easeby, removing a small pouch of powder from his belt and loading the single cavalry pistol he had permitted himself to bring along. "You and the rest of the party continue along the path ahead. I will wait here for our pursuer and catch up with you once I have spoken to him. If you hear a shot, send the stable lads back this way at speed. Do not come yourself, though, Nathaniel, and do not send Joshua. It is highly unlikely that anything will happen to me, but if it does, you will need to go to Huntingdon in my stead. Do you understand?"

"I understand, Richard."

"Good. You know enough of my methods to apply them in the matter of the Wenham woman. Get to the bottom of it, Nathaniel. There are no such things as witches save in the minds of men who refuse to look beyond the limits of their prejudice."

"Indeed, Richard, though your wit in these matters far exceeds my own. Please, be careful. I am not a good traveller, especially without company. I have always needed good conversation on the road."

Easeby smiled at that and led his horse to the gorse bushes. From there, he watched as the party continued ahead without him.

***

Nathaniel Wright allowed himself ten minutes or so before calling a halt to the small band. They turned to look back along the path behind them.

To his relief, no shot had been heard, but he did not want to travel out of hearing range. He resolved to wait where they now stood for whatever might transpire.

Shading their eyes against the sun, which was beginning to dip lower towards the West, they eventually discerned the figures of two horsemen approaching them. They were not travelling at great speed, which gave Nathaniel some hope that all might yet be well.

From his shape and height, and the distinctive chestnut colour of the horse he was riding, it was clear that one of the figures was Sir Richard. The second rider was much smaller and leaner. He certainly did not have the look of a desperate criminal. It was only as they drew closer, though, that recognition began to dawn on Nathaniel and Joshua Cooper.

It was the figure of Rebecca Standish.

10
The White Hart

Despite her wilful disobedience, Easeby found he could not stay angry with the girl for long. Indeed, he almost admired her resourcefulness and determination.

Under gentle interrogation, she admitted that she had slipped into the stables whilst the party had been preparing for departure and taken a young mare, together with a saddle and the necessary tack. Her father was a farrier and she had lived around horses all her young life, often riding them after they were re-shod to make sure the fit was a good one. She had a natural, calming way with them, and the mare had shown no signs of taking fright.

Having already stolen bread, cheese and some weak ale from the kitchens during the night, she had simply waited a short time after their departure before following on their trail. Whilst they had enjoyed the comfort of the inn on the first night, she had camped under the stars with nothing but a couple of blankets and the clothes she was wearing for warmth. She seemed to have suffered no physical harm from the experience.

Joshua Cooper was delighted and mortified in equal measure to see her. He looked warily at Sir Richard, waiting to see what would happen now.

"What is to be done with the girl, Richard?" asked Nathaniel Wright. "This presents us with something of a dilemma."

"Indeed, it does, Nathaniel. It seems we have only two options: either we send her back, or we allow her to come with us, at least as far as Doncaster. If we choose the first option, what is there to stop the girl simply turning and following us once again as soon as we are out of sight?"

"That is true, Richard. We could send one of the stable lads back with her, but that would leave us short-handed and the horses over-burdened."

"And I wouldn't put it past the girl simply to give the lad the slip and come back to us anyway!" added Sir Richard.

He strode ahead to the top of the ridge where the party had been waiting for him, and surveyed the land ahead of them.

It seemed they had at last reached the summit of the climb. From this point, the land levelled out and appeared relatively flat in the direction of Huddersfield, where they planned to spend their second night. From Huddersfield, the track fell away gradually, descending the eastern flank of the Pennines and snaking its way onwards towards Barnsley and Doncaster.

"At least the girl can ride," he said eventually, his mind finally made up. "Master Cooper, the girl is in your charge. If she disobeys one more instruction, it is you that I will hold responsible; do you understand me?"

Joshua Cooper reddened and nodded his head, giving Becky a sideways glance that did not altogether exude confidence.

"Very well," continued Easeby, "the girl will come with us as far as Doncaster at least. I will decide then what is to be done with her." He turned again, as though surveying the onwards path once more, though in truth it was more to conceal the trace of a smile that was fighting to break out on his face.

***

The White Hart was a large, rambling tavern-house situated on the Great North Road, just to the south of the town of Doncaster. What began as a small country inn had grown quickly in size as the number of travellers from north to south and south to north had grown. It now serviced a constant flow of foot travellers, riders and the small number of commercial stage wagons that had begun to ply their trade up and down the road.

Still, few in number, the demand for these wagons and coaches had grown rapidly: more rapidly than the supply of vehicles, in fact. Many entrepreneurial townsfolk living close to the North Road had realised there was profit to be made from converting whatever ramshackle vehicles they owned to ferry passengers for payment.

It was in the evening of their third day from Rufford that Sir Richard and his party arrived at the inn. Their journey had been a good one, without further incident, and they had made much better progress than either Easeby or Nathaniel had dared hope. Rebecca Standish proved herself a very useful addition to the group, and Easeby noted with satisfaction how well she and Joshua Cooper worked together. They were forever scurrying around, preparing the group's journey-meals, packing and unpacking provisions and even helping the stable-hands feed and tend the horses during their stop at Huddersfield.

Joshua also revealed himself to have a fine singing voice, a talent Sir Richard had previously been unaware of. The boy entertained them for long hours on the road with simple songs delivered in a rich, tenor voice that belied his sixteen years. From where he had learned such things, Easeby had no idea. His capacity for remembering words was unexpected and impressive, and the party proceeded for long periods in silence, with just the sound of Joshua's voice to accompany them on their way.

Sir Richard and Nathaniel shared a large room on the first floor of the inn, looking directly out over the courtyard. Following discussions with the landlord, it had been arranged for Becky to share a garret-room with a group of serving girls who lived-in at the tavern, whilst Joshua and the three stable-hands were housed in bunks in the stable block.

Having refreshed themselves with warm water, delivered to them in a large copper jug, Nathaniel and Easeby went down to the large public room, which was packed with fellow travellers and local residents. There, they intended to have something to eat and drink. Joshua was already waiting for them in the bar room. Easeby noted that Becky was already busy, scurrying about and helping her roommates for the night, serving ale, porter and food to the company. Not for the first time, he found himself admiring the girl's industry and initiative; neither had the landlord failed to take note, and he stood now with his hands on his hips, looking on appreciatively.

"A good worker, that one," he said to Sir Richard, as he showed them to seats at the end of a large table in the corner of the bar. "I'd be happy to take her off your hands if you ever wanted rid of her."

"Alas, we have already tried that!" joked Sir Richard. "The girl seems determined to follow us, and I fear you would not enjoy the benefit of her services for long once we had left."

Joshua Cooper looked at his master but kept silent. Could this mean that Sir Richard had already determined to allow Becky to continue with them to Huntingdon? It seemed there was some hope at least, and he dived ravenously into the plates of ham, mutton and potatoes that were brought from the kitchens and laid out in front of them. It was only after his fifth mouthful that he looked up and noticed Sir Richard and Nathaniel looking at him disapprovingly.

"I am not aware that we have yet said grace, Master Cooper!"

Joshua reddened and bowed his head as Nathaniel recited the words: "Blessed are we for this, your bounty, oh Lord! Amen."

***

As the evening drew on, the noise and chatter in the bar grew deafening. Sharing their table was a particularly raucous group that seemed to be engaged in some sort of game. The game involved three wooden cups and an ochre-coloured pebble.

Easeby had been watching the game for some time, with an arched eyebrow and mild curiosity.

The principal conductor of proceedings was a dark, handsome-looking man, brightly dressed and somewhat different from the rest of the group, who were intently following every movement of his hands.

The man placed the pebble under one of the wooden cups and then proceeded to shuffle them quickly so that each cup might be left resting in a different position to where it started. The game was simple enough. The group of men took turns to wager a penny coin on which of the cups had the pebble beneath it. If they guessed correctly, they won back their stake and a further coin from the man. If not, he kept their stake, always careful to lift the cup and show the whereabouts of the pebble whilst doing so.

Having won the first few rounds at the man's expense, the group's enthusiasm for the game grew quickly and a large crowd had gathered, each man keen to take his turn; but the man then went on a winning streak of his own. No matter how closely they watched the movement of the cups, no one seemed able to guess correctly, and the pile of coins on his side of the table had begun to grow large.

The mood became discernibly more tense, and the landlord glanced over nervously in their direction. The man seemed to sense it, too. Eventually, he stretched and yawned theatrically, feigning tiredness.

"Well, it is high time I took my leave of you, good gentlemen. Don't be too concerned. I have been uncommonly lucky this evening and I am sure you will fleece me in turn whenever I am back this way again."

There were grumblings of disquiet as he rose to take his leave, silently congratulating himself on having timed his departure just right. That was until Sir Richard Easeby rose to his feet.

"I have been watching with interest, sir. The game is quite fascinating. Please, may I play one game before you take your leave?"

The stranger hesitated. He knew better than to push his luck. When a crowd had begun to turn, that was the time to take his leave. It had always been his rule.

"Thank you, sir. I would have been delighted to let you win a penny from me; but, as I said, the evening is late and I really must be going."

"Nonsense. Just one final game will not detain you too long, surely? Here, let me make it worth your while."

There was a gasp amongst the assembled crowd as Easeby pulled a gold crown from his pocket and placed it on the table in front of him.

"I wager this crown against your winnings for the evening. What do you say? You cannot have won more than twenty pennies, I would guess. A crown is what, five shillings?"

The man eyed the crown greedily as it glinted on the table in front of him. What were rules for if not to be broken on occasion? If this fool was mad or drunk enough to wager a crown, then so be it.

"Very well, sir. I see your means are matched by your resolve in the matter. I am a poor man and can ill afford to lose twenty pennies, but I am also a sporting one. The wager seems fair. Just one game, though, winner takes all; agreed?"

"Agreed," answered Sir Richard, seating himself opposite the man as the three cups were lined up once more and the pebble placed beneath the centre one.

A hush fell across the whole room as even more people crowded around to watch the proceedings.

"Now, watch carefully, please, sir; perhaps not too carefully, though, if you'll beg my leave. As I say, I am a poor man and I dare say my twenty pennies are worth more to me than your crown is to you!"

With that, the stranger quickly shuffled the cups with a well-practised flourish. Every eye in the room followed their movement; every eye, that is, except those belonging to Sir Richard Easeby. He did not watch the cups at all, but instead sat back, nonchalantly watching the man sitting opposite him. The stranger was so intent on his shuffling, that he did not even notice this curious lack of interest.

"Now, sir," said the man, "be sure to choose wisely. Which cup hides the pebble?" He glanced again at the crown on the table in front of Sir Richard; such a pretty coin, he thought to himself.

Easeby stared at each of the cups in turn. There was the gentle hum of excited anticipation from the crowd. Many of them had placed side bets of their own on the outcome. Easeby remained silent and still.

The man started to grow impatient and agitated. "Come, come, sir, choose a cup if you will! I must be leaving. I do not have all night. Make your choice!"

At last, Sir Richard spoke:

"I do not believe the pebble to be under any of the cups, sir. I believe it to be in the palm of your right hand. There it will stay until I have chosen incorrectly. You will then allow it to roll from your palm as you lift one of the remaining cups to reveal it to me. It is a trick, sir; a simple sleight of hand."

11
South

The man was lucky to escape with his life, and it was Joshua Cooper he had to thank for that. As he bolted for the door, Joshua stuck out a foot to trip him, sending him flying into a heap on the floor.

In the mêlée that followed — a frenzy of flying fists and tangled bodies — the man was able to crawl free of the scrum and make it to the door unnoticed, shuffling on his elbows and knees. From there, he rose to his feet and ran to where his tethered horse was waiting. Jumping into the makeshift saddle, he quickly disappeared into the dark November night.

It was only when Sir Richard climbed onto the table and fired a blank round of powder from his pistol into the ceiling above them that the fighting ceased and the man's escape was discovered. Two or three of the duped victims ran to the door, but the man had already disappeared.

"Be at peace, everyone!" shouted Sir Richard, all eyes turning on him. "The fraudster has gone and I imagine will never dare show his face in these parts again. Every man who has lost money this evening will be recompensed. Form a queue to this table and Master Wright and I will return your coins."

The whole process took nearly half an hour. There was much debate and argument as to who had, and had not, placed a wager and on how many games each man had gambled. At times, it seemed as though more fighting might break out. Inevitably, the twenty pennies left behind by the swindler did not cover half of the claims, and Easeby found himself substantially out of pocket by the time the last man had left.

"And this, sir, is for the trouble and damage caused," he said finally to the landlord, tossing him the gold crown. "I trust it will cover your expenses and I am sorry for the inconvenience."

The landlord, who had been standing with a face like thunder throughout the whole escapade, brightened in mood considerably.

"Never you mind, sir. I am just sorry the crook escaped, that's all. I'll have lads waiting for him if he dares show his face around here again! That was quite something, though. How on earth did you manage to work it out so quickly? It seems he had us all fooled except you."

The room had largely emptied of customers and Easeby reflected ruefully on how he had become the centre of attention when discretion was required above all else. Still, what was done was done and couldn't be helped. Getting to the bottom of conundrums was in his nature, and he held a deeply ingrained antipathy towards fakery and foul play. There was no question the incident could have played out any other way.

"It's a question of probability, that is all," said Easeby, responding to the landlord's question. "The odds of a winning streak like that, in a game of chance, are so miniscule as to be virtually impossible. Once you understand that, the possibility it is a trick becomes a certainty.

"It was then just a case of observing the man to work out how the trick was contrived. His routine was exactly the same on each occasion. The pebble was always placed, or rather not placed, under the centre cup with his right hand. When he shuffled the cups, I noticed that his left hand always seemed to move more assuredly than the right, as though the latter was somehow inhibited. I guessed it was because he was shielding something in the palm. The final step was to turn the cup slightly towards himself rather than towards the player as he made the reveal. Again, it was always with his right hand, allowing the pebble to drop the short distance from his palm as he did so. It gave the illusion the pebble had been under the cup all the time.

"The rest, I imagine, is just timing and speed, honed through practice. It is a skill, though not a very admirable one. A quick enough hand will always deceive the eye, and men are inclined to believe what they think they see rather than what they actually do see. At least, that has always been my experience."

The landlord, no less impressed for the simplicity of the explanation, stood them another round of drinks and it was nearly midnight before the group of travellers finally retired to their beds.

***

The vehicle identified by Easeby's outrider belonged to a local farmer called Moses Brooke. It seemed sturdy enough, though somewhat lacking in comfort. The only concessions were two long wooden benches running the length of the wagon on either side and a roughly sewn canvas canopy, supported by four curved iron hoops, to protect the passengers from the worst of the weather. The price demanded was extortionate, but the best on offer.

Moses Brooke was a surly giant of a man. He complained bitterly when the destination of the journey was revealed to him. Huntingdon was further than he had ever travelled in his life before and at first, he refused the commission point blank.

Sir Richard had predicted the problem and instructed Neville Chandler, his messenger and outrider, not to disclose the real destination until he had himself arrived to lead the negotiation, yet still Brooke remained unmoved. There was no way he was going to be away from his farm for that length of time; neither would his wife ever allow it, and there was an end to the matter.

"Might I make a suggestion, Richard?" asked Nathaniel, when the discussion had reached a dead-end and Moses Brooke was preparing to return home with his wagon.

"Of course, Nathaniel. If we do not resolve this soon, we will need to ride to Huntingdon on horseback, and I for one still ache from the three days we have already spent in the saddle."

Nathaniel reached for his own saddle-sore back in sympathy. Riding long distances was a young man's pursuit, and neither he nor Easeby could claim the benefit of youth these days.

"Well, it seems to me that Mr Brooke is quite justified in his concerns; but at the same time, our own predicament remains unresolved. Mrs Brooke requires the company of Mr Brooke and we require the company of Mr Brooke's wagon. If he could be persuaded to allow us the use of it for a few days, then perhaps the matter is not without satisfactory resolution. Ned Jones is quite capable of driving a horse and cart — I have seen him do so myself on many occasions — and we have our own horses. There is no need to deprive Mrs Brooke of her husband or Mr Brooke of his steeds."

And so it was agreed. The price paid for the rental of the wagon was the same as had previously been agreed for the wagon, horses and driver. In addition, a deposit was paid covering the full value of the wagon, to be returned to Easeby upon its safe return. There was also an additional fee to cover the loss of further business to Mr Brooke whilst the vehicle was out of his possession.

All in all, the price was substantial and well beyond anything Nathaniel had budgeted for, but that could not be helped. Moses Brooke, at least, seemed fully satisfied with the transaction.

The change in circumstances also required a change of logistics. It was decided that Ned Jones would continue to Huntingdon with the main party, whilst Timothy Wellens and Benjamin Farrier returned home to Rufford with the spare horses.

Neville Chandler, on the other hand, was to remain at the White Hart and wait there for the return of the group from Huntingdon. He would then ride back to Rufford to summon the return of the stable hands to Doncaster with fresh mounts for the group's homeward journey.

***

By the time the arrangements had been made, it was close to midday as the company finally set out on the journey south. Driving the horses was Ned Jones, with Joshua Cooper sitting alongside him.

Seated behind them, on the rough, uncomfortable bench seats, were Sir Richard Easeby, Nathaniel Wright, and to Joshua's obvious delight, Rebecca Standish.

On the latter point, Sir Richard had long ago reconciled himself, though on the matter of the hard benches, he doubted he ever would.

12
Wood Walton

Sarah Wenham remained calm and unflustered as she draped a woollen shawl across her shoulders and opened the heavy wooden door to Jacob Smog and Malachai Harkiss.

"There is a man upstairs in urgent need of medical assistance," she told them, matter-of-factly. "His name is Abel Carter and if the physician is not called for immediately, there is every likelihood he will die. He has a wife at home and there are enough widows already in this parish. Unless any of your travelling companions wields a surgeon's knife as well as he does a torch, might I suggest my servant be allowed to go for him?"

This was not the welcome the magistrate had expected.

"What ails the man, madam? Is he feverish, or some accident perhaps?"

"No accident, Mr Smog. He is bleeding to death."

"Bleeding to death? How so, if not an accident?"

"I had cause to bite him, Mr Smog. He is injured, very badly."

"What new devilry is this?" exclaimed Harkiss, forcing his way past Sarah and into the house. "Seize the woman, Mr Smog. Do not allow her to escape!"

Harkiss ran to the oak-panelled staircase and upwards, taking the steps three at a time.

Sarah Wenham showed no signs of fleeing. Neither did she struggle as two townsmen stepped forward to take her by the wrists, her face maintaining a studied calmness throughout.

Outside, the torchbearers slowly fanned out to form a ring encircling the whole of Wood Walton Manor. The effect, it seemed to Sarah, was like one of the giant St Catherine's devices from Mr Babington's *Pyrotechnia*: a circle of flame blazing brightly against the dark November sky. The analogy seemed apposite in the circumstances, and she smiled to herself grimly.

"Please, Mr Smog, allow Luke to go for the physician. I have done what I can to stem the man's bleeding, but I fear it is not enough. His life may be draining away whilst your companions entertain themselves with their torchlight display."

"I suggest you do as the woman says," said Malachai Harkiss, returning quickly and grim-faced from the chamber upstairs. "It is likely we will have a murder on our hands this evening unless the physician attends the man quickly. His life-blood is already much spent. It is no ordinary, mortal injury. Bring the woman inside. We have many things to discuss, she and I."

Jane Newton and Anne Stenton sat at the top of the staircase, watching and listening with horrified fascination to the strange drama below. They pressed their bodies tightly together for comfort and warmth, sharing a single blanket draped across their shoulders.

Luke, recently returned from the village, was now with Annabel Leach, assisting the physician as he attended to Abel Carter.

Sarah Wenham was seated on a rough wooden chair in the middle of the room. She had been tied with a rope and was unable either to stand or lift her arms. The fire, coaxed back to life, burned greedily in the large, open fireplace, and the shadows of the three figures flickered and danced on the wood-panelled walls.

The voices below were clear and loud enough for the two girls to follow every word:

"My name is Malachai Harkiss, Sarah Wenham. Do you understand why I have come?" The voice was that of the tall stranger. Neither of the girls had seen the man before.

"I understand very well, sir."

"Yet, you do not seem surprised. Why is that so?"

"Because I know your business, Mr Harkiss. You have come because you are a stupid man, and those who have followed you here are more stupid still."

Their mistress's voice was clear and defiant, which cheered the girls a little and made them smile to each other, though weakly. They knew her well enough to have expected no other manner of response.

Malachai Harkiss started at the words, and it seemed for a moment as though he might step forward and strike their mistress. He breathed in deeply, regaining his composure. Jacob Smog, the third person in the room, sensed it, too, and quickly intervened:

"Come, come, Mrs Wenham! Please maintain some civility. Mr Harkiss wishes only to ask you some questions. You will do yourself no favours in this matter if you do not behave reasonably."

Sarah suddenly flashed with anger. "Civility, Mr Smog? It is civil to assemble a rabble and march on the home of an innocent woman? It is reasonable to tether her like an animal and restrain her inside her own house? Is this what passes for civility and reasonableness in your understanding, Mr Smog? Clearly, your sensibilities are very far divorced from mine!"

"Listen to her words, Mr Smog! Heed the manner of her response! See how she contrives to present herself a victim! These are the paroxysms of a cornered devil!"

"I am very sure you are more acquainted with the paroxysms of devils than am I, Mr Harkiss, but let us not jump to conclusions. The woman has the right to defend herself against the charges. That is the law.

Please, Mrs Wenham, answer the point. You do not seem surprised to see us here. Why is that?"

Sarah fixed the magistrate with a cool, penetrating stare. The disdain in her voice when she finally spoke cut deep and sharp, like a knife slicing through the pelt of a young deer.

"I am neither deaf nor blind, Mr Smog. I hear the things that are said about me and I see the suspicion on the faces of my neighbours as I go about my business. If people wish to believe such things, then there is nothing I can do. If I ignore them, my silence tacitly confirms the suspicions. If I rail against them, I behave as though I am a cornered devil, as Mr Harkiss so eloquently puts it. Either way, I am assumed guilty and Mr Harkiss becomes a wealthy man at my expense, and at the expense of many others like me. That is why I am not surprised to see you, Mr Smog."

"Your neck, Mrs Wenham! What is that mark on your neck?" The question came abruptly and out of nowhere, surprising both Sarah and Smog. Harkiss approached Sarah, lifting her chin with his fingers to examine the small, red lesion he had just noticed.

"Mark, sir? I am aware of no mark. What is the meaning of this?"

"The meaning is clear enough, madam. Each of your kind carries a similar scar. It is made by a demon as he suckles on the flesh."

"You talk in riddles, Mr Harkiss. I am not some poor peasant woman, to be terrorised by your flights of fancy. If there is a mark, it is there at Abel Carter's doing."

"Ah, yes, Mr Carter; and what was Carter doing in your chamber, Mrs Wenham? What ruse did you use to lure him there and what curse did you place upon him?"

"Curse, sir? It is I who am cursed. I am alone in the World, abandoned like prey to any man whose lust and entitlement exceeds his senses. I am the victim in this matter, Mr Harkiss, not Abel Carter!"

"You are the victim, Mrs Wenham? A man is bewitched and lured to your chamber, yet we are to believe it is you who is the victim? Tell me, madam, which of you now lies on the floor of your chamber, bleeding to death?"

There was a short silence; when it was broken, it was not by Sarah Wenham, but by the physician as he pushed his way past Jane and Anne and descended the staircase.

"Not bleeding to death, sir. The man had already lost too much blood before I arrived. He is dead."

13
The Library

Ever since she was a young child, Sarah had been an avid reader. She insisted on being taught Greek and Latin along with her brothers, falling into a tantrum when her father at first refused. But Sarah had always been a wilful child and he eventually acceded, hiring a private tutor for the purpose of teaching his precocious daughter.

Thomas Wenham had also been happy to indulge his wife's passion, and the library was his wedding gift to her; shelf upon shelf containing every volume he was able to acquire. He spent a small fortune on the project during the period of their engagement.

On their wedding night, he tied a blindfold around her eyes and led her by the hand into the room he had previously kept locked whenever she visited. On occasion, she had asked him the reason, and Thomas had smiled and told her she would find out soon enough.

Instructing her to count to three, her husband loosened the blindfold and Sarah gasped in awe at the array of books suddenly revealed to her. From Plutarch to Aeschylus, Plato to Aristotle, Anselm to Aquinas, Homer to Ovid, Chaucer to More; there were printed volumes covering every aspect of human enquiry, verse and philosophy.

She had loved her husband that night, more than she ever imagined possible, and considered herself the most blessed woman on earth. It was a love that prevailed even after his death.

***

Sarah was untied from the chair early that morning and allowed to move freely about the ground floor of her home, but always with an escort. Most of the townspeople had dispersed and returned to Huntingdon now that the woman's capture had been secured; but a small number remained to keep guard. Four roamed the perimeter of the house and two others were billeted inside, where they made themselves at home in the kitchens and the larder.

Jacob Smog was also keen to remain, overseeing the collection of "evidence" and ensuring that he alone received credit as the director of the operation. He claimed Sarah's chamber as his own and found the bed very much to his liking, once the linen had been changed and all traces of Abel Carter's blood removed.

Jane Newton, Annabel Leach and Anne Stenton were also ordered to remain at the house; under no circumstances, were they permitted to leave the grounds of the estate. Harkiss made it clear to them that they were also under suspicion, by way of association, and that they were likely to share whatever fate befell their mistress unless they repented and testified against her.

The girls were terrified, and Annabel, the most God-fearing of the three, prayed long into the night for their deliverance.

Luke Simmons alone escaped the curfew. He proved himself of too much use, running errands to the village at the behest of the occupiers.

***

"And what do we do now, Mr Harkiss?" It was noon and Jacob Smog and Malachai Harkiss stood alone in the library whilst the household went about its business. Sarah had retired to a couch in the parlour to sleep in front of the fire, accompanied by Anne and watched closely by one of the guards.

"As I told you before, the evidence against the woman is largely circumstantial. It is doubtful any jury would convict her without harder evidence, even were I to direct them to do so. She has made it clear she denies the charges and there is no other route I am permitted to take than to order a full trial. We may even need to wait for the arrival of the assizes, unless the case is sufficiently clear-cut that I might try it myself."

Not for the first time, Harkiss looked at the magistrate with something resembling disdain.

"We watch and we wait, Mr Smog. We watch through the night and if nothing transpires, we watch again tomorrow and the night after that if needs be. Eventually, the demon will reveal itself and betray its mistress. You must have patience and resolve in these matters. We do the Lord's work, you and I, and Lucifer himself will try to sow seeds of doubt in our minds. Fear not, Mr Smog; if we remain strong and trust to the mercy of God, our labours will not be in vain. Have faith!"

Jacob Smog did not at all like the idea of being kept from his bed for nights on end.

"But I am the magistrate, Mr Harkiss! Even were the matter clear-cut, which it is not, I am not permitted to give evidence against the woman. I am either witness or judge; I cannot be both!"

Harkiss could barely conceal his contempt.

"That is quite so, Mr Smog. I am familiar enough with the law of this land to understand the obstacles it contrives to place in the way of justice. Many times, I have witnessed the guilty walk free because of such technicalities of law. Always, they go on to spread their contagion, mocking us as they do so. We must be wary of such impediments, sir. It is why your assistance is of such value!"

The last word was said with such sarcasm that Smog assumed he had misheard; to a vain man like himself, it is only flattery that ever truly registers.

"Then what do you suggest, sir? It will require more than your testament alone to see the woman convicted."

"Again, you are ahead of me, Mr Smog! Your mind races forwards like a greyhound in pursuit of the hare! We need the assistance of three women of the village to act as watchers and to sit with us through the vigil of the night.

"As it happens, I have two of the names already: Ruth Carter, the widow of the dead man, and Catherine Monk, who I know to have interest in the case. The third I am happy to leave to your discretion, Mr Smog. It must be a woman of sound mind and resolute character, though. Someone who knows Sarah Wenham, but is not close enough to her to be swayed by the tricks the woman will doubtless conjure."

"Then might I suggest Elizabeth Salt, Mr Harkiss? I believe the woman's husband to be missing since yesterday. She may also have interest in the case."

"Missing, you say? Is that so? Then Elizabeth Salt it shall be, Mr Smog. I trust entirely to your judgement in the matter. I already observe it to be quite as sharp as your wit."

Once again, the sarcasm went unregistered.

14
Starlings

It was dusk on the evening following Sarah Wenham's arrest when the three women found themselves summoned to attend the house under the legal authority of Jacob Smog. Smog's jurisdiction stretched to the village of Wood Walton and beyond, and his name and face were well known in the village and the wider parishes.

They met at the church and then proceeded along Church End in the direction of the manor house. As they did so, the women became aware of a large flock of birds gathered on the fences, stone walls, tree branches and felled oak stumps lining the lane. From the shrillness of their calls and the colour of their plumage — seemingly black from a distance, but with subtle shades of turquoise, blue and green on closer inspection — they quickly identified the birds as starlings. Though not at all rare in these parts, the women had never before seen them gathered together in such number.

Still the creatures continued to come; ever growing numbers perched and watched as the women drew closer to the gates marking the entrance to Sarah Wenham's estate. They occupied every available resting place on either side of the lane, and the women quickened their pace in silence, unable to give expression to their shared sense of disquiet.

It was a mood of nervous unease, and such things defy explanation.

***

Elizabeth Salt walked at the centre of the group. It was already nearing the end of the second day since Jonah had set out for Huntingdon, and still there was no news of him. Jacob Smog confirmed that their appointment had not been kept, but what could that mean? Known always for his punctuality, and familiar as he was with the route, there could be little doubt that something ill must have befallen him. Elizabeth was beside herself with worry and was determined to find answers. She had long harboured suspicions, and those suspicions pointed to the door of Sarah Wenham.

Ruth Carter walked to the left of Elizabeth. She was the wife and now widow to Abel Carter. She had received news of her husband's death late the previous night from Luke Simmons, servant to Sarah Wenham. She listened to the boy in silence, the circumstances unclear and barely registering. The lad was clearly unable or unwilling to say too much, but in her grief, Ruth had already begun to weave the threads of a narrative in her mind.

For months, Abel had been infatuated with the woman, and it became clear that Sarah Wenham had cast some sort of spell over him. What had he been doing in her house last night and what sorcery had caused his fatal injury?

Grief and jealousy competed for primacy in Ruth's mind, and when the message came from Jacob Smog that the witch-finder had arrived and her services were called for, she seized the opportunity without question. If justice was to be done, Ruth Carter would be at the centre of it, and whatever influence she could exert, it would be to see the woman pay for her crimes.

The third member of the group was Catherine Monk, the quietest and most reserved of the three. Catherine's son Tobias, a lad of seventeen, was recently returned from the war, broken in body and spirit.

Tobias had fought at Naseby, though on the opposite side of the conflict to Thomas Wenham. He served in the parliamentary army as an infantryman. Of the events and circumstances of the battle, he said little either to Catherine or to his father, Mathias. Piecing together the fragments as best they could, they deduced that he had taken a musket-ball in the face during the very early stages of engagement. The wound had left him blinded in the right eye and with the whole of his right cheek shattered; a disfigurement he was unable to come to terms with.

Discharged and returned home to his parents, the lad now did nothing but sit and stare into the vacant space ahead of him, very rarely speaking.

Mathias was a farmhand, not a craftsman; nevertheless, he was skilful with his hands and he fashioned a leather mask for the boy, covering the whole upper-right quarter of his face. His mother wept when Tobias first wore the thing, but from the first, he would not be parted from it and wore it even when he retired to his bed.

When Sarah Wenham heard of the boy's injuries, she took great pity on him. Empathising perhaps because of her own loss, she began to visit and sit with Tobias each week, bringing him fruits from her garden and reading to him from the Bible and other books from her library. She imagined at some point that she might even teach the boy to read, when his mind had become more settled and he was able to focus more clearly.

Tobias responded little to her efforts, but he tolerated her visits, as did Catherine, who had been grateful and flattered at first for their neighbour's charity; but when the rumours about Sarah became louder and more difficult to ignore, Catherine grew wary of the association and suspicious of the woman's motives.

One morning in early October, she met Sarah at the door of the family's small cottage and told her she was grateful for all she had done but would prefer she no longer visited her son. Sarah did not seem surprised and took the news graciously, handing Catherine a basket of pomegranates to give to Tobias. The fruits were still rare in England and it was only with care and patience that Sarah had managed to cultivate a small number of the trees in a sheltered corner of her private garden. The fruits she handed to Catherine that morning, were from the first crop the trees had yielded.

It was some time shortly after Sarah's visit that day that the nightmares began. Every night thereafter, Catherine and Mathias were awoken to the sound of their son's screams. His nightgown drenched in sweat, the boy sat bolt upright in bed, his single unmasked eye wide in terror and his fists clenched so tightly together, Catherine could scarcely prise them apart.

Night after night and week after week, it was the same; and instead of getting better over time, the episodes increased in intensity and violence. The boy seemed demented with fear, as though a curse had been placed upon him.

During the summer months, news of Malachai Harkiss, and the purge of the witches across Cambridge and the eastern shires, started to arrive in the village from travellers and pedlars journeying the North Road; Catherine's mind became fixed. Maybe the things they said about Sarah Wenham were true. Something must be done to save her son from his torment, and if sorcery lay behind it, then the culprit could only be Sarah Wenham.

Her friend, Ruth Carter, had learned her letters from Edward Donne, the physician, whilst working as a housekeeper for him. One day, the two women sat together and penned a short note, addressed to Harkiss:

Sir,
    Please come to Wood Walton in the county of Huntingdon. We are much assailed by wickedness. We are afeared of a woman called Sarah Wenham and have reason to suspect her a witch.

Ruth signed the letter and Catherine added her mark. They then handed the note to a journeyman trader, passing through on his way east towards Cambridge. The women had little hope that the message would find its way to the witch-finder, but at least they had tried, and for the next few weeks they forgot all about it.

***

When the murmuration began, it was sudden and caused the women to start and then cower with fright.

    With a single, perfectly timed synchronicity, the starlings soared as one into the sky above Sarah Wenham's estate. There, they formed a black cloud that seemed to pulsate with life, like a beating human heart. Where the birds had once perched along the sides of the lane, not a single one now remained.

The cloud rose ever upwards, becoming thinner and funnel-shaped as it did so. Snaking in movement, the funnel swayed from side to side before arcing at its apex and plummeting downwards to where the three women stood. The beating of the wings was deafening as the birds swooped past them. The cloud then split in two before rising again, each half mirroring the other as though engaged in some strange courtship ritual.

The two halves swayed from left to right, sashaying around each other for maybe thirty seconds before coming together to form a single black cloud once more.

And so, the pattern began again: the tapering funnel, arcing above the heads of the women and then falling and swooping past them before splitting, dancing and finally re-merging.

Perhaps twenty times or more, the pattern was repeated in near identical fashion until, at the final arc, the birds scattered and, swooping downwards, disappeared within seconds into the trees bounding Sarah Wenham's estate.

The three women looked at each other, their eyes wide with wonder and amazement. They had seen similar things before, but never on this scale and never in a manner appearing so orchestrated and contrived. If the display had been a welcome devised for their benefit, then it was a fearsome welcome like none they had ever known before.

Without a word to each other, they passed through the gates of Sarah Wenham's estate, observed by a host of roosting starlings.

Unseen from a window on the upper storey of the house, another figure had also watched the display. He stood now deep in thought, impassively contemplating the spectacle he had just witnessed. The figure was that of Malachai Harkiss.

15
Vigil

Harkiss explained the purpose of the vigil to the three women as soon as they entered the house. Their suspicions were vindicated by everything he had seen and heard since his arrival at Wood Walton, he advised them. They had done right to send for him. As far as he was concerned, there was little doubt that the woman practised witchcraft, or that she had enlisted the three young girls to assist her.

All that remained was the final, conclusive proof. It would be the appearance of her demon. It was difficult to know in what form it would manifest — each case was different — but, eventually, it would most certainly come.

Their role was a simple enough one: to sit with him through the night and observe the woman, bearing witness to the demon's arrival and then testifying to it before a court of law. He could not know for sure when it would happen, or indeed whether it would be this night. They should prepare themselves for the possibility of a long vigil. This, they should do in the knowledge it was the Lord's work and they should take solace in that whenever their spirits wavered.

They were not to be afraid. He himself would be present throughout the long hours and he had sufficient experience of these things to protect them, if necessary, whenever the moment came. On this, they must place their trust in him entirely.

Finally, on no account were they to heed the woman's words, for she would surely try to deceive them and dissuade them of her guilt. They must remain resolute and determined, taking their lead only from him.

***

It was growing dark as the group gathered in the library of Sarah Wenham's house. Candles had been lit, filling the room with a dim half-light. The room was large, second in size only to the reception room where Harkiss and Smog had first interrogated Sarah the previous night. A small fire burned cheerlessly in the hearth, barely warming the occupants against the cold November night.

Sarah sat in the centre of the room, with Annabel, Anne and Jane each occupying a small stool at their mistress's feet. Chairs had also been placed at the four corners of the room. Elizabeth Salt, Ruth Carter and Catherine Monk occupied three of these. The fourth chair was left for Malachai Harkiss, though rarely through the night did he make use of it. Instead, he paced up and down the room, surveying and appraising the books lining the walls.

Two guards were stationed outside the library door, with instructions not to allow anyone but Harkiss and Jacob Smog to enter or leave until first light.

Smog had himself been present for a short while, but quickly became tired of the vigil and retired to Sarah's chamber to sleep, leaving instructions that he was to be awoken only if something important transpired during the night.

"You have uncommonly eclectic reading tastes, madam. Do all of these books belong to you?"

Harkiss held a volume of St Thomas Aquinas's *Summa Theologica* in his hands as he addressed the question to Sarah, turning the pages casually and only cursorily reading from it.

"Indeed, they do, Mr Harkiss. They were a gift from my husband. I draw much comfort from learning and the beauty of the written word."

"The things we love tell us what we are."

Harkiss recited the words from memory, his eyes half closed as he did so.

"Were not those the words of St Thomas, Mrs Wenham? Indeed, there is much to be learned about a man from the things he holds dear. On that, at least, I think Aquinas was right."

"To one who has faith, no explanation is necessary. To one without faith, no explanation is possible."

Sarah fired the response back instantly, with the assuredness that comes from close familiarity with a text.

"Those were also St Thomas's words, I believe, Mr Harkiss."

The quickness of the response took him by surprise. He was rarely accustomed to being out-quoted on questions of theology, and never by a woman.

"Be careful, madam! There is blasphemy in those words. It is our duty always to strive to understand the will of God, and to do so from introspection and the examination of our consciences alone. That is the essence of the contract between man and the Divine."

"There is no blasphemy, sir; just the application of logical method to the question of faith."

"Faith is not the subject of logical enquiry; nor can it be understood by the methods of papist priests and pagan philosophers, madam. We should not look to fanciful interpretations for our salvation; especially those taken from the mouths of idolaters, wearing baubles and robes."

"I am sure on this, as on all matters, you are correct, Mr Harkiss. It seems to me that on matters of fanciful interpretation, I could do worse than defer to you."

"Silence, woman! You test my patience too often. Remember why you are here! I advise your time would be better spent in silent reflection rather than malicious wordplay."

Harkiss looked around him, taking in once again the sheer volume of books adorning the room.

"I know you for what you are, Sarah Wenham. I have met many of your kind, and the clever words of Aristotle and Aquinas will not save your mortal soul from retribution. Only the Lord our father, in his infinite wisdom, can do that."

"I am sure St Thomas would admit the possibility of fallibility in his method, Mr Harkiss. Perhaps that kind of humility is something you might also learn."

There was a gasp from the other occupants of the room as Harkiss strode forward, striking Sarah powerfully across the face and forcing her neck backwards and to the side. There, she held it quite still, defiantly waiting for a second blow to come. Harkiss raised his hand, preparing to deliver it, but then hesitated, eventually allowing his hand to fall back to his side.

"Be silent, madam! You have the devil's tongue in your head. One more word, and I will cut the thing from your mouth."

Annabel began to sob uncontrollably and Anne and Jane tried gently to comfort her, though they themselves had tears in their eyes. Catherine and Elizabeth, who had leaped instantly to their feet as the blow was delivered, slowly retook their seats, a look of fear passing fleetingly between them as they did so.

Only Ruth Carter looked on impassively, the faint trace of a smile on her face. It was a smile of silent satisfaction.

***

The night was a long and uncomfortable one. The fire had long since burned low, and only once did Harkiss allow Annabel to add more logs to it, bringing short respite from the bitter cold. The three girls dozed fitfully on the cold wooden floor, whilst Sarah could find only a minute or two's slumber at a time. The chair was hard and hurting her back and it was impossible to find a comfortable position for more than a few minutes. She sat with her fingers resting on Annabel's head. The girl felt feverish to the touch.

In three corners of the room, Elizabeth Salt, Ruth Carter and Catherine Monk were nodding, their chins falling and coming to rest on their chests. Occasionally, they woke themselves with a start and rubbed their eyes, focusing again on the woman seated in the centre of the room; but their eyes quickly became heavy again and their heads once more began to fall.

Only Malachai Harkiss remained fully awake throughout the night. He continued to pace up and down the room, the even pattern of his steps rhythmically lulling the women further into sleep. Through the large window running the full length of the library wall — an extravagant luxury, speaking loudly the extent of

Thomas Wenham's wealth — the darkness had deepened to its blackest hue, signifying that the hour before dawn had arrived. All was silent, save for the occasional screech of a barn owl. There was no beauty in its call, just the shrill, murderous siren of a predator in search of prey.

When Harkiss first heard it, the owl seemed some distance away and the sound barely perceptible; but now it drew closer and the screeching grew louder and more persistent. He strode slowly to the window, cupping his hands against the latticed glass to see more clearly.

At first there appeared to be nothing, but then he saw it: a small white shape swooping and diving just yards from the house. The bird seemed distressed in some way, its flight erratic and frenzied, and Harkiss watched it with silent fascination.

Sarah also heard the animal and turned her head to look, though she could see little from her seated position in the middle of the room. Elizabeth, Ruth and Catherine also stirred.

"What is it, sir?" asked Elizabeth, standing and walking towards the window. "An owl, perhaps?"

Ruth and Catherine also stood, following her.

"Yes, it is an owl. An unholy creature: watch how it dives and swoops. It is seeking something."

"I cannot see it, sir. Please show me…"

Elizabeth did not have time to finish the sentence. With an almighty thud, the creature flew at the glass, cracking a single pane and then falling to the ground outside, where it lay, flailing and flapping its wings.

Everybody inside the library started at the force of the collision. Annabel and Jane both screamed in fright, awoken abruptly from their sleep.

"Have pity on the poor creature, Mr Harkiss!" cried Sarah Wenham, getting to her feet. "Please, go outside and see what can be done for it. It may be just stunned or badly injured. Help the poor thing, sir!"

Harkiss turned to face her, a look of triumph on his face. "I will do no such thing, madam. It has come. The thing is surely your demon, returning to its mistress."

Part Two
The Trial

16
Dragoon

Sir Richard Easeby and his party were nearing the town of Newark, little more than a day and a half from Huntingdon, when they noticed a rider approaching them at speed. The rider was headed north, dressed in military uniform. When at last he reached them, Sir Richard recognised him as the dragoon who had first brought Cromwell's message to Rufford.

"Greetings, Corporal, our paths cross again! What news do you have?"

"Through design rather than accident, Sir Richard, I rode north hoping to intercept you. I come directly from Huntingdon, where your services are urgently needed. The woman is arrested and awaiting trial in the town."

"And what of your commander, Corporal? Did he receive my response? What action has he taken on the woman's behalf?"

The dragoon looked warily at Easeby's companions. "By your leave, Sir Richard, I think these things are best discussed in private. There is much to tell and it is sensitive in nature. I have my orders."

"Very well, Corporal. Everybody here has some awareness of the task, but I will not test the matter further; time is short. Ned, Joshua, Becky; please stay with the wagon. Nathaniel, you may join us."

"Your ears only, Sir Richard, if you please."

A flash of anger passed across Easeby's face.

"Corporal, Nathaniel is my clerk and trusted assistant in all matters. His discretion is beyond reproach and his knowledge of law considerable. On this, I am insistent. Nathaniel will join us to hear what you have to say. Those are my terms."

The dragoon hesitated, but sensing Easeby's resolve, finally acceded.

"Very well, sir. Please, let us walk a while. My back is sore from riding and it would be good to stretch my legs!"

When they were at last some distance from the wagon, the dragoon relaxed a little and began to talk.

"I reached Commander Cromwell with your reply just over a week ago, Sir Richard. He was greatly relieved to receive it and bids me convey his gratitude. The war takes much out of him, I think."

"A war of his own making, Corporal. Things did not need to come to this. Your master knows very well my views on the matter. It is why he and I are no longer on civil terms, though we were once very great friends."

"I urge you to be careful, Sir Richard! I am asked only to convey messages to you, and this is what I do. Remember, though, I am also a soldier in the parliamentary army. It is the king that caused this war, not Fairfax or Cromwell or any of those on our side."

"Wars are never entirely the fault of one side, Corporal. A man cannot wrestle by himself or strike up an argument in an empty room. I support the cause, but not the means. On this Cromwell and I have long differed; that is all. But we are not here to discuss politics, you and I. Please, proceed with your news."

"As you say, Sir Richard, I have not ridden these miles to parlay with you on politics. The situation is grave and we do not have the time, even if we had the inclination.

"Commander Cromwell heeded your request and wrote at once to the magistrate of the town — a man called Jacob Smog — telling him of your imminent arrival and ordering him to stay the woman's trial until you got there. I took the message to Huntingdon myself and was asked to report back immediately on how the message was received."

"And how was the message received, Corporal?"

"Badly, Sir Richard. This Jacob Smog is a conceited little man, full of his own self-importance. Forgive me for speaking bluntly, but that is the truth of the matter. He raged like a madman when he read the message. He told me the commander no longer has any jurisdiction in the town and no right to interfere in its legal affairs. He intends to proceed with the trial immediately."

"That is not possible," said Nathaniel Wright, who had been listening to the exchange with great interest. "The charge is a capital offence and must be referred to the assizes for trial. The woman cannot be tried for the crime in a magistrate's court. This Jacob Smog grievously exceeds his authority."

"In normal times, you would be right, Nathaniel; but these are not normal times," replied Easeby. "The assizes are much interrupted because of the war, and their progress through some of the worst-hit shires has stalled completely. In clear-cut cases, magistrates have been given latitude to try and sentence the accused themselves. It is seen as a way of relieving the burden on the courts and clearing the prison-houses."

"But that is madness, Richard! It means a woman may hang on the authority of a junior justice of the peace."

"Indeed so, Nathaniel, but this whole war is madness; the crime of witchcraft is madness; the legally sanctioned killing of one human being by another is madness. We live in an age replete with madness, Nathaniel, and reason and goodwill are in precious short supply."

"I fear there is yet more bad news, Sir Richard," continued the dragoon. "The witch-finder — this Malachai Harkiss — was with the magistrate when I delivered the message. I fear he holds great sway over him and seeks to both flatter and cajole him into doing his bidding. He is a formidable man, Sir Richard; that much was obvious to me. He has something unsettling about him."

"What do you mean by 'unsettling', Corporal?"

The dragoon hesitated, as though struggling to find the right words.

"I do not know how better to describe it; he has a certain presence, sir. He does not say much, but when he does speak, it is always with an authority that makes men take notice. It is not just Sarah Wenham who is now accused. Three of her servants — young girls — have been locked up and are to stand trial with her. Jacob Smog appears to be in thrall to the man."

"This is grievous news indeed, Corporal. What are the charges against the girls?"

"The same as their mistress, sir. They are accused of witchcraft. He believes them to be accomplices to Sarah Wenham. All four have been taken to the prison-house in the town to await trial."

Easeby stood silently for a while, as though gathering his thoughts. Shielding his eyes from the late autumnal sun, he stared down the length of the Great North Road, which seemed to stretch interminably ahead of them. Nathaniel and the dragoon followed the direction of his gaze.

Away to the side, Rebecca Standish could be seen, gathering wild herbs from the side of the road, perhaps even within earshot of the conversation.

At last, Easeby spoke.

"Has a date been set for the trial, Corporal?"

"It has, Sir Richard. I rode at haste from Huntingdon, hoping to find you, for that reason. The court meets the day after tomorrow."

17
Rebecca

The dragoon insisted on riding back with them as far as Huntingdon to ensure nothing further delayed their journey. On occasion, he grew impatient with the rate of progress and urged Ned to quicken the pace. The boy reluctantly acquiesced. He was concerned for the horses and heeded the instruction only for a few minutes before relaxing the reins again, allowing the beasts to return to their normal walking pace.

Conversation between Ned and Joshua Cooper had long-since become exhausted, and they now rode side by side in silence at the front of the wagon.

Behind them, sheltering beneath the canopy, the passengers bumped and jolted on their makeshift benches as the wagon struggled monotonously forward along the badly rutted road.

Sir Richard Easeby had been studying Rebecca for some time and he eventually rose from his place alongside Nathaniel and moved across to sit with the girl. After a few moments, he began to speak to her in a hushed tone:

"I believe you were eavesdropping on our conversation with the corporal, Becky. I asked you to stay with the wagon."

Becky blushed a bright scarlet. "I was not eavesdropping, sir! I was gathering some bitter cress from the side of the road. I like the taste; that is all. It is peppery and good in potage."

"It is entirely possible to gather herbs and listen at the same time, Becky. Do not be defensive; I am not angry with you. Did you hear the conversation? Be truthful with me, please. That is all I ask."

"I heard some of it, sir, yes. I am sorry."

Easeby smiled and nodded. "Good, that's as I thought. And tell me, Becky, what did you make of what you heard?"

"I don't know what to say, sir. It is not my place to speak of it."

"It is your place, Becky, because I have asked you the question. What did you make of the corporal's news?"

Rebecca Standish hesitated, unsure of how much she should say.

"Well, sir, I was thinking of those poor girls who have been arrested with their mistress."

"What of them, Becky?" Sir Richard seemed genuinely interested in what she had to say, and the girl began to relax a little.

"I was thinking how terrified they must be, sir. It seems to me that if they are innocent of the crime, it must be a horrible experience for them. I mean, being locked up in a prison-house and not even knowing why you are there. Having some stranger come along and say such horrible things about you when you have done nothing wrong, and then some magistrate telling you that you are to stand trial and that you'll probably hang! I can't imagine how that would make me feel, sir!"

Easeby nodded and continued to study the girl closely.

"But I am asking you to imagine, Becky. Put yourself in their shoes, just for a moment. How would you feel?"

"Well, at first, sir, I'd be properly terrified, like I said. I wouldn't want to talk to nobody or eat or anything."

"I think you are right, Becky. That is exactly how you would feel at first, but what then? What after the initial shock had gone? What would you feel then?"

"Well, I don't really know, sir. I suppose I would begin to feel angry and cross and think everything was unfair."

"And what if it wasn't just you, Becky? What if there were other people who had also been accused of the same things? How would you feel about them?"

"That depends, I suppose, sir. If I knew them very well, I suppose I'd feel sorry for them, too."

"And if you didn't know them so well? If they were people you just worked with, and you hadn't known them for very long?"

"That would be different, sir. I suppose I might begin to wonder whether they had done something wrong and I was now getting the blame for it. That would make me feel really angry."

"And if you were really scared and really angry, what might you then do, Becky? Tell me, please. You are of an age with them. I'm an old man, at least to your eyes, and my mind would undoubtedly work differently to yours in similar circumstances. Tell me what you might do."

"Well, sir, I reckon I'd know that I was innocent and that would make me suspicious of them. I'd probably do anything to make it look like they were guilty and I wasn't if I thought that would save me."

"Quite so, Becky. Do anything or say anything. Might you even say things that weren't true?"

"Like what, sir? I'm not a liar!"

"Nobody is saying you are, Becky, but I am asking you to imagine yourself in a situation where you are very angry and very scared and desperate to save yourself. What then?"

Becky considered the question carefully for a long time.

"Well, sir, I suppose if I knew for a fact that I was innocent, but there was a chance the others were guilty, I might begin to think about some of the things I'd seen and well — you know — they might seem different to me then. I might begin to imagine things, if you understand me? Read things into what I had actually seen that I hadn't thought of at first."

"So, not lie exactly, but interpret things in a different way? Is that what you mean?"

"Yes, sir, exactly that. And then I'd probably tell somebody about those things if I thought it might save me."

Easeby smiled and nodded, before changing the subject.

"And what do you make of the corporal, Becky? Did his story make sense to you?"

"Well, it mostly seemed to make sense, sir."

"Mostly, Becky? Which bits didn't make sense?"

Again, Becky hesitated, unsure of how much she should say; but it was clear Sir Richard was not playing games with her. The question seemed genuine enough.

"Well, sir, it's not so much what he did say, but what he didn't say, if you know what I mean?"

"I think so, Becky, but explain it to me."

"Like when he said he rode straight here from Huntingdon as soon as he found out when the trial was going to be. That didn't make sense."

"Why not, Becky? What was wrong with it?"

"Well, sir, earlier he said that this Commander Cromwell had asked him to pass on his thanks to you, but how could he have known the corporal was going to see you? His errand was just to deliver a message to the magistrate and then report straight back to him. It was only when the corporal found out how soon the trial was going to be held that he decided to try to find you. Those weren't his orders. There must have been something else that he didn't tell you."

Not for the first time in their short acquaintance, Easeby arched his eyebrows and regarded Becky with a look of surprised admiration.

"You think somebody is playing me for a game, Becky?"

"I don't know about that, sir. It just didn't make sense. That's all."

"Quite so, Miss Standish. You have an uncommonly clever mind. I am glad you decided to come along."

18
The Summons

Isaiah Felt was a wealthy man. He had made his fortune a long time ago, investing in adventurous schemes to drain tracts of local fenland. The risks had been substantial and he had needed to borrow much of the money, but the rewards had proved greater still. Large grants of the resulting farmland were signed over to him as a return on his investment. These, he immediately broke up into smaller plots, renting them out to local tenant farmers at fiercely exorbitant rates.

For the most part, the harvests had been good during the intervening years and the tenants could just about afford the rents and earn a meagre living for themselves on top. When the harvests failed, however, things were very different, and the harvest this year had been particularly bad.

Already, Felt had begun to receive pleas for forbearance from many of his tenants. These, he very rarely entertained, of course, having grown used to the handsome income he now enjoyed.

There was only one other landowner in the district of Wood Walton whose holdings matched those of Isaiah Felt in size, and that had been Thomas Wenham.

Unlike Felt, Wenham's estates had been inherited from his father. They occupied the only sizeable plot of land in the area not to have been reclaimed from the fens. It was prize agricultural land, and Felt had long coveted it.

When Wenham died earlier that year, Felt had seen an opportunity. He was growing old, and a life dedicated to business affairs meant that he had never quite got round to the question of finding a wife. Nearing the age of sixty, he now found his mind increasingly turned to the matter of inheritance. He had no heir and he was damned if his lands were going to fall to the Crown on his death, or to whatever authority substituted the Crown when this war was finally over.

Sarah Wenham was a handsome woman, of that there could be no argument, and Felt stumbled on the idea of dispatching two birds with a single stone. By marrying the widow, he would acquire the means of procuring an heir, whilst at the same time combining the two estates as one. In this way, he would become the master of one of the largest landholdings in the whole of Huntingdonshire and substantially add to his already considerable wealth.

It was clear the woman would struggle to maintain her estates without experience or male guidance, and there was no man more experienced or more willing to guide than Isaiah Felt.

The solution was so obviously beneficial to both of them, it never once occurred to him that she would say no; yet say no she did.

Spurned, insulted and aggrieved, Isaiah Felt had hated the woman from that moment on. He retired to his study following the rebuttal of his proposal and there, over a period of many days, he plotted another route.

***

It was a cold, dank day in mid-November and Felt was in his study, going through his accounts for the second time that morning. Yet more tenants had defaulted on their rents and his temper grew increasingly frayed. No matter how many times he totalled the figures, they continued to show the same result: an ever-expanding column of outstanding debtors.

Growing impatient with the task, he snapped the ledger shut with a heavy thud and turned his attention instead to the letter, recently placed on his desk by his clerk. Turning the thing in his hands, he inspected the magistrate's seal carefully through his eyeglasses, before taking a knife and slicing it through.

Unfolding the single sheet, he laid it on his desk and holding the eyeglasses an inch or two from the page, he began to read:

Under pain of prosecution, the persons here named are required to attend the magistrate's court in the town of Huntingdon on the 18th day of this month of November 1645, that day being Saturday.

They are summonsed to bear testimony in the case of Sarah Wenham of this shire and three of her housemaids, namely Jane Newton, Annabel Leach and Anne Stenton, who are charged with most grievous acts of witchcraft and murder.

The persons hereby summonsed and noted as such in the court records being:

Malachai Harkiss esq

Isaiah Felt esq

Edward Donne, Dr

Catherine Monk

Elizabeth Salt

Ruth Carter

Proceedings commence at nine o'clock sharp and tardiness will not be tolerated.

By order of Jacob Smog,

Magistrate.

Felt read the summons through for the third time, before refolding it and placing it in the drawer of his bureau. He had known, of course, that Harkiss had come to Wood Walton. He witnessed the procession of torches through the village with his own eyes and deduced that the letter he had written to the witch-finder many weeks ago had been received and acted upon.

What surprised him, though, was the speed with which events now seemed to be unfurling. It was just ten days since he had witnessed the crowd marching to Sarah Wenham's home and already the case had been passed to trial. Why the haste? It was, of course, entirely to his benefit that things should be moving at pace, but Isaiah Felt was a man who liked to feel in control of events, and he was beginning to doubt that he still retained control over this particular matter.

That made him uneasy as he stood and paced about the room.

The other perplexing part of the summons was the reference to murder; what murder? He had mentioned nothing of murder in his letter to Harkiss, nor did he raise the question of the three house-servants who had also been charged, according to the summons.

For a moment, he experienced a brief sensation, perhaps recognisable as a pricking of his conscience. How might he feel if three innocent girls were to die?

He had no belief in witchcraft, of course. It was all superstitious nonsense; but enough people did believe for the fate of the girls to be cast in considerable doubt. It was that very superstition that informed the whole basis of his plan.

At last, he ceased his pacing. Damn the woman to hell! It was unfortunate and unplanned, but if there were to be collateral victims, they could not be blamed on him. None of these things would have been necessary, had the woman consented to be his wife. The fault was entirely hers, and if they hanged, he would not have any of their blood on his hands.

The fault would lie with Sarah Wenham alone.

19
The Pricking

The events at Wood Walton moved swiftly following the vigil and the appearance of the demon.

For the second time in as many days, the physician, Edward Donne, was called to the house of Sarah Wenham. There, in his presence, each of the four accused women was ordered to strip and their bodies carefully inspected by Harkiss.

Jacob Smog, awoken from his sleep, was also present to oversee the legality of the proceedings. If there was also a lascivious look in his eyes on occasion, then he was careful to ensure that no one noticed.

Every last birth-mark, mole and scar were recorded in exact detail by the physician, its precise location indicated and sketched in a folio under the instruction of the witch-finder. A large pin was then employed to prick at the marks. Those that immediately yielded blood were left blank in the records, whilst those that did not were underscored and coded with a star next to the description.

Anne, Jane and Annabel, terrified and full of shame, shivered with cold and fear throughout the examination. Only Sarah Wenham managed to maintain her composure and dignity throughout the proceedings, fixing the physician with an icy stare as he dutifully recorded the marks on her body.

"Which part of your oath is served by this charade, Doctor? What area of science are you seeking to advance?"

"I do only as I have been instructed by the magistrate, Mrs Wenham. I take no joy in the task."

"I do not believe the same can be said of your colleagues, sir."

"Be silent, woman!" hissed Malachai Harkiss. "With each protestation, you reveal your nature more clearly."

"You are correct, sir! My protestations reveal my nature precisely, just as this specious examination reveals yours."

"Silence, woman! Mr Donne, make note of this mark in the greatest detail, if you please. The lesion on her neck has grown and darkened since I first noticed it."

With his back to the physician, Harkiss took the pin and inserted it into the lesion, causing Sarah to flinch. As he removed it, a small drop of blood appeared on the tip, which he quickly wiped on his sleeve.

"Does the lesion bleed, Mr Harkiss?" asked Jacob Smog.

"No, Mr Smog, it does not. Mark it with a star in the records, please, Dr Donne."

***

The prison-house in Huntingdon occupied a small stone building, adjacent to the courthouse. The first two floors contained the jailor's quarters and a number of small interview rooms, whilst the cells themselves were housed in the basement, which could be reached directly from the courthouse via a short, dimly lit tunnel.

The cells were small, cold and damp and completely devoid of natural light save for a small half-window high up, which opened out at street level. The windows were heavily barred and offered the prisoners little by way of sunlight. When it rained heavily, water would flow in from the street above and cascade down the walls, sometimes causing the cells to flood, so that the occupants found themselves ankle-deep in foul-smelling water.

On occasion, children would lie on their stomachs in the street and peer down into the darkness below, hoping to catch sight of the wretched occupants; but there was rarely anything of note to be seen.

It was a place of despair, known locally as "The Pits".

***

On conclusion of the examination at Wood Walton, the four women were driven the short distance to Huntingdon in a cart. Anne, Annabel and Jane were placed in a cell together, whilst Sarah was allowed the adjacent cell to herself.

To their surprise, the jailor, a tall, sinewy man called Adam Crook, they found to be uncommonly kind and courteous. He gave them each a small loaf of bread to eat from the prison stores and fresh water from the well. These small acts of kindness gave them some comfort, especially the three girls, though when the cell doors were closed behind them, they found themselves squinting in the bare half-light and the reality of their situation hit them hard.

Annabel lay down immediately on the hard wooden planks, lifted just inches from the floor and serving as her bed. She refused to be consoled by Jane and Anne, though they tried repeatedly. Taking turns to sit beside her, they brushed her hair from her face and urged her to have courage; but still the girl sobbed uncontrollably.

Her weeping continued long into the afternoon. The day began to wane, and what little light there was, grew dimmer until it disappeared completely. Eventually, Annabel grew quiet and Jane and Anne thought her asleep.

In the absolute darkness, their sense of hearing became sharper and every sound from the street above them echoed loudly on the bare walls.

They could also hear the movements from their mistress's cell, next door. Her feet were pacing the cold, stone floor; walking up and down the length of the room and occasionally stopping for a short while, before beginning again. The three girls lay each on their own bed, a woollen blanket pulled tightly to their chins as they shivered against the cold.

Eventually, the pacing stopped and after a few seconds, they heard the faint sound of Sarah's voice. She seemed to be incanting in a language they did not understand:

Pater noster in caelis;
Sanctificetur nomen tuum,
Adveniat regnum tuum;
Fiat voluntas tua,
in terris sicut in caelis.
Panem nostrum quotidianum da nobis hodie.
Et dimitte nobis peccata nostra
Sicut nos remittimus delinquentibus contra nos peccatum
Ne nos inducas in temptationem
sed libera nos a malo.
Quia tuum est regnum, et potestas,
et gloria,
aeternus et umquam.

"What is that?" whispered Anne.

"I don't know for sure," replied Jane. "I think it might be the Lord's Prayer in the old language. I have only heard it spoken like that a few times before. We used to have a tutor when I was very young and he said those words to us but told us we mustn't tell anybody he'd done so. It was a secret between us."

"Why not? Why weren't you allowed to say anything?"

"He said that some people didn't like it and that we could get into a lot of trouble. He liked it, though, and I liked him."

"The mistress shouldn't be saying it like that then; not if there are lots of people who don't like it. She'll get herself into even more trouble!"

"I know, Anne. It sounds nice, though, doesn't it?" replied Jane. "It's prettier than in English, somehow."

"Perhaps, but she's in enough trouble already, and so are we. Why does she have to do that? I wish she wouldn't!"

Annabel, who had been silent until then, stirred in her bed. She had been listening carefully to what the others had been saying.

"I know why," she whispered. "It's because she's a witch, that's why."

20
Opening Address

Saturday morning dawned cold and crisp. The first frost
of the late autumn season had blanketed the fields and
pastureland in a gossamer-white sheen, like a gown
draped carefully across a bride's bed on the morning of
her wedding. A single black crow perched high on the
sill of the magistrate's chamber window, squawking
and flapping its huge wings as Jacob Smog relieved
himself into his piss-pot.

Today promised to be a memorable day, and the
magistrate was up and about his business early. He
breakfasted alone in his room on eggs and gammon,
washed down with claret wine, before dressing himself
in his favourite black winter robe. The gown was lined
with miniver fur and had cost the court exchequer a
small fortune. Strictly speaking, he was not of sufficient
rank to wear such a garment, but Jacob Smog was never
one to allow such things to stand in the way of an
ostentatious display of authority.

Already, he had resolved to commission a portrait
of himself wearing the robe as soon as this case had
concluded. The work — 'Jacob Smog, Magistrate and
Deliverer of Huntingdon' — would take pride of place

in the courthouse, where it would be admired and revered for generations to come.

Posterity would be less kind to Malachai Harkiss, of course. The witch-finder would be dismissed from memory as a minor player soon enough, disappearing back to wherever he came from with nothing but the twenty shillings owed to him in his purse.

Manningtree, did he say? Smog had never even heard of the place!

Nor did Jacob Smog intend the proceedings to be lengthy. The witnesses were few in number and their testimony straightforward. The evidence, though unorthodox, was sufficiently compelling to ensure a swift conviction in the current mood; and whilst Sarah Wenham had shown herself sufficiently articulate to weave a few distractions into proceedings, Smog was not without the occasional rhetorical flourish of his own.

With a fair wind, the thing should be done and dusted by mid-afternoon. To be on the safe side, he had acceded to Harkiss's request that the witch-finder be allowed to lead the cross-examination himself. The man was not at all to Smog's tastes, but there could be little doubt he was charismatic and had a way of influencing people, which could only prove useful in a court of law.

Better still, Smog received notice late last evening that one of the girls, Annabel Leach, had signalled her willingness to give evidence against her mistress in return for her own life. That would not only expedite matters, but had the advantage of allowing Smog the chance to show his magnanimous side. The people always loved that kind of thing, and he had long since learned that the courtroom was a theatre where performance was everything.

All in all, it was in an entirely satisfactory frame of mind that Jacob Smog left his house and made his way the short distance to the courthouse. If, at one point on the journey, a young child ran up behind him and made crude gestures behind his back to the merriment of his fellows, it was not something that Smog noticed.

***

The courtroom was packed to the rafters as the four women were led through the short tunnel from the prison-house and into the dock. Every available seat in the public gallery had been claimed as soon as the doors were opened, and the late arrivals now crowded into any standing space they could claim. Many were left standing outside, disappointed.

The mood was one of feverish excitement, which did not altogether displease the magistrate. There was nothing Jacob Smog enjoyed more than an audience, and there was no better audience than a febrile one. He ordered the courtroom doors to be left ajar so that those outside could listen to proceedings. As a result, a bitter cold filled the room, causing those not benefiting from a fur-lined robe to shiver and complain.

"Court rise!"

There was a loud shuffling of feet as all present obeyed the barked instruction. Jacob Smog waited a few moments, as was his custom, before entering from a door to the rear of the court and taking his seat. The delay was for effect, of course; a technique he had honed over many years of practice. It was always important to maintain a sense of theatre, and there should never be any doubt as to the principal actor in these proceedings.

Having rehearsed his opening address conscientiously the previous evening, he was determined to enjoy the moment fully. Surveying the packed courtroom slowly and deliberately until satisfied that every eye in the place was focused on him, he began:

"Gentlemen of the jury, these are dark times and we are forced to confront them with nothing but our fortitude to defend us. The women you see before you are charged with the most grievous crimes imaginable. They are crimes against nature, against God and against the laws of this land, both sacred and temporal. They are charges that, if proven, can carry only one sentence; that of death."

There was a buzz of excitement and whispered conversation at that point. Smog allowed it to die down of its own course before he continued:

"You will hear many things today that will stretch the very limits of your understanding. It is not your role to pre-judge these things, but to rely solely on the evidence presented before you; that is the oath you have sworn to on appointment to this jury. If convicted, the women can do you no harm, and it remains 'if' until you have determined the matter conclusively. In the event of their conviction, the sentence will be executed at speed and without delay; on that you have my word."

Jane and Anne glanced nervously at each other at that point, the eyes of each reflecting the panic of the other. Annabel's eyes remained firmly fixed to the floor.

"Three of these women are charged with facilitating and concealing acts of maleficia under instruction of their mistress, Sarah Wenham. They are puppets in a play of her devising, but that does not diminish the charges against them or the consequences of their guilt should the charges be proven.

Their fate, gentlemen of the jury, is inextricably tied to that of their mistress. It is Sarah Wenham who is alleged to be the orchestrator of these things. It is she who is the puppeteer, and you should labour under no illusion as to the heinousness of the crimes of which she is accused."

At this point, Jacob Smog produced a rolled parchment from the folds of his gown. He proceeded to unroll it and began to read the contents out loud, as though seeing the words for the first time.

"The charges against you are four-fold, madam." He now addressed Sarah directly. Her eyes remained fixed on his throughout and at no point did she show concern or fear. Rather, she lifted her chin slightly, holding her head high and signalling her defiance.

"On the first count, it is alleged that you bewitched and lured Abel Carter of the village of Wood Walton to your chamber and there contrived his murder by means of emasculation. How do you plead to the charge, madam?"

"Not guilty, Mr Smog."

"You will address me as 'sir' or 'your honour' in this place, if you please, madam; take note of that, if you will. On the second count, it is alleged that you bewitched Tobias Monk of the village of Wood Walton, providing him with charmed fruits from your garden and causing him to become deranged and demented of mind. In that condition, he remains to this day. On this charge, how do you plead?"

"Not guilty, Mr Smog, your honour."

There was a murmur of laughter at that point, causing Smog's face to flush a dangerous violet.

"Silence in court! It is JUST 'your honour', madam! You will show me my due respect!"

"Due respect indeed, Mr Smog. I believe I was doing precisely that."

The laughter this time was louder and more prolonged.

"SILENCE IN COURT!" Jacob Smog sensed he was beginning to lose control, and that was not at all in the script he had prepared.

"One more sign of insolence, madam, and I will hold you in contempt of this court, for which the punishment is grave!"

"Grave, sir? And will that grave punishment come before or after you have hanged me, Mr Smog?"

This time, the laughter was tumultuous. Even Jane and Anne allowed themselves the faint traces of a smile.

"Madam, you will not obstruct the business of this court with your clever wordplay. Answer to the charges only!" Smog adjusted the sleeves of his gown before continuing:

"On the third count, it is alleged that you caused the failure of crops by the use of witchcraft with the aim of personal profit, thereby causing depravation and hunger to the people of these parishes. How do you plead?"

This time, Sarah sensed the mood changed and all heads were turned to look at her. This was a matter affecting many in the courtroom and not something to be joked about.

"Not guilty, sir."

Smog sat upright, relieved that decorum had been restored.

"Good. Much better. On the fourth and final count, it is alleged that you corrupted the girls standing with you in the dock. You enlisted their help in perpetrating these acts of witchcraft. How do you plead, madam?"

"I am innocent of the charge, sir, as are they."

"Gentlemen of the jury, you have heard the pleas of Mrs Wenham. She has also pleaded the innocence of the girls who stand accused with her. I can tell you now that one of those girls has signalled her intention to plead guilty and will be called to give evidence against Mrs Wenham. The pleas of all three girls will be recorded formally only after the fate of their mistress is decided, to encourage the others to reflect carefully before doing so. Only in that way may they avail themselves of whatever clemency the court may determine."

There was a murmur amongst the crowd as the magistrate spoke those words. Smog knew that the reference to clemency would play well with the public, even if he had no intention whatsoever of adhering to it. Anne and Jane looked at each other and then at Annabel, who was still staring at the floor.

"Annabel! How could you?" whispered Jane.

"I will have silence in this court!" Jacob Smog intoned threateningly, confident now that his authority had been fully restored.

"The case for the prosecution will be put to you by Mr Malachai Harkiss of the county of Essex, and he will cross-examine each of the presented witnesses. Listen carefully to their testimony, gentlemen of the jury. Justice will depend on it.

"Mrs Wenham, I understand you will be providing your own defence and intend to cross-examine the witnesses on your own behalf. Is that the case?"

"That is so, sir, yes. Nobody else has been made available to me."

At that point, the affirmation was immediately contradicted by a new voice, adding itself to the proceedings:

"Actually, that is not the case, sir. With her leave, I will be representing the woman; the girls also."

The interruption came from an unexpected source. A man of middling age had jostled his way to the front of the courtroom and now stood at the bar, from where he carefully studied the magistrate in an altogether disconcerting manner. Jacob Smog did not recognise the man at all.

"And who in the name of damnation are you, sir?"

"My name is Sir Richard Easeby. I am master of Rufford Hall in the county of Lancashire. I understand you were advised to expect my arrival. Forgive me the delay; it has been a long journey and these are difficult times in which to travel at speed."

21
Adjournment

Nathaniel Wright slowly made his way through the scrum of bodies to stand next to Sir Richard at the bar of the court. The entrance of the two arrivals caused such a stir that people were now standing in the gallery to get a better look, and a loud atmosphere of excitement threatened to overwhelm the proceedings completely.

"Silence! Silence! I will have order in this courtroom!"

Jacob Smog was bellowing at the top of his voice, his face crimson with rage.

"What is the meaning of this intrusion, sir? This is a courtroom, not a summer fair!"

Sir Richard bowed deeply.

"Indeed not, sir, and again I beg your forgiveness. The manner of my entrance was not as I intended, but your sergeant-at-arms seemed somewhat reluctant to pass you the news of our arrival. I can assure you, it is not my custom to barge my way into a courtroom in this way, but you will understand this is a matter of considerable urgency. There are lives at stake and I have been asked to defend the charges against these four women in accordance with the law. That is all."

"I believe I made myself quite clear to Master Cromwell's messenger, sir! He has no jurisdiction in this town. It is my place to decide what does and does not take place within this courtroom."

There was a further flurry of excitement at the mention of Cromwell's name, and Smog was once again required to call for silence. Eventually, the noise subsided sufficiently for Sir Richard to respond.

"You are correct, sir, but the extent or otherwise of his jurisdiction is of no interest to me whatsoever. You can rest assured that I would not have travelled these many miles had it been simply to represent Master Cromwell in this place. Under the laws of this land, these women have the right to legal representation. If they consent to it, I place my services, and those of my clerk here, at their disposal."

"Only if I consent to it, sir!"

"With the greatest possible respect, your honour, the decision is not yours; nor is it Oliver Cromwell's, come to that. It is theirs alone."

This was not at all in Jacob Smog's plans for the day. The matter was to have been settled quickly and with minimum resistance, notwithstanding the occasional barb from the tongue of Sarah Wenham. The appointment of defence counsel would only serve to delay proceedings. There was also something in the deportment of this Sir Richard Easeby that worried Smog: an air of controlled assuredness that came with knowledge and experience of such matters. It did not bode well.

"Sir, your manner of arrival and the interruption of this court's business has been noted and I fully intend to charge you with contempt as soon as this case has concluded. On the matter of your proposal, however, I do see fit to make your offer available to the women in the interests of justice."

"With respect, the matter is not one of court discretion; it is the law," replied Easeby.

"I will not be lectured on the subject of the law in my own courtroom, sir! You are here under my forbearance and had I not been a fair man, I would have had you evicted from this place already. Be of no doubt, I will have you removed immediately if you test my patience further. Do I make myself clear?"

"You make yourself perfectly clear, sir."

Jacob Smog nodded and turned to the women in the dock.

"Mrs Wenham, you have heard this gentleman's proposal. Is it your wish to avail yourself of his representation during this trial?"

Sarah had been watching and listening to the developments with keen interest, not least the manner of Sir Richard's responses to the fool, Jacob Smog. He exuded a calmness that she found soothing and reassuring, though she could not have explained why.

"I do not know, sir. I have never met the gentleman before. I know nothing of his qualifications for the task."

"As do none of us, madam! My advice to you is to decline the offer, but the choice is entirely yours."

"Sir, may I approach the lady for just a short moment?" asked Easeby, keen to act quickly before she wavered.

"Very well, but be quick about it!"

Easeby bowed towards Smog and made his way towards the dock, which was raised a few feet above the ground and on a level with the magistrate's seat. Leaning and reaching upwards, he handed Sarah a small piece of paper, which she took, unfolded and read carefully. The words were written in an assured and accomplished, if somewhat hurried, hand:

The case is a charade and I do not believe you guilty. I will demolish all charges against you. You have my word.

Sarah read the message twice and then fixed Easeby with an inquisitive look. He sensed that she was appraising him and returned the look without blinking. He had scribbled the note hastily as they approached the courthouse, having arrived in Huntingdon to find the trial already begun. It was a desperately weak plea, he knew, but all that he could manage in the time available to him. He could only hope it was enough.

Leaning forwards, Sarah silently mouthed a single word to him:

"How?"

Easeby smiled, reassuringly, before responding in the same manner, mouthing the words:

"I do not know yet, madam."

For many long seconds, Sarah continued to study Easeby, before eventually relaxing her shoulders and nodding.

"It seems I have no option but to place my trust in this gentleman, your honour. Sir Richard will represent me and the girls, too, unless they indicate otherwise."

The three girls all shook their heads, though Annabel with less certainty than Jane and Anne.

"Then we are all decided, sir."

Easeby gave Sarah a relieved smile, nodding and hanging his head to signify his thanks, before abruptly turning to face Jacob Smog once again.

"With your permission then, your honour, I request an immediate adjournment to this trial whilst I consult with my clients and prepare their defence. There is much I need to discover about the circumstances of the case."

Smog had been fearing this, but knew it was inevitable and predictable. What was even worse, he could think of no, good reason, to decline the request. It was a reasonable one, though incredibly inconvenient.

"Very well, sir, if you must! How long do you need?"

"I would need the rest of today, sir, as an absolute minimum; and as it is Sunday tomorrow, I assume the court will not meet on the Sabbath. That would give me forty-eight hours to prepare. It is still precious little time, but will have to suffice."

Jacob Smog sighed theatrically. Again, the request was not unreasonable, but the prospect of a two-day delay tested his patience to the limits. Alas, it could not be helped. Why had he set the trial date as a Saturday?

"Very well, Sir Richard. You may have your forty-eight hours, but not a moment longer. I shall retire now and consider the matter of your contempt for this court's proceedings. You have not heard the last of it. This court is adjourned until nine o'clock Monday. Everybody, go home!"

With those words, Smog rose from his seat and exited the courtroom abruptly through his private entrance, feeling disgruntled and not a little out of sorts. The portrait would have to be put on hold for a while longer, he reflected ruefully.

To the rear of the courtroom, Malachai Harkiss sat watching the developments with a silent contempt.

22
The Cut

Outside the courtroom, Joshua, Rebecca and Ned stood amongst the crowd waiting for Sir Richard's return. It seemed the whole town had congregated there, and they could scarcely hear a single word through the open doors, let alone catch a glimpse of what was happening inside. The snippets of information occasionally passed back from those nearer the front were confused and difficult to make sense of.

Rebecca felt herself jostled and squeezed in the crowd and began to feel faint. The dragoon had departed after clearing a path for Sir Richard and Nathaniel to enter the courtroom, presumably to carry news of their arrival at Huntingdon back to Oliver Cromwell.

Rebecca looked around to attract Joshua's attention, but they had long since become separated. He was now some yards ahead, standing alongside Ned. She could just make out the backs of their heads through the mass of bodies.

Conscious of the child she carried and concerned for its safety, she determined to push her way back through the scrum of bodies and towards the outer edges of the crowd. It would be thinner there and she might be able to breathe more freely. She thought of the wagon, which they'd left some distance away, and decided to make her way towards it. She would wait there for the others to join her.

Rebecca was small and slight, and the task was not an easy one. People grew angry and ill-tempered as she pushed against the tide of bodies, cursing and pushing back at her as she tried to free herself from the tumult. On more than one occasion, she felt in danger of losing her footing and began to panic, imagining what might happen were she to fall.

Eventually, she reached a place where the crowd grew thinner and she could stop to catch her breath and take her bearings. Looking around, she spotted a dark, swarthy man standing slightly away from the rest of the crowd, watching her in a dark, threatening way. He spat onto the cobblestones, before purposefully striding towards her.

Rebecca panicked and looked about her for somewhere to escape, but it was too late. Within seconds, he was on her, grabbing her roughly by the arm and causing her to scream with pain. The grip was strong and tight; and, struggle as she might, she could not free herself.

"Well, well, well! What have we here?"

"Let go of me, please, sir! I have done you no ill."

"Is that so? I wonder about that. Come to watch your sisters hang, have you?"

"Let go of me! You are hurting me!"

"No, young missy, I'll not let you go. I know every face in this town and I don't know yours. Word got out about our little discovery here, has it? Thought you'd come and weave one of your spells to get them out?"

The people close by had begun to take notice and were moving towards them, keen to find out what extra excitement the day might have to offer. Amongst them was a brightly dressed figure, incongruous against the drab puritan dress of the rest of the townspeople.

"What's going on, Samuel Parr?" asked one woman. "Who is this?"

"It's another one of them in there, I reckon, Meg Tyler," Samuel Parr answered, nodding in the direction of the courthouse. "I caught her spying just now. She tried to escape when she saw me watching her!"

Meg Tyler stopped in her tracks, uncertain whether she should approach any closer.

"A witch, you mean? Do you think so? She's nothing but a young slip of a lass."

"You can never tell by looking at them, Meg. What's she doing around here if she hasn't come to help them? I've never seen her before, have you?"

"No, I haven't, now you mention it. That Mr Harkiss will know, though. He saw through that Sarah Wenham in a couple of days, they say. Keep hold of her, Samuel, and don't let her go!"

But Rebecca had already heard enough. Twisting her arm as far as she could to face Samuel Parr, she kicked out at his groin with all her might. The kick was perfectly directed and he howled in pain, releasing his grip sufficiently for her to break free and run.

**

Inside the courtroom, Jacob Smog had just adjourned proceedings and people were beginning to flood out into the open air. Those standing nearest the door reluctantly moved aside to make room for them, eagerly enquiring as to what had just happened and why the trial had finished so early. The scene was rapidly descending into chaos.

Joshua Cooper and Ned Jones turned to look for Rebecca, but could see no sign of her. Panicking a little, Joshua pushed his way through the crowds, calling her name, with Ned following close behind.

"Becky! Where are you, Becky?"

In the distance, Ned spotted a man who seemed to be bent double, struggling for his breath. A small crowd of people had gathered around him and, just beyond them, a couple of figures appeared to be fleeing the scene, one small and the other much larger. It seemed certain they were not fleeing together, but that one was in pursuit of the other. What's more, the larger figure was quickly gaining on the smaller one.

Ned grabbed Joshua by the shoulder and pointed in their direction.

"Look over there! Isn't that Becky, Josh?"

At a lightning pace, Joshua was off, covering the yards as though his life depended on it and leaving Ned floundering in his wake. Within ten seconds, he had halved the distance between himself and the two figures and was now close enough to see that the second figure — brightly dressed and somehow familiar — held a knife in his hand.

Lunging forward with a dive, the man caught Becky a blow to her ankle, causing her to stumble and fall to the ground. He quickly knelt above her sprawling body, both their chests heaving with exertion. Becky continued to struggle and in the split second before Joshua crashed into the man, there was a glint of steel, like the blue flash of a kingfisher seen out of the corner of the eye.

Such was the force of the collision, the man was instantly winded and Joshua had little trouble pinning him to the ground, his hand grasped tightly to his throat.

"You!" Joshua exclaimed, recognising him instantly as the fraudster from the White Hart Tavern in Doncaster. "What the hell are you doing here?"

"That is my business! Get off me, you oaf, you're choking me!"

Beside them, Becky knelt and picked up the knife, which had fallen to the ground in the struggle. The blade was red and she felt a dull soreness in her abdomen. Looking down, she saw the first traces of blood begin to flow from a wound across her stomach.

23
Pyramus Peake

Sir Richard Easeby knelt beside Rebecca, stemming the flow of blood with a length of linen torn from the sleeve of his shirt.

"Damn it!" he whispered under his breath. "We do not have time for this."

The wound at least was not as bad as it first appeared. The man had slashed rather than stabbed at her, and the flesh had not been fully pierced; just cut. That was something.

"Ned, run to the town and find a physician! The wound will need stitching, I think, but I do not believe any serious harm has been done. Go now, as quickly as you can!"

Ned obeyed the instruction, running back in the direction of the courthouse. Joshua remained straddling the culprit, pinning him to the ground. The rest of the crowd of onlookers had slowly drifted away, including Samuel Parr and Meg Tyler. They had blended back into the crowd as soon as they saw the party of strangers approaching from the courthouse. There were few enough gentlemen in the town, and they had little appetite for finding themselves on the wrong side of this new arrival. The manner of his dress told them all they needed to know.

"Should we not send for the constable, Richard?" asked Nathaniel Wright. "This man should be taken into custody. He has crossed our paths twice already. He's a thief and, but for the grace of God, a murderer, too."

"You are almost certainly right, Nathaniel, but let us pause for just a moment. The man may yet be of use to us. Are you able to sit, Becky?"

"I think so, sir. It is sore, but already the blood has lessened, I think."

"Good girl. Here, take this and hold it tight against the wound!"

Easeby tore a second strip of cloth from his other sleeve and handed it to Rebecca.

"The physician will be here soon and will doubtless wish to stitch it. It will hurt, Becky, but you must be brave. Do you understand?"

She nodded her agreement and nobody present doubted that brave was exactly what she would be.

Seeing her comfortable and out of immediate danger, Easeby turned his attention to the stranger.

"What's your name?"

The stranger struggled against Joshua Cooper's weight, but, unable to free himself, he relaxed back to the ground.

"None of your fucking business; that's my name!"

"I think you were right after all, Nathaniel. Please, go and find the constable."

"Pyramus fucking Peake, all right? My name's Pyramus fucking Peake!"

"That's better! Thank you, Mr Peake; and tell me, how do you come to find yourself in the same town as us? It is quite some coincidence, don't you think? I'm a logical man and I really do not believe in happenstance like that. Why did you follow us here?"

"Why do you think? You owe me twenty fucking pennies; remember? I saw you on the road near Newark and recognised you, but you had some military cock with you, so I followed you here and waited for him to go."

"As it happens, it is you who owes me, Mr Peake. I was left considerably out of pocket following your little sporting game. I paid out nearly double to the people you duped and gave a crown to the landlord to pay for the damage. I very strongly advise you not to pass that way again, by the way. He is not at all pleased with you."

"That's your own damn fault then, isn't it? Nobody asked you to pay the fuckers. I can't be held to blame if the World's full of arseholes that can't see turds for shit."

Joshua had heard enough and landed a punch right in Pyramus Peake's stomach, causing him to retch and vomit.

"Joshua, I might forgive you one display of violence, but do that again and I cannot promise the same forbearance! I have never fought violence with violence and I have no intention of starting now. Do you understand me?"

For the first time in his life, Joshua thought to contradict his master, but relented, and nodded his head in acknowledgement. Easeby turned his attention back to Pyramus Peake.

"Why did you attack this girl? What harm has she done you?"

"I didn't mean to cut her. I was just trying to catch her. Someone called her a witch and I thought there'd be profit in it for me if I stopped her escaping."

"A witch? Who called you that, Becky?"

"I don't know, sir. It was just some man in the crowd. He grabbed hold of me and wouldn't let me go. He said I was with the women in the courtroom and then everybody else started to join in. It was horrible! I kicked him in the balls and tried to run away, but this one caught me and tripped me up."

Easeby sighed deeply and not for the first time in Nathaniel's acquaintance with him, a look of world-weary despair passed across his face. After a few moments, he spoke words intended only for his own ears:

"So, it has begun already? Suspicion spreads from man to man like a parasite feeding off the ignorance of fools."

Pyramus Peake eventually broke the ensuing silence:

"I didn't mean to cut her, I tell you. She struggled and the knife slipped. I don't know the girl and had no cause to hurt her. I just saw money to be had catching her. That's all there is to it."

Easeby studied the man for a long time and then nodded.

"Very well, Mr Peake. You are a sporting man. I have a new proposition for you."

"Proposition? What proposition? What the fuck are you talking about now?"

"I will not turn you over to the authorities…"

"But, Sir Richard!"

Joshua could not contain himself any longer, interrupting his master mid-sentence. Easeby held up his hand to silence him.

"Be quiet, Joshua. I have not finished."

He continued, addressing the man still pinned to the ground:

"I will not turn you over to the constable, Mr Peake. What's more, I will return your twenty pennies and a gold crown on top of that, like the one I wagered against you at the White Hart. My only condition is that you do certain things for me over the coming few days, at any time of my asking. Do you consent?"

Pyramus Peake eyed him suspiciously. "Things? What things?"

"Don't worry, Mr Peake. They are things in keeping with your usual occupation; nothing more."

"You're talking in bloody riddles. What things?"

Easeby smiled. "Deceit, lies and theft, Mr Peake; that is all."

24
A Discovery

It was still dark as Luke Simmons saddled a horse and set out on the short journey from Wood Walton Manor to Huntingdon. It was Saturday, and Luke had determined he would go as soon as he learned of the date set for the trial.

Left to his own devices since his mistress's arrest, he had continued to go about his chores as best he could. He spent most of the intervening period keeping the house and grounds in some sort of order in the hope that Sarah would soon return with the others and that things would return to normal.

Why he had not also been arrested, he did not know, and preferred not to contemplate. For many days, he remained fearful that they would return for him, but eventually the days assumed their own rhythm and the fear slowly subsided.

He remained vigilant and avoided venturing beyond the bounds of the estate as much as possible. It was safer to keep himself to himself for the time being, and it almost seemed as though people had forgotten he was there. It was on a very rare trip to the village, sticking to the shadows and eavesdropping on conversations, that he overheard two women discussing the trial date.

Luke struck the North Road just as dawn was beginning to break, and by the time he reached the halfway point of his journey, the sun was well above the horizon. It promised to be a clear, bright day, though cold and frosty, and the surrounding fenland, usually cheerless and drab, presented itself dressed in a white, ethereal beauty.

Looking to the East and shielding his eyes against the low sun, he spotted a dark shape that appeared to be floating on the marshy waters of the fen. On a normal day, the thing would have been camouflaged against the darkness of the water, but today it stood out against the white gossamer of the frost blanketing the wetland shrub.

It was perhaps twenty yards or so from the road; too far for Luke to risk wading out for, but close enough to discern what the shape was. It was the muddied, high crown of a man's hat with the distinctive feather of a pheasant tucked into the outer headband.

Luke knew of only one man who wore such a hat, and that was Jonah Salt.

**

Ever since Jonah's disappearance and the vigil at the manor, Elizabeth Salt had become firmly convinced that the two events were somehow linked and that Jonah had become another of Sarah Wenham's victims.

The magistrate himself had confirmed that his planned meeting with Jonah had not taken place, first alerting Elizabeth to her husband's disappearance.

Malachai Harkiss, on learning of the disappearance, had asked her for a description of her husband. He told her that he had passed a man fitting the description on his way to Huntingdon in the dense fog just a couple of days before. He, too, seemed convinced that Sarah Wenham had a part to play in the disappearance, but without proof of Jonah's death, he was reluctant to add it to the list of charges. He did not want the case against her compromised by the inclusion of unproven allegations.

"I will deliver you the neck of the culprit, madam, with or without your husband's body," were his precise words.

"I sympathise with your loss, but have faith that the woman will hang anyway. We have sufficient evidence without the additional charge. Be at peace and pray for the deliverance of your husband's soul into heaven."

Elizabeth felt ignored and powerless. Each night thereafter, she lit a candle in her window in memory of Jonah and grieved alone. Often, she imagined his face in the flames of the hearth fire. It seemed in those moments that he was calling to her from the torments of purgatory.

At those times, she remembered the strange, choreographed dance of the starlings, and the unearthly thud of the owl flying into the library window during the vigil. She also recalled the distress of Sarah Wenham at the bird's anguish. It was more distress or anguish than the witch had shown for any of her victims, and a deep determination for vengeance began to consume Elizabeth's every waking hour.

Sarah Wenham would hang; and, when she did, Elizabeth would be at the front of the crowd, watching the woman's feet kick out against the empty air.

***

For Ruth Carter, the death of her own husband affected her differently. Whereas Elizabeth had nothing to confirm her bereavement beyond what she felt in the pit of her stomach, Ruth had the very real evidence of her husband's mutilated body; and yet, where Elizabeth's grief was deep and inconsolable, Ruth appeared sanguine to the point of coldness.

To those who knew her best, it appeared that Ruth continued to go about her daily business unaffected. She demurred adopting widow's weeds, preferring instead to wear her customary plain gown and coif. Neither did she take a single day away from her work, but seemed concerned only by the rumours of her husband's infidelity, which had gained currency amongst the goodwives of the village. Those rumours left their mark on Ruth to the extent that she adopted a fixed, steely expression whenever she passed her neighbours, their conversations trailing off into silence as she did so.

Ruth had become the subject of sympathy, and as a proud woman, sympathy was something she found hard to take; but more difficult even than sympathy, she had become the subject of gossip, and that she could never reconcile herself to.

"Poor woman! Not just a widow, but the widow of a faithless husband."

The widow part did not cause her pain, but the faithless part most certainly did.

Ruth's desire for vengeance against Sarah Wenham matched if not exceeded that of Elizabeth Salt, and it was the delicate flavour of vengeance she savoured the night of the vigil.

***

Arriving early, Luke was one of the first to enter the courtroom. He took a seat far away from the front-most rows, in the most discreet place he could find. His view was partly obscured by a large pillar, which suited him well enough. He could not see the magistrate's seat at all, which also meant that the magistrate would not be able to see him. His position also gave him a perfect view down onto the dock, where he was able to watch Sarah, Jane, Anne and Annabel throughout the proceedings.

Like everybody else in the courtroom, the arrival of the stranger, Sir Richard Easeby, had taken Luke by surprise, and he listened with growing excitement to the words exchanged between Easeby and the magistrate. From his position high above the dock, Luke was able to see the man's face clearly when he approached the dock to hand a note to Sarah. There was something in the calm intelligence of the face that gave Luke some cause for hope. Perhaps it was a forlorn, foolish hope, but it was hope nonetheless.

After the adjournment, Luke waited some time for the court to clear before taking his leave and making his way back towards Wood Walton, determined to return again on Monday.

As he approached the halfway point, he looked eastwards once more to search out the hat he had seen earlier that morning. He had already decided he should tell Elizabeth Salt about it and wanted to fix its precise location in his mind; maybe marking the spot with a large stone on the road so they could easily return to it.

Luke looked out across the fen for many long minutes, and though the weather remained clear and bright, there was nothing to be seen. The hat seemed to have vanished into thin air.

25
The Interview

The prison-house was bitterly cold and Sir Richard and Nathaniel shivered against the dampness as Adam Crook, the jailor, unlocked the small interview room and allowed them to enter. It had reached mid-afternoon and already the weak November light had started to fade outside.

They had stayed with Rebecca until the physician arrived with Ned and confirmed the wound superficial, before taking their leave. Sir Richard was anxious to speak to his client as soon as possible and asked Nathaniel to accompany him to take notes. Joshua, in the meantime, was instructed to find lodgings for the party and under no circumstances to cause further argument with Pyramus Peake.

Sarah Wenham was already seated on a rough wooden stool, a woollen shawl pulled tightly across her shoulders. She rose to her feet as the two men entered, Crook instructing them to knock loudly when they were ready to leave. He then locked the door firmly shut behind them.

"Please, madam, do not rise," said Sir Richard, his eyes surveying the room inquiringly. It appeared empty, except for three stools and a small bureau desk.

"My name is Sir Richard Easeby. This is my clerk, Nathaniel Wright. We have travelled many miles to help you."

"I understand that, Sir Richard, but I do not understand how you heard about my case and I do not understand why you would want to help me."

"Somebody asked me to attend you, madam; an old acquaintance of mine. He is concerned for his reputation and the reputation of his cause."

"You mean Master Cromwell?"

"Indeed so, but it is not for the sake of Master Cromwell's reputation that I agreed to come."

"Why then, Sir Richard? What other possible reason would bring you so far from your home?"

Easeby ignored the question, moving the subject quickly on. "Tell me, how long have you been in this place, madam?"

"It is hard to keep track, but it is twelve days since they brought us here from Wood Walton, I believe."

Easeby worked the calculation backwards in his mind and then nodded.

"That makes sense. The timeline at least is not open to question. And how are your, and the girls' health? Have they been treating you tolerably well?"

"I am not permitted to see Jane, Annabel and Anne, sir. Today in the courtroom was the first time I have

175

done so since we were brought here, so I cannot answer for them. My own health is good and I thank you for your concern. Mr Crook is as kind to me as his position allows. I am fed and given sufficient water, though I am sometimes required to share the food with the rats; they rarely think to ask me first, but I do not complain."

"And your spirits, madam? How are they?"

"Tolerable, sir. I am allowed my Bible."

"I am pleased to hear it. May I sit?"

"Of course, sir! Forgive me my lack of courtesy. My mind is somewhat preoccupied at the moment, as you will understand perhaps."

Sir Richard pulled up another stool and sat opposite Sarah, beckoning Nathaniel to do the same.

"We do not have much time, Mrs Wenham, so allow me to come straight to the point. There are four specific charges levelled against you. The jury is predisposed to believe those charges, I believe, and find you guilty. People have been badly affected by the war and by the failure of their harvests. At such times, they are not inclined to think rationally. They are content when easy explanations are presented to them, and superstition is the easiest of all to accept. It does not require evidence, just enough people to think the same way to normalise it. Superstition is the prosecuting counsel in this case, madam."

"Then it appears you have had a wasted journey, Sir Richard!"

"Forgive me for speaking bluntly, Mrs Wenham. I do not wish to alarm you, but it is important you understand the nature of the task. We must never underestimate our enemy. We do, however, have one advantage over them that is ours alone to exploit."

"And what advantage is that, sir?"

"It is the law itself, madam. The law requires that the prosecution must prove the charges against you beyond reasonable doubt. That is the only way the jury can convict you."

"You have yet to have the pleasure of meeting Mr Harkiss, sir! He is not a man to entertain the slightest possibility of doubt."

"That may be the case, madam, but remember this: we need just one piece of evidence of sufficient weight to sow the seed of doubt in the jury's minds; one piece of evidence for each of the four charges. That is all that is required. We must not be deflected from the task of finding it."

Sarah listened intently. There was nothing Sir Richard said that had not already gone through her mind a thousand times, but it had never before presented itself in such logical order. There was an almost beautiful simplicity to his words:

"And then there is the question of deportment. We must not allow ourselves to be seen as disdainful of the charges; that will only play into their hands. No matter how preposterous the evidence against you, it must be treated with respect. Each witness must be treated as though they are telling the truth, though perhaps, in some way, mistaken. Each interjection by Mr Smog must be treated as though it is the most insightful contribution imaginable."

Sarah allowed herself a brief smile at that point; a smile Easeby returned, sharing the joke.

"In short, Mrs Wenham, you must remain focused and trust yourself to the strategy. You must not waver from showing your humility under any circumstances. Do you understand?"

Sarah relaxed. She was beginning to feel more at ease.

"You ask a lot of me, Sir Richard, but I have already entrusted my fate to you. It would not seem sensible to consent to your representation but not listen to your advice."

"Indeed not, Mrs Wenham, and thank you for your trust. I promise you that I will do everything in my power to disprove the charges against you. Now, we have much work to do this day. The things you tell me now, I will have only until Monday morning to investigate. Please answer the questions I ask you very precisely. My clerk will take notes, if you do not mind?"

Sarah nodded her assent, and, taking his cue, Nathaniel produced a quill, a small bottle of ink and some paper from his small, leather satchel bag.

"Now, Mrs Wenham, we will deal with each of the charges in turn. Firstly, tell me, please, how you came to know Abel Carter and also, what you know about his wife."

26
The Falcon

It was late in the evening when Sir Richard and Nathaniel emerged from the prison-house and made their way to the Falcon Tavern, on Market Hill. Joshua had found rooms there and left word with Adam Crook to inform his master. They were exhausted, but there was still work to be done before they could think to retire to their beds. Most importantly, tasks needed to be assigned for tomorrow; their only opportunity to gather what was needed before the trial was reconvened on Monday.

They found the others congregated in a quiet corner of the bar room. Ned, Joshua and Becky were deep in conversation, whilst Pyramus Peake sat slightly apart, flipping coins from the edge of the table and catching them in his palm; a task he repeated with nerve-fraying persistence. He had been annoyed to find so few customers in the tavern and therefore very little opportunity to make money; just one of the reasons Joshua thought the place ideal.

"Becky, how is the wound?" asked Sir Richard, pulling up a chair and sitting down with them.

"It is fine; just a little sore, thank you, sir. The physician says it will heal quickly. It did not need many stitches."

"And…?" Sir Richard arched his brow and nodded at her belly, not finishing the sentence.

"He says there is no damage to that either, sir," replied Becky, catching his meaning immediately. Only Ned looked a little confused, whilst Pyramus was not paying sufficient attention to become distracted from his game.

"I am glad; very glad indeed. It is a great relief. Do you feel well enough to do something for me tomorrow, Becky? It is not a strenuous task."

"Of course, sir. I would sooner mop the floors than sit around idle!"

"That won't be necessary, Becky. It is far more important than that. I want you to go to the prison-house with Nathaniel first thing in the morning. Speak to the three girls and find out everything you can about what they know. You are a similar age to them. I think they will be more open with you than with me. In particular, pay close heed to Annabel Leach. She is the one that concerns me the most. Do you remember what you said about the dragoon?"

"You mean about the things he did and didn't say, sir?"

"Exactly that, Becky. When you report back to me, I need you to tell me not just what she says, but whether you think there are things she is holding back. I am looking for your honest opinion of the girl. Do you understand me?"

"I think so, sir. I will do my best."

"I know you will, Becky, and do not be afraid of the place. It is unpleasant there, but Nathaniel will be with you all the time, and the jailor, Adam Crook, is not a bad man in my estimation. You have nothing to fear."

"Thank you, sir."

Easeby then turned to Ned Jones.

"Ned, I am sorry. I know you have had a long journey, but I need you to ride out again tomorrow. It is an errand of the utmost importance. Lives will depend on the outcome."

"Of course, Sir Richard. Where am I to ride?"

"To Cambridge, Ned. It is twenty miles or so from Huntingdon. I need you to find the college called Sidney Sussex, which is my old college there, and ask for Dr James Dee. He is a very old friend and student colleague of mine. He now teaches at the college. I will give you a note to deliver to him. He must return with you, Ned, and he must be here in time for the trial on Monday. I just hope to God he is in Cambridge. I have no concerns that he will heed the call if he receives it. Set out at first light to give yourself every chance of finding him. I cannot stress too much how critical this is."

Ned straightened himself in his seat, his face flushing with pride.

"You can rely on me, Sir Richard."

Easeby nodded and rested his hand on Ned's shoulder.

"Everything depends on it, Ned. Ride quickly, but ride surely." He then turned to Joshua Cooper.

"Joshua, your task is perhaps the most difficult of all, because I need you to do something that is not in your nature."

Joshua looked alarmed.

"What, Sir Richard?"

"I need you to lie, Joshua. Not a wicked lie, but a necessary one. Go to the village of Wood Walton. It lies just a few miles north of here; we passed it on our journey this morning, I believe. I need you to find the home of Mathias and Catherine Monk. They have a son called Tobias, who is recently returned from the war. He is much affected by it.

If the mother is there, tell her you are an old comrade of his come to pay him your respects. It is likely it will be the only way she will allow you in to see him. She is very concerned for his health and her instincts will be to do anything she thinks might help him.

Do whatever is necessary to get some time alone with him. Speak to him about his injuries, about the war, about Sarah Wenham, and report back to me everything he says, and also what you make of him. He is the biggest conundrum in the case, so this is very important."

"I will do my best, Sir Richard, but what if they see through the lie? What if this Tobias gives me away as soon as he sees me?"

"That is indeed a possibility, Joshua, and why I say you have the most difficult task. I think the boy is probably starved of company, though, and will be glad for the distraction. I do not believe he will give you away. We must pray so."

Joshua looked concerned, but nodded his agreement.

Easeby turned finally to Pyramus Peake. "Mr Peake, that brings me finally to you."

Pyramus looked up from his coin flipping. "A gold crown, right?"

"A gold crown, Mr Peake. Tell me, does house-breaking feature in your long list of accomplishments?"

Pyramus looked angered for a split second and seemed about to say something scathing, but then thought the better of it. A gold crown is a gold crown, after all.

"That depends who's asking, doesn't it?"

"I do not have time for games. Do you have experience in the field, yes or no?"

"I may have had occasion to practice the art, yes. Purely to recover belongings wrongly deprived of me, you understand?"

"I understand perfectly, Mr Peake. In fact, I believe we both understand each other very well."

"There you're wrong! I can't fathom you out at all. A fucking enigma is what you are!"

"Then listen very carefully, please; it is vital you understand this. I need you also to go to Wood Walton, but not at the same time as Joshua. The timing of your visit is of critical importance. Go to the cottage of a woman called Ruth Carter and hide out of sight. Tomorrow is Sunday and she will certainly go to church at some point in the morning. She is a recent widow and lives alone now, so there should be no one else about. Once you have seen her leave, enter the house, being careful not to do any damage. It is important she does not know you have been there. Do you understand?"

"Don't tell me how to do my job! I know how to break into a bleeding house!"

"Good. You are looking for anything hand-written: letters, notes, verses, anything of interest. Collect them all and bring them to me. Do not disturb anything else. Do not steal anything else. Tell me, can you read, Mr Peake?"

"Yeah, I'm a fucking scholar, ain't I? You can tell just by looking at me. Of course I can't fucking read!"

"Perfect. Just bring the things to me."

"And what are you going to be doing whilst we're all out working our arses off and risking our necks in a noose, eh? Seems like you've given everyone a bloody job except yourself!"

"I have an appointment with someone, not that he knows it yet."

"An appointment with whom, Richard?" asked Nathaniel.

"With Mr Malachai Harkiss, Nathaniel, who else? It is high time I made his acquaintance."

27
Sermon

Sir Richard Easeby rose early and made his way to All Saints in Market Square, passing a clattering of jackdaws on his way into the church. It was not the first time he had been there, and he now recalled the first occasion he visited the place with Cromwell, whilst students together at Cambridge. The two men were very great friends in those days and Cromwell had wanted to visit his father's tomb, asking Easeby to come along with him for company. The year was 1618 and his father, Robert Cromwell, had died just a year earlier. He was interred inside the church, the same building in which Oliver himself had been baptised nineteen years earlier.

Easeby remembered vividly how Cromwell had railed against the ostentation of the building, with its gothic arches, stained-glass windows and alabaster pulpit. Even in those early days, his austere puritanism had begun to show, but it was not his religion that caused their later rift. A man of peace to his core, Easeby argued vehemently against escalation in the argument with the king. Cromwell had chosen a different path, and their relationship became strained and finally broken all together.

Five years ago, the last words were exchanged between them, and those words had been bitter and full of anger. Sir Richard regretted the rift, but knew that it had become inevitable and unavoidable. It was a matter of conscience to both men.

Easeby arrived early and took a seat at the rear of the church to survey the congregation more discreetly as they entered. It was perhaps twenty minutes or so before he noticed a man enter alone. He was youngish — Easeby estimated him to be between twenty-five and thirty years of age — tall and with a slight stoop. He was dressed in the serious, even severe fashion of the puritans, and Easeby noticed how the congregation turned to whisper to their neighbours as the man walked the length of the aisle to take a seat on the front-most pew. Mr Harkiss had clearly made quite an impression already on the townsfolk of Huntingdon.

It was widely anticipated that he would be the star of the show at the reconvened trial tomorrow. For now, though, it was his performance today that was of primary interest, for Harkiss had been invited to preach a sermon at the morning service.

Outside, the weather was in stark contrast to that of yesterday. Where Saturday had been clear, crisp and bright, today it was dark, cheerless and gloomy. A blanket of leaden clouds hung low over the town, smothering it in a dismal half-light; heavy, impenetrable and morose.

The chosen readings that morning fitted the mood of the weather, being taken from the Book of Jonah. The congregation sat in rapt silence as they heard Jonah refuse the Lord's command to travel to Nineveh, a city inflicted with much evil. Fleeing instead in a boat and pursued by a storm summoned by God in vengeance, the congregation sat on the edge of their seats as they heard how Jonah was thrown overboard to pacify the Lord and still the storm.

The final reading — the swallowing of Jonah by a mighty whale, followed by his captivity for three days and three nights, his repentance and the final release from the belly of the fish — were given to Harkiss to deliver.

Easeby sat and listened intently. He had heard many gifted orators before, but Harkiss was a breed apart. There was a musicality and rhythm to the way he pronounced each verse that wove a spell over his audience, drawing them in and leading them in a carefully choreographed dance. It felt almost as though they themselves were huddled inside the whale's belly, praying for forgiveness. The violence of the fish's retching as Jonah was vomited from its mouth, Harkiss delivered with such forcefulness that those on the front-most pews found themselves cowering in fear.

When he had finished reading, there followed a period of carefully contrived silence. For what must have been half a minute, Harkiss stood aloft in the pulpit, surveying the faces arranged in front of him. His gaze wandered slowly from pew to pew. Eventually, his eyes landed on Easeby, a look of recognition passing briefly across his face. The two men held each other's gaze for a few seconds; then, drawing himself up to his full height, Harkiss addressed the congregation once more. This time the words he spoke were his own:

"Friends, I have travelled many miles to come to this town. In many ways, I am Jonah and you are my Nineveh. There are things of wickedness here and I come to do God's work.

"Unlike Jonah, though, I do not look to shirk the task. There will be no storms here, no whales, no fear, no repentance and no redemption. There will be only justice and retribution. This I promise you."

There was a murmuring of excitement amongst the congregation. Heads nodded in agreement.

"He has them eating from his palm," thought Easeby, as Harkiss continued:

"I look amongst you and I see many God-fearing faces. I see your faith and your desire for deliverance from this evil. It is written in your eyes and it gladdens my heart to see it.

"I need tell you, though, brethren, there is one amongst us who does not share that hope. Like me, he has travelled many miles to be here. He comes from the godless lands of the North, and where I travel to see justice done, he travels to thwart it."

At those words, there was an exclamation of outrage from many corners of the church. Heads turned in all directions to search out the enemy amongst them. Easeby, sitting at the back of the congregation, remained calm and unmoved.

"Where the devil finds his foothold, he seeks out the weak and the faithless to assist him in his dealings. He places false words in their mouths; words intended to deceive us. They are sweet words, my brothers and sisters, and clever words; be wary of them! Do not entertain them!

"These tricks, Satan has deployed since the beginning of time, even on our Lord Jesus himself in the desert of Judea. Remember in the gospels how he contrived to tempt the Lord to turn the stones into bread to satisfy his hunger; to leap from the Holy Pinnacle so the angels might catch him and break his fall; and yes, even to bow down and worship Satan himself in exchange for lordship of the kingdoms of the Earth!

"These are the ways of Satan: lies, temptation and deceit. Do not succumb to those words, brothers and sisters!

"There are twelve amongst you who will be sorely tested tomorrow. Satan's emissary will sow seeds of doubt and suspicion in your minds. He will contrive to confuse you with falsehoods and lies. He will play upon your sympathies, exploit your kindness and debase your judgement with his trickery. He will weave such threads of deception that you will feel yourself trapped in a web, not knowing how you might escape."

The congregation was now becoming agitated and febrile. Many got to their feet, shouting "no" and "never!" Harkiss lifted the palm of his hand above his head to quieten them, pausing a while until they had done so.

"Don't be afraid, brothers and sisters. I come here to see justice done and to spare you these things. I will guide these twelve back to the truth should ever I see them waver. For know you this: the emissary of Satan is just a man. He has no mystical weapons to harm us if we stay strong and resolute. If we do that, my brothers and sisters, his clever words will scatter worthlessly like so many grains of sand through the fingers of his hands!"

The whole congregation stood, shouting and waving their hands in adulation. Only one remained unmoved. Taking his opportunity amongst the noise and excitement, Sir Richard Easeby calmly rose and made his way to the door of the church and out into the dismal grey of the November morning.

He had long since heard enough.

28
Nightshade

Sir Richard slowly made his way back to The Falcon, his mind deep in thought. There were just a few hours before he could expect the others to return from their allotted errands. Ned, he knew, would be the last to return, though the news from Cambridge was perhaps the most critical of all. He could only hope that Ned would find James Dee and that his old friend would heed the call.

For now, the few hours he had alone were preciously important. Climbing the rough wooden stairwell to his room on the first floor of the tavern, he locked the door behind him and lit a candle. He then took a large piece of paper and laid it on the small dressing table he had repurposed as a desk. Moving the candle to the centre of the desk, he focused his eyes on the flame, slowing his breathing as he had taught himself and shutting out the noise and chatter of the tavern yard below.

Having stared at the candle for ten minutes or so, he finally picked up a quill and, dipping it into a pot of ink, drew the outline of a circle in the upper left quarter of the paper. Inside the circle he wrote the words:

"Charge One: Abel Carter."

He then drew three further circles in the remaining quarters, and inside each, wrote in turn:

"Charge Two: Tobias Monk."

"Charge Three: Harvest."

"Charge Four: Coven."

Returning then to the first circle, underneath the words Abel Carter, he wrote:

"Ruth Carter; Lust; Jealousy; Literacy; Blood; Edward Donne?"

Moving to the second circle, underneath where he had written Tobias Monk, Easeby added the words:

"Mother; War; Madness; Solitude; Kindness; Fruit?"

In the third circle, beneath Harvest, Easeby wrote the words:

"Fenland; Isaiah Felt; Inheritance; Crops; Library; James Dee?"

To the fourth circle, he added the names of the three girls, Jane, Anne and Annabel, and the boy, Luke Simmons, who Sarah Wenham had mentioned during their interview. Why had Luke not also been arrested? He placed a question mark after Luke's name.

Finally, Easeby drew a fifth circle in the centre of the paper, overlapping in part with each of the other four. Inside the fifth circle, he wrote just three names: Sarah Wenham, Malachai Harkiss and Jacob Smog. Then, as an after-thought, he added a fourth name: that of Oliver Cromwell.

Satisfied finally with the diagram in front of him, Sir Richard put down the quill, closed his eyes and began to think.

***

Nathaniel and Becky were the first to return to the tavern, and it was Nathaniel's soft rap on the door that stirred Sir Richard from his meditation. How long he had been contemplating the sketch, he did not know, but the time was now well past midday. He wasted no time on welcomes.

"How did you find the girls? How are their spirits?"

"As well as can be expected, Richard," replied Nathaniel. "They are young and very afraid; that is the most that can be said of them. I do not believe they fully understand their situation. They know only that their fate is tied inextricably to that of their mistress."

"And what do they say of her? Do they doubt her innocence?"

Nathaniel and Becky exchanged glances at that point.

"Jane and Anne remain devoted to Mrs Wenham, Richard. They claim to have no cause for suspicion. I believe they retain every faith in her innocence."

"You do not include Annabel in that, Nathaniel? What of her?"

"Annabel is a different case entirely, Richard. A wedge has been driven between her and the other two girls, I believe. She has been separated from them on the order of Malachai Harkiss and is now in a cell of her own. Adam Crook said it happened on Friday night; on the eve of the trial."

"I feared as much. Did you manage to speak to her?"

"We did, but only after we had spoken to Jane and Anne. They warned us that Annabel was much changed by the experience. Where she was a happy and funny girl before, always quick to make practical jokes, she has become dark and sullen and subject to very wild swings of temper. That was exactly how we found her. At first, she refused to speak to us or answer any questions. I think had Becky not been with me, she would not have opened her mouth at all."

"And when she did, what did she say?"

"Wicked things, Richard. She claims to have been ordered to collect herbs and wild flowers, which her mistress then used to brew potions. She says that the potions come from books kept in the library at Wood Walton Manor and that Mrs Wenham locked herself away reading those books for days on end. Jane and Anne were always the first to go out foraging, but Annabel was afraid for her life and felt obliged to help them. She claims they collected mandrake, which was used as a potion to seduce Abel Carter, and other nightshades that were used to poison Tobias Monk and send him mad with hallucinations."

Sir Richard flushed with anger. "God's truth! How could a girl know such things? Someone has placed those ideas in her mind!"

"Indeed, Richard. That much was obvious; but would a jury see through it? I fear there is more to tell."

"More? What else, Nathaniel?"

"She says that she has heard Mrs Wenham incanting in the devil's tongue and speaking a language that she does not understand. She claims to have heard it many times, most recently whilst they have been in the prison-house. Annabel believes her mistress is casting spells on her to prevent her speaking the truth. She claims to fear for her life."

Sir Richard turned to Becky. "Tell me, Becky, do you believe these things? What were your impressions of the girl?"

"I do not believe her, sir. She is lying."

Nathaniel and Sir Richard both stared at the girl, taken aback by the assuredness of her response.

"How so, Becky? How can you be so sure?"

Becky shrugged her shoulders. "Nightshades grow in chalky soil, sir, and fenland is often very chalky. My grandmother knew a lot about herbs and wild flowers, and she taught me about them and where they grow. There must be lots and lots of chalky soil here, so there must be nightshades growing everywhere."

"That may be so, Becky, but surely that makes the story more likely to be true?"

"Forgive me, sir, but no. Everybody who knows nightshade knows that it is poisonous. If it's so common around here, you wouldn't need to read a library book to find that out, would you?"

Easeby and Nathaniel looked at each other. Nathaniel arched his brow, whilst Sir Richard smiled freely for the first time in many days.

"Indeed, you wouldn't, Miss Standish. Indeed, you wouldn't!"

29
Tobias Monk

Tobias Monk stood in the centre of the small, simply furnished room and stared warily at the stranger in front of him. Joshua had been relieved to find Catherine and Mathias out when he knocked on the door. It was Tobias himself who opened it to him.

"Who are you? What do you want? My parents are just at church. They will not be gone long."

Joshua noted how nervous the lad appeared to be. He guessed him to be perhaps a year or two older than himself and still wearing his bed gown, though the hour must have been well past ten in the morning. The most striking thing about him, though, was the leather mask covering his right eye and the whole upper right side of his face.

"My name's Joshua. I am a friend, Tobias. I do not mean you any harm. I just wanted to talk to you for a while, that's all."

"Talk to me about what? Who sent you? They discharged me. I didn't run away! My mother has the papers signed by my officer to prove it if you don't believe me!"

Joshua smiled, he hoped reassuringly, though he felt less than comfortable himself.

"I don't want to see any papers. It wouldn't help me if you showed them to me anyway. I can't read, except the few letters that Nathaniel taught me so I could write my name. He says he's going to teach me properly some time so I can help him with the copying, but I don't think I'm clever enough. What about you? Can you read?"

Tobias looked slightly ashamed. "No, but I know what the papers say because the officer that wrote them told me. They say that I'm discharged because of my injuries and that I served the cause bravely and with honour. That's what they say, and nobody can say otherwise!"

"I don't doubt you, Tobias. Nobody doubts you. What happened to your face?"

Tobias instinctively lifted his hand to the mask, taking a couple of steps backwards.

"None of your business! Who are you and how do you know my name? Why would I want to talk to you about it?"

"I'm sorry, Tobias. I was just interested, that's all. We don't have to talk about it if you don't want to. My master, Sir Richard, doesn't believe in the war and he wouldn't let me or any of the others sign up to fight, so I don't know anything about it."

"Sir Richard? Who is he? He sounds like a bloody royalist!"

"No, not a royalist, Tobias. He used to be good friends with Oliver Cromwell himself. He doesn't take either side in the war, and that's the honest truth. He did meet the king, though. That was long ago, before the fighting started. He tried to argue for peace and the king knighted him for it. That's when he and Cromwell fell out. That's all I know about it."

"The king's a traitor! Any friend of the king is a traitor, too!"

"He isn't a friend of the king, I told you! He just tried to stop them fighting. Sir Richard's a good man."

Tobias hesitated and then slumped onto a chair.

"You want to know about war? Well, I'll tell you. War is about marching through miles of shit to stand in a field and get your face blown off. You're terrified half the time and too tired to be terrified the rest of the time. In the end, it's a relief to get hit by a musket ball or stabbed through the stomach, because that means you can lie down; and when you lie down, you don't have to fight any more. You just lie down and try to go to sleep, but they stamp all over you. Other men trying to get to the front to get their own faces blown off, so they can lie down, too. That's war, and they can stick it up their arses!"

"I'm sorry, Tobias. Like I said, I have no idea."

"No, you don't. Nobody does. Nobody tries to understand. Nobody except her, that is."

"Who, Tobias? Who tried to understand?"

"The one they call a witch. She's the only one who listened."

"You mean Sarah Wenham, Tobias?"

"Yes, Mrs Wenham. Her husband was in the battle, too. I think she felt sorry for me."

"That's why we've come, Tobias. Sir Richard is going to speak up for her at the trial tomorrow."

"My mother is one of those who calls her a witch. She stopped her coming around to talk to me. I don't want to get into any more trouble."

Just then, the door opened and Catherine Monk entered the cottage, followed by the large, forbidding figure of Mathias, her husband. Tobias cowered slightly, whilst Joshua froze, his heart beating quickly inside his chest. It was Catherine Monk who broke the silence.

"Who is this, Toby? What's he doing inside the house?"

***

It didn't take long for Pyramus Peake to identify Ruth Carter's small cottage. Changing for the day from his customary bright outfit into a plain smock to pass himself off as a travelling labourer, he simply walked into Wood Walton, whistling and in plain sight.

Easeby had told him where he might find the woman's home, having been given directions by Sarah

Wenham. They had been straightforward and easy to follow.

Finding a small copse close to the house, Pyramus checked that nobody was around, before slipping into the trees and out of sight. He found a large oak tree and hid behind it. From there, he was able to keep a close eye on the cottage.

It was only an hour or so before he saw the door open and Ruth Carter emerge, locking it behind her with a large metal key. She then headed off in the direction of the village and the church.

Pyramus remained hidden until the woman was out of sight, before emerging from the trees and walking up to the front door. Taking a small length of wire from his pocket, he inserted it into the lock and after a couple of seconds, heard the satisfying click of the mechanism being released from the inside.

Looking around again to make sure nobody was watching, he quietly opened the door and slipped inside, closing it again quickly behind him.

Pyramus Peake took a deep breath and looked around the room he now found himself in, allowing himself a short moment of satisfaction. It had been a while since he had picked a lock, and he was relieved to discover that he hadn't lost his touch.

Once he began his search, it did not take him long to find what he was looking for. Beside the bed was a small cabinet. Going through the drawers one by one, he noticed one that appeared shallower than the others, though from the outside it was of the same depth. Rapping the bottom of the drawer with his knuckles, he was rewarded by a hollow sound confirming the existence of a false bottom.

Made of boxwood, the bottom of the drawer was loosely fitted into two grooves running along the sides. Taking his knife and sliding it down the side, he easily prised the bottom upwards and out, revealing a shallow compartment underneath. Inside was a pile of letters, all seemingly written in the same scrawling style. There was also a small pot of ink, some blank pieces of paper, a silver cross and a quill.

Slipping the letters and cross into his smock and tightening his belt to hold them in position, Pyramus carefully replaced the bottom of the drawer and slid it back into the cabinet. He then went through the rest of the contents of the room, but found little else of interest. There was certainly nothing else worth stealing, he reflected ruefully, as he made his exit, carefully locking the door again from the outside.

All in all, he had been inside Ruth Carter's cottage little more than twenty minutes. Not a bad morning's work, he thought. Easeby would get the letters he wanted. Pyramus Peake would get his gold crown and keep the cross for himself.

***

Sir Richard sat resting his chin on the tips of his fingers as Joshua told him about his meeting with Tobias Monk.

"And that's when the lad's parents returned home?"

"Yes, sir. Like I said, Mathias just stood there with his hands on his hips; but Catherine, the mother, looked like she might take a swipe at me at any moment. That's when I told them what you'd said, about me being a friend from the war just passing by. I was terrified, but Tobias didn't give me away. He backed up my story and that's when I left."

"That is as I thought, Joshua. The boy is starved of company."

"I'm sorry, sir, that I didn't have the chance to ask him more about Mrs Wenham. I daren't stay any longer. I'm not sure Catherine Monk really believed either of us."

"Don't worry, Joshua, you have done well enough. You've told me everything I need to know."

30
A Reunion

Sir Richard grew increasingly agitated as the evening drew on. There was still no sign of Ned Jones, and it had long since grown dark. What if he hadn't managed to find James Dee, or what if his old friend had simply refused to come to Huntingdon? Easeby knew the former was far more likely than the latter, but the effect of either would be exactly the same: a significant hole in his defence of Sarah Wenham. The woman would likely hang.

He paced the room above the tavern yard restlessly, whilst Nathaniel sat at the small dressing table, reading again the letters stolen by Pyramus Peake from Ruth Carter's cottage. They at least had calmed Sir Richard for a while, completing as they did another part of the puzzle, but that had been many hours ago now.

"Be calm, Richard. There is nothing more we can do but wait. Ned is a good lad and if Dr Dee is in Cambridge, he will find him."

"I should have gone myself, Nathaniel. Damn it! The task was too important to burden a young boy with."

"You cannot be everywhere at once, Richard. The work you have done today throws sufficient doubt on at least two of the charges to make the jury pause to think. We know that the fourth charge concerning the girls falls away if the other charges are unproven, so that is not something that need concern us."

"But that still leaves the most substantive charge, Nathaniel. The case against her hangs on the question of the harvest, and there only James can help us. The rest is reasonably dismissed, but the failure of the crops is perplexing and affects almost everyone in those parishes. They are angry and fearful, Nathaniel, and that is a dangerous combination. They will have their scapegoat and they will sacrifice her happily to the gods of revenge and superstition."

Nathaniel thought to change the subject.

"You've yet to tell me about the witch-finder, Richard. How did you find the man? Is he as the corporal described him?"

"Even more so, Nathaniel. The man has the skill of an orator and the gravitas of a preacher. I wish I knew more about him. I have tried to reason it in my mind. What brought him to Huntingdon? We know that he received a summons from Ruth and Catherine, but I do not believe that the word of two peasant women alone would bring him all this distance: so, who else? There must have been someone of more prominence."

"Then that is likely to be Isaiah Felt, Richard. We know from Mrs Wenham that the man is a rich land agent and has long coveted her property. He has much to gain by her death, I think. She has no heirs, so the property will certainly be sold after her death and probably at a discounted price. Only Felt would have the capital to buy it."

"You are right, Nathaniel. I have no doubt at all that Felt is central to the case, but still, I think there is more than that. My mind continues to return to what Becky said to me about the corporal on our journey here."

"You mean about there being things that he did not tell us?"

"Precisely that, Nathaniel. She is an uncommonly clever girl. She's astute and determined. I think she has the ability to see through people in a way most people do not. I have spent a long time thinking about those words ever since she spoke them. Why is Cromwell so determined that it should be I who defends the woman? What makes the case so important to him that he sends a dragoon to ensure my safe arrival? The more I think about it, the less clear it is to me how his reputation might be tarnished by the woman's death. Of all the many lawyers in England, why does it need to be me?"

"You think too much at times, Richard. What other motive could there possibly be?"

"Oliver Cromwell is a man of many sides, Nathaniel. He does nothing without a purpose, and usually there is more than one. He was always the same, even when we were young and carefree at Cambridge. If ever he invited you to go boating with him, it was always because he wanted you to steer whilst he fished. It was never just for the enjoyment of your company, though we enjoyed each other's company very much in those days. Imagine this for me, if you will, Nathaniel. What if it was not just I who was asked to come to Huntingdon?"

"I do not follow you, Richard. Who else would he have asked?"

"What if he asked the witch-finder also to come?"

"Malachai Harkiss? Why would he invite both of you, Richard, one to prosecute the woman and the other to defend her? That does not make sense."

"That is what I am trying to work out, Nathaniel. Whatever the reason, I am sure it is more than just the sport of pitting us against each other."

Their conversation was interrupted by the sound of horses' hooves on the cobblestones of the tavern yard below. Walking quickly to the window and leaning out, Sir Richard saw the familiar figure of Ned Jones dismounting with a practised leap, before running to assist a second rider who was also dismounting, though in a far less assured manner. The man was of middling age and wearing a long, fur-trimmed scholastic robe, wrapped tightly about him to ward off the bitter November chill.

Unable to contain his joy, Easeby cried out into the darkness, his breath steaming in the cold night air as he did so:

"James! James Dee! Thank God you have come! Well met, my friend! Well met!"

The man looked up at the window, his face intelligent, lined and smiling. He dusted himself down theatrically, before removing his black velvet cap, punching it back into shape and replacing it on his head.

"Richard Easeby, what the devil are you doing dragging me to the back of beyond on a night like this? This had better be good!"

***

Nathaniel paid his respects to James Dee and then politely took his leave, leaving the two old friends together. They had embraced warmly, slapping each other on the back many times, and it was clear their conversation would last well into the night. There was much to catch up on, and then there was the issue of the case to discuss. It warmed Nathaniel to see his master so relieved, and he went to find Ned to congratulate him.

After they had eaten in Easeby's room and exhausted the telling of old stories about their time together at Cambridge, the two men began to talk seriously. It was James Dee who brought the conversation around to the matter in hand.

"Your note intrigued me, Richard, but it gave me precious little to go on. You are in the business of saving witches' necks these days, it seems. I have heard about these things: women persecuted and put to death on the word of these witch-finders. It chills me to the bones. Tell me what it is I can do for you."

"The matter touches on your area of specialism directly, James. This town and the surrounding parishes have been blighted by a failed harvest, worse than any in living memory. Everybody is affected, with the exception of Sarah Wenham. Her crops have flourished in spite of all. In these times of superstition, people look for someone to blame, and Sarah Wenham is an obvious target. You are a scientist, an agriculturalist and a scholar. There is nobody who understands such things better than you. I need an explanation, James. I need something backed by science and reason to explain these things, and I need it tomorrow."

"Tomorrow? Hell's teeth, Richard, you do not ask much of me!"

"I know, James, I know. I am sorry."

"You must have given the matter a lot of thought of your own, Richard. Have you spoken to the woman about it? What does she say?"

"Believe me, I have thought of little else since I arrived here. I have only what my own reason tells me. There are two separate issues, I believe. The two appear to be connected, but not necessarily so. There need be no logical causality between them."

"Logical causality? You speak more like a scientist than I do these days, Richard! Explain what you mean."

"I mean this. The first issue is the success of Mrs Wenham's harvest. The second is the failure of everybody else's. The assumption is that the two must be related, but what if that is not the case? What if they occur completely independently of each other and their concurrence is pure coincidence?"

"That is certainly possible, Richard. Causality is almost always assumed. It is rare that it can be directly observed."

"Precisely my point. Now, on the first issue, I have made some progress talking to Mrs Wenham. She is a learned woman, James. She reads much and on very varied subjects, including agriculture and science. I need you to tell me everything you know about the Dutch system of rotation. It was something she says her husband began and she improved upon."

James Dee laughed. "That would be an absolute pleasure, Richard. I bore my students rigid on the subject every single day. I have never once had anybody willingly ask me to tell them about it, though!"

Easeby clapped his hands above his head. "Thank God for that, James! That is like music to my ears. I promise to be the most attentive student you ever taught!"

"That is not my memory of you from our student days, Richard, but I will take you at your word. A four-crop rotation over time would certainly give you an advantage, but it does not begin to address the second and more substantive issue, the absolute failure of everybody else's crops. What does Mrs Wenham say on that subject?"

"You are right, James. On that, I have only one thread. I hope you will be able to help me weave it into a pattern."

"Go on, Richard. I am listening."

"Mrs Wenham's land is the only sizeable estate to the North of the town that is not reclaimed from the fens. The estate has always been above the level of the water."

James Dee leaned forward, resting his chin on his crossed hands.

"Is that so? Now that, Richard, is very interesting indeed. You do realise that much of the land in these parts was reclaimed only very recently, perhaps no more than forty years ago? I have heard tell that the engineering works were very poorly performed."

"Who executed those works, James? Do you know?"

"It was a consortium project. There were many private investors. They were keen to finish as quickly as possible so they could see a fast return on their investment. The sums involved were eye-watering. They cut many corners, it is said."

31
The Testimony of Ruth Carter

Sir Richard and Nathaniel breakfasted together in the downstairs room of The Falcon. It was Monday 20th November, the morning of the reconvened trial.

Despite the importance of the day, Nathaniel found his master in surprisingly good spirits. He ate heartily and spoke warmly of his affection for Joshua, Becky and Ned. They had each grown substantially in his estimation since the beginning of the journey South, and he was increasingly satisfied that Joshua and Becky would make a very fine couple. Their devotion to each other was clear, and warmed even an old, cynical heart like his own, he joked.

As arranged, James Dee did not breakfast with them. He had risen very early, whilst it was still dark, and ridden with Ned and Joshua northwards towards Wood Walton. There was one final errand to be performed, and only the two old friends knew its nature, having determined the plan late the previous evening. Easeby's only concern was that James would have sufficient time to undertake the task and return to attend court later that day. The adding of his name to the roster of witnesses would be Sir Richard's first task as soon as he arrived at the courtroom.

Out of the bar room window, Nathaniel and Sir Richard could see Becky busily helping to collect logs from the wood store in the tavern yard. The weather had taken another turn for the worse and a light fluttering of snow had begun to fall. It was the first snowfall of the season, and it was not yet winter.

***

Malachai Harkiss got to his feet and approached the woman in the stand. The court was again full to the brim, and if anything, the sense of anticipation was even greater today. The sermon in All Saints Church the previous day had only served to whet their appetite more keenly.

"Your name is Ruth Carter, is that so, madam?"

Ruth Carter seemed undaunted by her appearance in court. She held her head high and did not once seek to avoid Harkiss's gaze. This was her moment, and she was going to savour it to the full.

"It is, sir, and my husband was Abel Carter. He was a good man and a loving husband. That is until SHE set her sights on him."

"She, being Sarah Wenham, Mrs Carter?"

"Yes, sir. He never looked at another woman until her husband got killed. That's when she put her spell on him. Anyone here will tell you the same. Everybody noticed it."

There was a murmur of assent from some corners of the court, and Jacob Smog felt the need to make an interjection of his own.

"Silence, please, ladies and gentlemen. Remember this is a court of law. It is not your place to be heard; only those in the witness stand are here for that purpose. Continue, please, Mr Harkiss."

"You saw a change in your husband then, madam? It seemed to you that there was some devilry at play?"

Sir Richard leaped to his feet. "With respect, sir, Mr Harkiss is leading the witness. She never used that word."

"Nonsense, sir! We all know why we are here! Devilry is at the very heart of the charges against her. I will remind you that I am the sole adjudicator here. The question is in order and I will allow it. You may answer Mr Harkiss's question, madam."

"Yes, sir, it was devilry. Why else would he suddenly change like that? Why else would he sneak out of the house and go to the manor that night? She lured him there with tricks and potions. It's as plain as the nose on your face! Why would he go there, if not because she'd bewitched him? Why else would he let her do that to him?"

The meaning of the last remark was lost on no one in the courtroom. The manner of Abel Carter's death had long since become common knowledge.

"Why indeed, Ruth Carter?" Malachai Harkiss drew himself up to his full height and turned to address his next remarks to the jury.

"The devil comes in many forms and guises, gentlemen. He seeks out our weaknesses and uses them to bend us to his will. We are all men of flesh and blood. He knows the power of lust, as does his agent there in the dock. There is no doubt she lured him there. You have heard it from the testimony of his wife, herself. She lured him there, gentlemen, to seduce and then murder him. She did that for no other reason than her own spite and the satisfaction of the act itself. She emasculated him! Imagine that for one moment, gentlemen. What more potent symbol of devilry could there be than to mutilate that belonging to another woman by the ordinance of God's holy estate of marriage? It is an evil thing. It is a wicked thing. It is the act of a witch and a succubus, of that there is no doubt."

The remarks were followed by complete silence in the courtroom. For the second time in as many days, Sir Richard observed the power of the man's words over his audience. He looked over to the dock with the intention of catching Sarah Wenham's eye, but was discouraged to see that her head was bowed. He silently willed her to maintain her faith.

It was Jacob Smog who finally broke the silence.

"Sir Richard, do you have any questions for this witness, or am I permitted to let her go and recompose herself? This ordeal must be distressing for her."

217

Sir Richard rose to his feet. "I do, sir, but I promise I will be quick. I do not wish to extend her ordeal any longer than is absolutely necessary."

"Oh, very well, man, but be as brief as you can! We must all show some humanity here."

"Thank you, sir. I am grateful for your forbearance. I can assure you that humanity is my primary concern in this and in all matters."

Slowly, he approached the dock.

"Mrs Carter, a very straightforward question, if I may. It requires only a yes or no answer. Are you able to read, madam?"

The question took everybody by surprise, not least Ruth Carter.

"Yes, sir, I can read."

There was a murmur of surprise in the courtroom. Even Jacob Smog seemed momentarily taken aback. For the wife of a common joiner to be able to read was scarcely a common accomplishment.

"There's no crime in that!" she added, feeling wrong-footed for the first time.

"Indeed, there is not, madam. In fact, it is a thing to be much commended. It is unusual, though, wouldn't you say? I wonder, madam, who was it that taught you to read?"

Ruth Carter was beginning to feel decidedly uncomfortable. She looked around, as though looking for help, but all eyes were now focused on her in anticipation of her answer.

"Let me assist you, madam. Might it perhaps have been Dr Edward Donne who taught you?"

Again, there was the unmistakable sound of surprised murmuring from the public gallery. Ruth Carter blushed, aware and afraid of the sudden scrutiny of her words. Eventually, she managed to whisper a barely audible response.

"Yes, he taught me."

"That is as I thought, madam, but what still confuses me is why a gentleman like Dr Donne might teach his occasional housekeeper to read. Can you enlighten me on that, madam?"

Ruth felt herself redden still further, and spat out her response rather petulantly.

"I don't know! Why don't you ask him?"

"Thank you, madam. That is precisely what I intend to do. I have no further questions at this time."

32
The Testimony of Edward Donne

Malachai Harkiss held up a large drawing, executed in the hand of Dr Edward Donne, for the benefit of the jury. The sketch was artfully and carefully rendered and contained a number of notations, each one signifying a particular mark on the body of Sarah Wenham. A large number of the notations were accompanied by a star, and underlined in a bold, scrawling hand.

"For the benefit of the jury, Doctor, could you explain, please, what these markings are and what those accompanied by a star indicate?"

"Certainly, Mr Harkiss. Each notation is a mark on the woman's body. At your instruction, I indicated their precise location in this sketch. Some are birthmarks, moles and such-like. Others are lesions caused by some other agent on the body, either internal or external. The markings accompanied by a star are those which, when pricked with a pin, did not yield blood."

Harkiss turned to the jury.

"And that is significant, gentlemen. The pricking of a mark is a proven method in identifying a witch. It is one I have employed on many previous occasions in my work. A natural mark will always bleed when it is pricked; an unnatural one will not. Those marks are most usually made by an incubus through the act of suckling on its mistress. Pay particular attention to the mark on the neck, gentlemen. I noticed that mark when I first met the woman. It is the largest of the unnatural marks on her body. It is a mark of great significance."

Harkiss then turned back to Edward Donne.

"Tell me, Doctor, did that particular mark yield blood when I inserted this pin into it?"

Harkiss drew a large, sharp pin from his coat and held it up for the jury to see clearly. The pin was a full six inches in length.

"No, Mr Harkiss, it did not. The star on the sketch signifies that quite clearly."

"Thank you, Doctor. I have no further questions for this witness, Mr Smog."

Jacob Smog bristled at the use of his name in court, but decided not to repeat the episode from Saturday, which had caused so much merriment. He was determined that there would be no repetition today.

"Thank you, Mr Harkiss. The witness is all yours, Sir Richard. Please be quick about it. We have much to get through, and the evidence here is incontrovertible, I think."

Easeby rose to his feet.

"Thank you, sir. On that point, we shall see."

He approached the witness stand.

"Dr Donne, I congratulate you on this drawing. It is very artfully done. You are a man of many talents, it seems."

Donne straightened himself, pleased with the compliment.

"Thank you, sir. Yes, drawing is one of my pastimes. I take great pride in it. I find it helps distract the mind."

"Distracts the mind indeed, Doctor. The drawing here is no simple sketch. You have taken very great care with it, I see. Was perhaps your mind so distracted that you focused more on your artistry than on witnessing the examination itself?"

"What do you mean, sir?"

"I mean this, Doctor: did you actually witness the act of pricking with your own eyes, or were your eyes more focused on the sketch you were producing, and instead, you took the word of Mr Harkiss as to which marks were bleeding and which were not?"

Malachai Harkiss leaped to his feet in rage.

"That is a scurrilous remark, sir! Gentlemen, see how he seeks to twist and pervert the truth with his trickery! He impugns not only my own integrity, but that of the good doctor here with that suggestion!"

"On the contrary, Mr Harkiss. I seek to impugn nobody's integrity, assuming there to be any integrity to be impugned, that is. I am only trying to establish exactly what Dr Donne is testifying to. Is it the evidence of his eyes or the evidence of his ears?"

Jacob Smog felt the need to interject again.

"Sit down, please, Mr Harkiss. The question is a fair one. I see nothing untoward in it. Answer the question, please, Dr Donne. Did you witness each prick with your own eyes or not?"

"I... I don't know, sir. I suppose it possible that I did not witness every single one."

"Not only possible, Dr Donne," replied Easeby, "highly likely, I think." He then quickly changed the subject.

"You attended Abel Carter on the night of his death, did you not, Dr Donne?"

"I did, sir. Unfortunately, the man had already lost too much blood from his injury. I was unable to save him."

"And when you found him, Doctor, what did you see? Had there been any attempt to stem the bleeding?"

"Yes, sir. Several bandages had been applied."

"Several bandages, you say? Do you know who applied those bandages, Doctor?"

Donne looked over at Sarah Wenham in the dock. The woman was staring straight back at him.

"I believe it was Mrs Wenham, sir."

"Mrs Wenham? It is peculiar, do you not think, that a woman accused of witchcraft would lure her victim into her lair, heinously bite him as might a succubus with murder on her mind, and then attempt to save his life?"

Easeby left no time for the question to be answered, allowing the point just sufficient opportunity to lodge itself inside the jury's minds. Instead, he immediately changed tack again.

"There was a period of some time, from your arrival at the house and the man's death, was there not?"

"Yes, sir. I was trying to save him, as I said."

"Is that so, Dr Donne? Or were you perhaps delaying whilst his lifeblood drained away? You were conscious of the unexpected opportunity it afforded you, were you not?"

Jacob Smog railed instantly at the question.

"That is outrageous, sir! You will withdraw that question immediately and you, gentlemen of the jury, will expunge it from your minds! Dr Donne is a witness here. He is not on trial!"

Easeby had been expecting that; indeed, it is what he had hoped for.

"I apologise, sir. Please forgive me. I will ask a different question then, if I may? Tell me, Dr Donne, how long have you known Ruth Carter, the man's wife?"

'I don't know, sir. What relevance is that?"

"If you do not wish to answer the question, I will have to answer it for you, Dr Donne. You have known her for two years, is that not so? She is your housekeeper."

"I suppose that would be about right, yes. It would probably be about two years."

"Long enough for you to teach her to read, in fact. We have learned from Mrs Carter's testimony that you did so. Why did you teach your housekeeper to read, Dr Donne? That is an unusual arrangement, is it not?"

"I... I don't know, sir. I just wanted to help her improve herself, I suppose."

"Is that so? May I offer an alternative possibility that is just as feasible? Is it perhaps that you were in love with her? Were the two of you, in fact, star-crossed lovers, communicating with each other in verse and letters of affection, because whilst her husband yet lived, those were the only means available to you?"

"You have no basis for that assertion, sir! How dare you?"

Sir Richard removed a pile of papers from his tunic and slammed them onto the witness stand in front of Edward Donne.

"On the contrary, sir. I have every basis for that assertion. I have the letters and verses themselves. They are all in your hand, Dr Donne, every single one of them. I submit them to this court as evidence."

33
The Testimony of Catherine Monk

Jacob Smog was forced to call a brief halt to proceedings. Easeby's questioning of the doctor had caused such a commotion in the courtroom that an immediate continuation was impossible until the atmosphere had calmed a little.

"It is not proper, sir, to submit material evidence without prior notification to me and to the court officers! How dare you, sir? May I remind you that you are already on probation for your behaviour in this place on Saturday?"

"The evidence is newly acquired, sir, and there was no opportunity for me to submit it to you earlier. I apologise for that, but there was no alternative."

"Very well, man. I will peruse the documents during this short break. In the meantime, nobody is permitted to leave this place. Sergeant, see to it that the doors are locked, please, and allow nobody in or out of this courtroom!"

With that, Jacob Smog rose brusquely and left the court, retiring to the small antechamber he retained for his personal use.

It was perhaps thirty minutes before he returned. Easeby was glad for the break in proceedings. Every second of delay was valuable time bought and might allow James Dee a greater chance of completing his errand and returning to the court in time.

Taking his seat once more, Smog addressed the court.

"I have looked at the documents submitted by Sir Richard Easeby. I have to inform the court that they are indeed written in the Doctor's hand and that they appear to be letters of endearment from him to Mrs Carter. How Sir Richard came by those letters is a matter I intend to get to the bottom of; however, for the purposes of the trial of Mrs Wenham, I see no reason why they should not be permitted as evidence. Gentlemen of the jury, you will be given the opportunity to examine the artefacts for yourselves during your deliberations at the end of this case. I know most of you and am content that there are sufficient amongst you able to read to render the things intelligible.

"Now let us continue these proceedings. Mr Harkiss, who do you intend to call to the stand next?"

Harkiss had sat throughout the short adjournment silently seething to himself, and his reply, when it came, sounded petulant and sarcastic.

"I call the woman, Catherine Monk. Her testimony at least cannot be twisted with clever words and deceitful sleights of logic!"

Sarah Wenham sat listening to Catherine Monk's testimony rapt with attention. Of all the charges against her, it was this one that caused her the greatest anguish. She had liked the boy, Tobias Monk, and felt empathy towards him. It was impossible to see him and not think of her husband, Thomas, left to die on the field with the rage of the battle all around him.

At Harkiss's prompting, Catherine told the court of her son's injuries and his state of mind. Whilst he had returned unusually introverted, it was only after Sarah started to show an unexpected interest in the boy that his condition seemed to worsen dangerously. As the rumours about Sarah began to circulate, Catherine had done only what any mother would have done in the circumstances and asked the woman to leave her son alone.

Sarah had agreed without argument and left the boy a gift of some strange fruit, the like of which Catherine had never seen before. It was immediately afterwards that the nightmares began.

"Mrs Monk, would you please tell the court about these nightmares?"

"They come every night, sir. It is a terrible thing to behold. It is as though he has lost his wits. He screams and writhes and oftentimes my husband has to restrain him to prevent him doing himself harm."

"Would you say it's as though the boy has a devil inside him, madam?"

Sir Richard considered objecting to the remark. It undoubtedly put words into the woman's mouth again, but he thought the better of it. The testimony on the charge of Tobias was sensitive and required very careful handling. Easeby had no desire to belittle the woman's anguish. That would only serve to increase the jury's sympathy for her, so he let the question pass unchallenged.

"Yes, sir! That is exactly what it is like."

"And you say that this began only after you prohibited the Wenham woman from visiting him?"

"Yes, sir. The first nightmare came that very night. He woke us with his screaming and he was drenched with sweat. We could not calm him no matter how much we tried. We scarcely could recognise him as our son, so terrible and demented he had become."

"Demented, you say, madam?"

"Yes sir, there is no other word for it. He is demented when the dreams come."

"And at your wits' end, cognisant that many in the village, for reasons of their own, thought the woman a witch, that is when you decided to call for my assistance? Is that so, madam?"

"It is, sir."

Harkiss now turned to the jury once more.

"Gentlemen, you have heard from Mrs Monk's own mouth her assessment of her son's condition. She has used a very specific word, gentlemen. The word was 'demented'. That is not a word I suggested to her, or put into her mouth. It is her word, not mine.

"The word has a very interesting etymology, gentlemen. It is from the Latin 'de mentis' and means quite literally 'out of the mind'. Her son has been driven out of his mind by the spell cast on him by Sarah Wenham.

"The agent of the spell was a fruit, gentlemen. It is a fruit not easily cultivated on these shores, yet Mrs Wenham has managed to cultivate it. What's more, the pomegranate is a fruit of evil reputation. There are Biblical scholars who now believe that the fruit with which Eve first tempted Adam was not an apple, as we are usually taught, but, in fact, was a pomegranate. The Ancient Greeks were also aware of its reputation for evil. It was with the help of a pomegranate that Hades stole Persephone, the daughter of Demeter and Zeus, and lured her to the underworld.

"Mrs Wenham is a scholar, gentlemen. I have seen with my own eyes the library of books she keeps in her manor house. She knows these classical myths. She also knows, gentlemen, that the Roman equivalent of Demeter was Ceres, the goddess of the harvest.

"Think of that, gentlemen. The symbolism is not a coincidence. It is quite deliberate, and the charges are linked, one to the other, by means of that symbolism. The crops failed, gentlemen, when Hades lured Persephone away, causing her mother to grieve for her loss. The Ancient Greeks believed that is why we have the winter months, devoid of growth and crops.

"No, gentlemen, there are no coincidences here. The choice of the pomegranate as the agent of her spell was quite deliberate. She relishes in the intertwining of her crimes; the failing of the harvest and the tormenting of a young boy's mind.

"She cast a spell on Tobias Monk by means of a pomegranate infused with nightshade and quite literally drove him out of his mind. And why, gentlemen? What crime had Tobias committed to offend her so much? It is only this: he fought in a battle on the opposite side to her husband. He survived the battle and her husband did not. He fought on the side of the common good, her husband on the side of a tyrannical king.

"It is spite, gentlemen; plain and simple spite."

***

There was complete silence as Harkiss resumed his seat. Whatever advantage Easeby had won by his revelations concerning Ruth Carter and Edward Donne was now in serious danger of unravelling. Harkiss had woven a spell of his own over the courtroom, and Easeby knew it. This was a critical point in the whole trial, and he would have to play his part with extreme caution. He rose slowly to his feet.

"Mrs Monk, the condition of your son leaves us all touched and saddened. I have no words of consolation I can offer that would even begin to ease your pain. I pray for your son's deliverance from his current torment."

"I thank you, sir."

"It is, however, my role here to make sure that those injuries are not compounded by a miscarriage of justice. I do not know your son, madam, but I am sure that is not something he would wish to see."

"Miscarriage of justice, sir? The only miscarriage of justice would be to see that woman walk free!"

"That, I fear, is for the jury to determine, Mrs Monk. It is not for you, or for Mr Harkiss or for me, come to that, to determine the outcome. The burden is theirs alone. That is how justice is done in this land. I am sure you understand that."

Catherine Monk did not respond. Instead, she remained silent and fixed Easeby with a proud look, which unsettled him slightly. He held her gaze for as long as he dared, before continuing.

"When your son returned from the war, did he speak to you about his experiences there?"

"No, sir. He did not want to speak to anyone about it. He still doesn't."

"Does the boy have friends in Wood Walton, madam? Lads his own age who he might have confided in?"

"No, sir. All the lads of his age went to war. They are all either dead or still fighting."

"So, there was no one at all?"

"No, sir. No one."

"I see; except that isn't entirely true, is it? Forgive me, madam, I do not mean to gainsay you, but Mrs Wenham showed an interest in him, did she not? You have already testified as much."

"Yes, sir. She came uninvited. I did not ask her to."

"I am aware of that, Mrs Monk. Indeed, she was not asked to come and yet come she did. Tell me, when Mrs Wenham first came to see Tobias, how did you feel about that? Were you angry or were you grateful perhaps?"

"I... I was grateful, I suppose; at first, anyway."

"I very much expect you were, madam. It was an act of great kindness, would you not say?"

"She deceived me, sir! She deceived us all!"

"And yet it was only when rumours — other people's rumours — began to circulate that you felt differently. Is that so?"

"I have a mind of my own, sir! I do not need anyone else to tell me what is best for my son!"

"Indeed, you do not, madam. You certainly would not listen to anyone else's advice on that matter anyway, would you?"

Jacob Smog interjected immediately.

"Be careful, sir! Mrs Monk is much traumatised by her experiences; that much is clear to anyone. You will treat her with courtesy and respect in my court; that is not a request, sir, it is an instruction. Show some empathy!"

233

"I can assure you, sir, empathy and respect are at the very forefront of my mind."

He turned to the jury.

"You see, gentlemen, empathy is a very important concept in this matter. It relies upon a degree of understanding of how another person feels. No matter how close we are to someone, or how deep our love for them may be, if their experiences are very alien to anything we have ourselves experienced, then empathy is a chimera. No matter how hard we try, it may always elude us. That is how it differs from sympathy. We can sympathise with someone without understanding the cause of their torment; but to empathise with them, that is a different matter."

Sir Richard turned back to Catherine Monk.

"Tell me, madam, were you ever present during the long hours that Mrs Wenham sat with your son?"

"No, sir. I left them alone. As you say, I was grateful at first for her attentiveness. There seemed no harm in it."

"So, it is fair of me to assume that you do not know on what subjects the two of them spoke?"

"I… I suppose so, sir, yes. She read to him. That much I do know."

"But they spoke, too, Mrs Monk. Mrs Wenham will testify to that herself when she is called to give evidence. I have spoken to Mrs Wenham, so I have an advantage over you, I am afraid. I know exactly the subject they spoke about almost exclusively. It is the subject your son could not bring himself to speak to you or his father about, Mrs Monk.

"The subject was war, and it was a subject your son desperately needed to talk about."

***

Sir Richard turned once again to the jury.

"You see, gentlemen, war is a terrible thing. Young boys grow up believing it to be a glorious, honourable adventure. They fight battles as children. Each boy has fought and died a thousand times by the time he reaches the age of ten and enjoyed every single one of those deaths. But war — real war — is not like those games at all, gentlemen. We all know that to be true.

"Tobias Monk, like many of his peers, went off to war with a feather in his cap and a spring in his stride; but the things he experienced when he got there left him injured not only in body, but also in mind. He experienced trauma of every conceivable kind, gentlemen. It is a trauma he still experiences to this day. It is the memory of blood, disease, filth and death.

"Many men are able to shut such things from their minds. They are not stronger necessarily, just able to forget more quickly. But for others, the scars take much longer to heal. The only hope in such cases is that time will eventually fade those images from their minds, a process that can sometimes be helped by talking;

especially, gentlemen, talking about them with someone capable of showing real empathy.

"Why could Mrs Wenham show that empathy when the boy's own parents could not? It is because she herself was suffering the pain of loss, gentlemen: the loss of her husband. Why did the boy's nightmares begin the day his mother sent Mrs Wenham away? It is because Mrs Wenham was his only means of escape from the horrors he had seen."

Sir Richard then removed something small and round from his tunic and, taking a knife, cut it into two pieces.

"We are asked to believe that the cause of the boy's torment is this, gentlemen; a pomegranate. It is said the fruit was infused with nightshade to drive the boy mad, as though everything he had seen was not sufficient to do that."

He squeezed one half of the fruit in his hand, causing the juice to drip through his fingers to the floor.

"See how it bleeds, gentlemen! See how its blood scorches the earth on reaching it! Can it be that it is exactly as Mr Harkiss describes it? Can it be that fruit can carry spells just as owls can be demons?"

He then took the other half of the fruit and, raising it to his lips, drank some of the juice, before letting the thing fall to the floor at his feet. He paused for a while, the courtroom again completely silent. Then, in a hushed tone:

"But no, it seems it is just a fruit after all, gentlemen. Not witchcraft; not devilry; not mystical contrivance; it is just a fruit."

Into the silence that followed came the unmistakable sound of sobbing; in the witness stand, Catherine Monk was weeping.

34
Snow

What had begun as a light flurry of flakes had quickly thickened into a full snowstorm, swirling about the town of Huntingdon and the surrounding fields and fenland. Inside the courtroom, cocooned and protected from the elements, Easeby remained ignorant of the blizzard for now; but outside on the road back to Huntingdon, the three horsemen rode hunched in their saddles, cloaks pulled tightly over their heads. The wind was blowing from the North and against their backs, which was perhaps the only blessing. The road ahead had long since disappeared beneath a carpet of white, and their progress became painfully slow.

"Be careful, sir!" called Joshua Cooper. "We must keep to the road. This is dangerous fenland and it is hard to know where the road finishes and the marshes begin."

Ned had taken the lead, with James Dee riding behind him and Joshua at the rear. Dee was not an accomplished horseman and on more than one occasion, Joshua had to ride up alongside him to take the reins and steer his horse away from the edge.

"How much further is it to Huntingdon, Master Cooper? I have lost all track of time and everything is so featureless in this storm."

"I do not know for sure, sir. I think we have passed the halfway point, so perhaps an hour or so at this rate. We dare not go faster."

"I am afraid I am slowing us all down! I have never been much of a rider. There is little call for the art on the college greens of Cambridge! Your master was always more accomplished than I at the outdoor pursuits, though neither of us was ever a match for Oliver. This damnable weather! Of all the days it chooses, it chooses the one where I most need God's speed!"

"You discovered everything you needed to at Wood Walton, sir?"

Joshua had earlier watched the man with bemusement as he strode purposefully across field after open field, the soggy earth often reaching the top of his boots.

"Yes, Master Cooper. I believe I did, but it will all be for nought unless we can reach Huntingdon in time. An hour, you say? God pray it will be soon enough!"

"Whoa, sir! Be careful there!"

Dee had again allowed his horse to drift to the side of the road, and this time the beast's front legs sank into the soft fenland earth, causing its rider to fall forwards and nearly out of the saddle. He saved himself from falling only by wrapping his arms tightly around the horse's neck. There, he remained perfectly still.

Hearing the commotion behind, Ned acted swiftly. Leaping from his saddle, he ran back to the stricken horse and grabbed the reins in his hands. Patting the horse gently on its haunches and whispering soothing words, he then slowly coaxed it backwards until its hooves reached the firm ground of the road once more. James Dee remained motionless in the saddle, his arms still wrapped tightly around the beast's neck, reluctant to relinquish his grip.

"Are you well, sir?" Joshua asked, concerned that James Dee appeared pale and unable to sit upright in the saddle. "Take a moment to catch your breath. That was a close thing!"

"You did well to hang on, sir. We'll make a horseman of you yet, perhaps," added Ned Jones, continuing to pat and soothe Dee's horse.

"It was the most curious thing," replied James Dee, finally recovering his breath and his composure.

"Why curious, sir? You lost sight of the road, that is all," said Joshua.

"Not that, Master Cooper. I heard a woman's voice, calling to me as I held onto the beast. Did you not hear it?"

"A voice, sir? There was no voice that I heard. A trick of the wind, perhaps?"

"Perhaps, but I swear I heard it speaking to me."

"Speaking to you? What did it say, sir?" asked Ned.

"It called me by my name, Master Jones. It was as though a woman was standing right next to me. She asked me three times where I was going and then wished me God's speed."

***

The other girls had long since retreated back to the refuge of the Falcon, but Rebecca Standish continued collecting logs, carrying them from the woodpile to the cover of the porch at the rear of the tavern. It was hard, back-breaking work, and the cold had numbed her fingers to the point where she could no longer feel their tips.

This was not her job, of course, but Becky had always found hard work the perfect antidote to worry. She had happily volunteered for the task, welcoming the opportunity to take her mind off the trial of the three girls she met yesterday. She had liked Jane and Anne immediately, and even Annabel, who she had quickly recognised as a liar, she felt some sympathy for.

Who knows what anyone would do or say in such circumstances? Becky liked to imagine that she herself would remain calm and truthful, but it was impossible to know for sure. Nobody can truly know until such moments arrive, and the girls were so young, hardly any older than Becky herself.

The snow had quickly grown deep on the cobbled courtyard and Becky found it increasingly difficult to keep her footing. There was a thin layer of ice beneath the snow, and as the covering grew deeper, the worst-affected parts became difficult to spot.

Lifting a particularly heavy log, Becky suddenly felt a stabbing pain in her abdomen. It came not from the scar, which had given her little trouble even with the heavy work, but much lower. It was like the pain she regularly felt when her monthly cycle began, but this time it was much worse.

She cried out in agony, allowing the log to fall to the ground. Bending over double, she lost her footing completely and fell into a heap on the floor, where she curled herself into a ball, fighting back the howls of pain as best she could.

In the spot she had just been standing, the snow had become stained red with blood. The blood had seeped from between her legs, and under her skirts it had flowed freely down her legs and gathered into a pool of crimson set against the pure white blanket of virgin snow.

35
The Testimony of Isaiah Felt

Once again, Jacob Smog was required to call a halt to proceedings as Catherine Monk was led from the stand and into the arms of her waiting husband. Not for the first time in a court of law, Sir Richard found himself feeling slightly ashamed.

Looking over towards Sarah Wenham in the dock, he saw that the woman, too, had shared in Catherine's anguish. If only someone had spoken to her about these things sooner, thought Easeby, much pain could have been avoided. It seemed a failure of common decency that it had to happen here, in a public court. Once again, he cursed the lack of time he'd been given to prepare the case more sensitively. He knew there was no longer any choice but to play the cards he had been dealt as best he could.

Nathaniel leant over to whisper to him.

"I have been watching the jury carefully, Richard. They were moved by your words. I even dare hope the case may begin to swing in our favour."

"It is an abominable thing, Nathaniel. I take no pride in it. I will never understand why people must inflict such pain on each other."

"It is not your job to defend the human condition, Richard. That would be too great a task even for you. Content yourself that there is some hope at least that Sarah Wenham may yet walk free."

"We are far from escaping the woods, Nathaniel. Harkiss will call Isaiah Felt next. It is the issue of the harvest that determines the case, and we run short of time. Where is James? I cannot delay and prevaricate forever. I have already tested Smog's patience to the very limits, I think. I dare not go further."

"He will come, Richard. Have faith!"

Whilst Sir Richard and Nathaniel were talking, one of the court officers approached Jacob Smog to whisper something into the magistrate's ear. There was a brief and animated exchange between the two, before Smog dismissed the man with a wave of his hand and called the court to order.

"Ladies and gentlemen, I have been informed that outside this place, a great blizzard has been raging for the past two hours. Already, the snow lies heavy on the ground and there is a risk that many of the routes to the town may soon become impassable.

"It is my intention to draw this trial to its conclusion as quickly as possible so that you may all return safely to your homes. We will deal briefly with the third of the charges against Mrs Wenham and then listen to her own defence testimony and that of Annabel Leach, her servant and co-defendant, on the subject of the fourth charge. That testimony, I believe, will be sufficiently damning to conclude the matter decisively. The jury will then retire to consider its verdict as expeditiously as possible."

Easeby exchanged a look of horror with Nathaniel, before quickly jumping to his feet.

"Your honour, I object in the strongest possible terms! This morning, I added the name of Dr James Dee of Sidney Sussex College, Cambridge, to the roster of witnesses. It is imperative that Dr Dee testifies in this case if justice is to be done. His knowledge on the subject of crops and harvests is unrivalled in all of England. It is critical to Mrs Wenham's defence!"

Jacob Smog had long since grown tired of Sir Richard Easeby. His face grew purple with rage and he growled his riposte with barely concealed contempt.

"Sir! On Saturday, you interrupted the proper progress of this court's affairs and caused me to adjourn it for a period of forty-eight hours. Today, you have stood in my court and impugned the integrity of Mr Harkiss. You then impugned the integrity of Dr Donne and all but accused the man of manslaughter. You have brought a woman of these parishes to tears, and now you demand that I risk the safety of everyone present to hear the musings of a college scholar — doubtless still in his bed — on the subject of blight?

"No, sir! If the man was central to your case, it was your responsibility to make sure he was here on time. He is not here, sir! I look all about me, and he is not here.

"If a central issue of Mrs Wenham's defence cannot be explored to your satisfaction, it is your fault, sir, not the fault of the court. I warned Mrs Wenham not to trust to you on the matter of her defence. It appears I was right to do so, and she was wrong to have ignored my counsel. I will delay no longer!

"Mr Harkiss, you may call Mr Felt!"

***

Malachai Harkiss had watched Easeby's methodical unpicking of the charges against Sarah Wenham with alarm. He had begun to fear a turning of the tide in court, and Jacob Smog's tirade against Sir Richard had come as a timely intervention. It was now down to Harkiss himself to ring the witch's final death knell, and he intended to do so as loudly as possible.

"Mr Felt, you are an esteemed landowner in these parts, is that not the case?"

Isaiah Felt savoured the use of the word "esteemed" and drew himself to his full, yet still rather diminutive, height.

"That is correct, Mr Harkiss. I am privileged to own several estates in the area. I do not farm them myself, but lease parcels of land to many local farmers at highly competitive rates. I cannot abide to see the land go to waste, sir."

"That is extremely public spirited of you, Mr Felt."

"I do not think of it in those terms, Mr Harkiss. I am a man of comfortable though not prodigious means. I make little profit from the rents; barely enough to cover my expenses, in fact. Rather, I consider it an act of charity, sir. The only debt I owe is to God. Charity is the means by which I repay that debt."

There was some incredulous laughter from the public gallery at that point, but both Harkiss and Felt remained oblivious to it.

"Many of your tenants have struggled to maintain payment of their rents this year, have they not, Mr Felt?"

"Alas that is so, sir. I see many of them in this court today and I take great pity on them. I know they do their best and I fear for their futures. The harvests have failed, sir. Not in forty years have I known such catastrophe. Not a man amongst them is unaffected and not a crop has escaped; wheat, barley, corn, all are similarly afflicted."

"To a charitable man like yourself, that must bring great anguish, Mr Felt."

"Indeed so. I have shown great forbearance in all cases, Mr Harkiss. I have waived and deferred more payments than I could possibly cite here. I deem it my moral duty to do so."

This time the laughter was louder, and Harkiss could not help but be aware of it. The man was not popular; that much was clear. He quickly moved the subject onto safer ground.

"You said that every 'man' has been affected by the failure, Mr Felt, but some of the land in these regions is now farmed by a woman, is it not? Am I to assume that she has suffered a similar fate?"

"Ah, now there you hit on a most curious point, Mr Harkiss! You refer, of course, to Mrs Wenham, and the answer is no, her harvest has been completely unaffected. Indeed, I believe she has enjoyed an excellent yield this year."

"Does that strike you as strange, Mr Felt?"

"Indeed, it does, sir, but I do not offer any supposition or reason for it. I know that many of my tenants have attributed it to witchcraft. I do not understand such things, Mr Harkiss. I am a man of the empirical world and prefer to limit my opinions to what I can see with my eyes and touch with my fingers. I leave more metaphysical matters to men such as you. I find it best to defer to expertise in matters of which I have no experience."

Harkiss turned to the jury.

"You heard those words, gentlemen. They are wise words indeed. Mr Felt does not understand witchcraft, gentlemen, so he defers to me. He is right to do so, just as I would defer to him on matters of finance. What he does understand, though, is the desperate plight of his tenants.

"Perhaps you are amongst that number? I do not know, but if that is the case, then you will surely understand the fear of privation, for that is what many of you will now be facing: privation and hunger.

"Famine is a terrible thing, gentlemen. The Lord himself knows this. It is why He rarely and so reluctantly uses it as an instrument of His punishment, as in the case of Egypt: 'And I will punish those that live in the land of Egypt, as I have punished Jerusalem, with the sword, with famine and with pestilence.'

"Think on those words, gentlemen. They are taken from the Book of Jeremiah. Mrs Wenham knows the Bible and she knows those words as well as I. But whereas I use them to venerate the Lord, she takes them and twists them to denigrate and mock Him.

"Mark my words, gentlemen. This privation — this famine — is not a curse brought on you by our vengeful Lord. No! This curse is hers in the making. She audaciously apes His designs. She takes a punishment used only sparingly by the Almighty and engineers it for her own ends.

"It is not the will of the Lord that your children will starve this winter, gentlemen. It is the will of Sarah Wenham. She is malicious and in thrall to the devil.

"There is no natural reason why your crops would fail and hers would not. There is no science, or chance, or law of probability that might explain it. Only witchcraft can do that, gentlemen.

"Sarah Wenham does not grieve or mourn the starvation of your children. She rejoices and profits from it. She monopolises the markets and drives whatever price she wishes, knowing there is not one amongst you to undercut her.

"Heed the words of Mr Felt, gentlemen. He is an empirical man and trusts only what he can see and touch. The winter will soon be on us and your barns and larders are bare. That much, any man can see with his eyes and feel with the hunger of his belly.

"I have no further questions for this witness, Mr Smog."

***

Sir Richard rose to his feet and approached the witness stand with slow, deliberate steps. They were designed in no small part to delay proceedings as long as he could.

On reaching the stand, he appraised Isaiah Felt for a few moments, tilting his head to one side and resting his fingers on his chin.

Felt was a small, ugly man and clearly had very few friends in this place. That much was clear from the incredulous laughter that had greeted his flattering self-portraiture.

That antipathy was to Easeby's advantage, and he had long since learned that in cross-examination, the lawyer must exploit every advantage open to him.

Eventually, Sir Richard broke the silence.

"Mr Felt, what on earth possessed you to imagine that Sarah Wenham would ever consent to be your wife?"

From all corners of the courtroom, there was a sharp intake of breath, accompanied by a number of gasps and loud murmurs. The subject of Felt's proposal to Sarah was known only to the two of them; she having wished to spare the man's blushes and he feeling humiliated and resentful.

Felt was completely wrong-footed by the question and could scarcely formulate a coherent response at all.

"I do not know, sir. You are being impertinent and preposterous!"

"Impertinent and preposterous indeed, Mr Felt! I mean you are what, sixty years of age? She is a young woman of twenty-five. I ask you again, what on earth possessed you to suppose that she would consent to such an arrangement?"

Felt began to panic. He looked over to Jacob Smog in hope of an intervention, but none came. Indeed, the magistrate seemed as curious about this unexpected line of questioning as the rest of the courtroom. He sat silently looking at Felt, waiting for his response. Neither did Harkiss rise to his feet. This was not a narrative he could reshape in any helpful way. The line of questioning would have to take its course.

Eventually, Felt realised that he would have to answer the question directly. He had already seen enough of Sir Richard Easeby to understand that he dared not lie outright.

"It was a serious and sincere offer, sir, if it is of any business of yours. The offer was made out of charitable consideration for the woman's future."

"And yet she turned you down flat, did she not, Mr Felt? How did the rejection make you feel?"

"Feel, sir? I felt nothing but concern for the woman."

"Is that so, Mr Felt? Mrs Wenham's estate is of considerable value, is it not? I imagine that a man of 'comfortable but not prodigious means' — your own words, Mr Felt — would have benefited greatly by acquiring that estate, would he not?"

"I am sufficiently secure, sir, not to require any financial support from Mrs Wenham's estate."

"Indeed so, Mr Felt. You are more than 'secure', in fact, due to the revenues you receive from your tenanted lands. You are, sir, prodigiously wealthy, are you not?"

"I take little interest in calculating my financial worth, sir."

There was a much louder and more prolonged peal of laughter from the gallery at that point, causing Jacob Smog to call for order. Eventually, the noise subsided sufficiently for Easeby to continue.

"I believe you presented a fully audited statement of combined assets to Mrs Wenham as part of your wedding proposal, Mr Felt. That is hardly the act of a man who takes little interest in calculating his worth, is it? Isn't the truth of the matter that you have long coveted Mrs Wenham's estates, and when her husband died, you saw the perfect opportunity to acquire them and add them to your already extensive portfolio?"

"I resent that insinuation, sir! The offer was made out of charity, as I already told you."

"And when Mrs Wenham turned you down, you felt humiliated, did you not, Mr Felt? Humiliated and thwarted."

"No, sir!"

"The truth of the matter, Mr Felt, is that you were so humiliated that you hatched another plan from the depths of your resentment. If Mrs Wenham was to die intestate and without heir, you would gain the opportunity to acquire the estates you have so long coveted at less than their market price. Is that not so, Mr Felt?"

Jacob Smog had now heard enough.

"Sir Richard, your capacity for scurrilous accusation surpasses itself. I see no evidence for these allegations whatsoever. What is more, sir, they shed no light at all on the failure of the harvests, which is the primary issue here. They do not begin to answer the question why all crops have failed save those of the accused woman."

"Forgive me, your honour. I believe on that point, I may be of some assistance."

This response came not from Sir Richard Easeby, but from a cloaked figure recently entered into the courtroom. He was covered in thick snow and his boots were caked in mud.

"And who the blazes might you be, sir?" bellowed Smog.

"Forgive me, sir. I should have introduced myself. That is uncommonly rude of me. My name is Dr James Dee. I am a scientist and teacher of natural philosophy at Sidney Sussex College in the town of Cambridge. I was told the court would be expecting me."

36
The Testimony of James Dee

The man in the witness stand was very different from any who had gone before on that day. Erudite, precise and knowledgeable, his responses to Sir Richard's questions brooked little scope for challenge from either Jacob Smog or an increasingly agitated Malachai Harkiss.

"Mrs Wenham practices something that has become known as the Dutch method of farming, Dr Dee. Could you explain to the court in very simple terms what that is, please?"

"That is correct, Sir Richard. It is given that name because it was pioneered in the Netherlands, where the land is very similar to this part of England. I inspected her fields myself, this morning. It is clear that the method has been employed for some years now, so I can only assume it was adopted first by her late husband."

"And how does it differ from our more traditional practices, Dr Dee?"

"It is a simple enough concept to understand. Traditionally, land is divided into three sections. Two of the sections are planted with different crops, whilst the third section is left fallow. After each harvest cycle, the order of planting is shifted along so that the second field is planted with the crop previously planted in the first. The field left fallow is planted with the crop previously grown in the second field, and this time, it is the first field that is left fallow."

"And what is the purpose of rotating crops like that, Dr Dee?"

"It is to prevent erosion of the soil, Sir Richard. Soil contains nutrients that crops need to grow. If you simply planted the same crop in the same soil year after year, those nutrients would diminish over time. Different crops feed off different nutrients, so by rotating the crops, those nutrients are allowed time to replenish. The fallow field speeds the replenishment process, but obviously reduces the overall yield each year by a third."

"But the Dutch system is different?"

"It is. Under the Dutch system, the land is divided into four rather than three sections, and no section is ever left fallow. Instead, it is four different crops that are sequentially rotated. The soil still has time to replenish its nutrients and the overall yield is maximised each cycle. There is one additional advantage in that it allows for the growing of a winter crop for the feeding of livestock."

"And that is the system employed by Mrs Wenham?"

"And her husband before her, yes. Over time, the benefits will begin to manifest as better and more reliable yields."

"Is there anything else you noticed that is particular to Mrs Wenham's lands, Dr Dee?"

"Indeed so, Sir Richard. Her estate lies on higher ground. It is, in fact, the only land in the surrounding area not reclaimed from fen water."

"Does that in itself give an advantage, Dr Dee?"

"Not necessarily, no. If fenland has been well drained, with proper engineering and irrigation, there is no reason at all why it should not yield as successfully as unclaimed land. Indeed, for certain crops, it may even be better."

"I understand; that is all perfectly clear, but this is particularly important, so answer this next question very precisely, if you please, Dr Dee. This morning you inspected not only Mrs Wenham's fields, but also those in the surrounding area; the fields that were reclaimed. Is that so?"

"It is."

"What did you notice about those fields?"

"They are extremely muddy, Sir Richard, as evidenced by the state of my boots; much muddier than those on the Wenham estate."

"And what did you deduce from that, Dr Dee?"

"That the drainage was badly done and the water is returning, Sir Richard. The peat level — the base level, if you will — is shrinking. Each year the level of the fields is sinking lower and lower and very soon they will be under water again unless they are re-drained in a more resilient way."

"And the effect on crops grown in those conditions?"

"The soil condition is very bad. It is no wonder that the harvests have failed this year. Indeed, it is a surprise to me that the crops have not failed sooner."

"Do you know when the land was first drained, Dr Dee?"

"I believe it was about forty years ago. I teach my students at the university about the methods they employed at the time."

"To teach them how it is done?"

"No, to show them how it should not be done."

Doctor Dee's testimony had caught the attention of everybody in the courtroom and it was listened to in complete silence. This was substantiated evidence, and everybody recognised its importance, not least Malachai Harkiss. Not a syllable spoken was left unheeded.

"Do you know sufficient of the history to tell the court how the drainage of those lands was organised, Dr Dee?"

"Of course, Sir Richard. Large consortia of investors were formed to pay for the works. They were, of course, keen to see a return on their investment as quickly as possible, so unfortunately many corners were cut. Each investor was rewarded with a grant of the reclaimed land to use as they saw fit. Some farmed the land themselves; others sold it on at a profit. Many held onto the land and leased it out to tenant farmers, charging them rent and giving themselves an annual income; a very considerable income in some cases."

"So, the failure of the crops today can be directly attributed to actions taken by those consortia forty years ago?"

"That is correct, Sir Richard. There is a very direct correlation."

"And in the lands around Wood Walton, Dr Dee, do you know the names of any of those investors?"

"I do, Sir Richard. By far and away the principal amongst them was a gentleman called Isaiah Felt. He borrowed and invested thousands of pounds, it is said."

Part Three
Retribution

37
Mob

The jury took just fifteen minutes to deliver its verdict of not guilty against Sarah Wenham and the three girls. The mood grew tense following the testimony of James Dee and loud arguments broke out in the public gallery whilst the jury was deliberating. When it finally returned its verdict, all hell broke loose. This time, the anger was directed not at Sarah Wenham, but at Isaiah Felt.

Jacob Smog had called a halt to proceedings following Dee's testimony. It was Smog himself who directed the jury to acquit the woman, and the deliberations therefore became a formality. The magistrate was experienced enough to understand that the testimony had swung the case decisively in her favour and there was little point continuing with the matter. More importantly, it was vital that he was not viewed as having taken the wrong side now that the circumstances had changed. The instruction to acquit was taken as much to rescue what he could of his reputation as in the interests of justice.

Neither Sarah nor Annabel's testimony was heard; if Sarah was not guilty of the other charges, then the fourth charge concerning the girls naturally fell away, as Nathaniel had predicted.

What happened next, though, nobody could have foreseen. A fistfight in the public gallery very quickly escalated into a full-scale brawl that soon spilled out of the courtroom and into the surrounding streets. For the rest of the day, an angry mob ran riot through the streets of Huntingdon.

Isaiah Felt was smuggled through the short tunnel linking the court building to the prison-house, and for his own safety was locked into one of the cells. The prison-house then became the focal point of the unrest, and many attempts were made to break down the gates and storm the building. Inside his cell, Felt sat shaking with fear. The mob's purpose was clear: they intended to lynch him.

Sensing the mood turn, Sir Richard led Sarah and the three girls from the dock and out into the blizzard still swirling outside. From there, he, Nathaniel and James Dee escorted them towards the Falcon Tavern. It was only when they reached the inn that they realised that Annabel was no longer with them. She must have slipped away somewhere along the short route, Easeby guessed, perhaps terrified of what her mistress might say, knowing that she had been willing to testify against her.

Sarah was desperate to try to find the girl, but the mob on the streets had already grown dangerously out of control and Sir Richard persuaded her against it.

"The girl cannot have gone far in this weather, madam. She will come to her senses and find her way here soon enough. Please, go inside and warm yourselves by the fire. I will retrace our steps and look for sign of her."

"I will come with you, Richard."

"Very well, James. I'll be glad of the company. Nathaniel, please stay here with the women. We will return as quickly as possible."

With that, Easeby and Dee turned and headed back into the blizzard.

***

Jacob Smog retired to his office to consider what to do next. To his surprise and anger, he found Malachai Harkiss waiting for him.

"What are you doing here, man? Don't you think you have caused enough damage for one day? Your hokum has brought disrepute to this town and a riot to the streets. You will please leave immediately! I wish never to set my eyes on you again."

"You fool, Smog! Don't you see what they have done? They have blinded you with their tricks. This was always their plan!"

"I have listened to you too long, Mr Harkiss. Your voice grates on me like that of a shrewish wife. Be gone before I call the constable!"

"You will live to regret this day, Jacob Smog. The woman has not finished with this town. Indeed, she is emboldened by your stupidity. There will be no redemption for you or for those you are charged with protecting through your office. She will continue to weave her spells and her malevolence as long as she lives. She will have her revenge on all of you. I have seen such things before.

"Mark my words, Jacob Smog! You have brought ill fortune this day, and when these things come to pass, I will heed the call of this town again; not out of pity, but because it is the will of God that I should do so."

"Get out, Mr Harkiss! Be gone, I tell you! You are no longer welcome here, sir."

Harkiss drew himself to his full height, casting a shadow on the wall twice as tall as the man himself. For the briefest of moments, Smog feared he was going to strike him, but instead the witch-finder simply turned on his heels and left, slamming the door behind him.

Outside, the noise of the crowd showed no signs of abating. Not even the snow seemed to cool their wrath, and for the first time in his life, Jacob Smog was at a loss to know what to do. The prison-house gates would not hold them back forever.

***

Easeby and Dee retraced their steps as far as the prison-house but could see no sign of the girl. They had reached the outer edges of the mob, perhaps now two hundred strong, and to their horror they saw that a large tree had been felled and was now being used as a battering ram against the prison-house gates.

"They will hang the man if they break through, James. In the name of all humanity, how does one wrong cure another?"

"There is nothing we can do, Richard. I fear they would not listen to us even if we tried. I have seen such things before, in Cambridge when the war started. Mobs develop a will of their own. They become more than the sum of their parts. One day, perhaps, someone will be able to explain the phenomenon. For now, it is beyond the knowledge of natural science."

Behind the gates, they could see Adam Crook standing resolute. He was remonstrating with the crowd between the charges of the battering ram.

"The jailor is a good man, James. See how he stands his ground. They will trample him to death if they breach the gates. Surely there is something we can do!"

"No, Richard. It is beyond us. No eloquent speech will calm them."

At that point, their conversation was interrupted by another sound. Faint at first, but growing louder at speed, the unmistakable sound of hooves on cobbles was approaching like a storm: not just one horse, but very many.

Suddenly breaking into sight to their left, a company of dragoons could be seen riding towards the crowd at full gallop. As they drew closer, some of the dragoons fired shots into the air, immediately scattering the crowd in all directions. Without breaking speed and with practised co-ordination, the rest of the company drew swords and divided into smaller units of four or five men. They then pursued the remaining groups of fleeing townsmen, dispersing them still further. Within five minutes, the streets had been cleared completely without a single man being killed or injured on either side.

From their vantage point away from the skirmish, Easeby and Dee looked on, marvelling at the trained precision of the exercise. It was no wonder that the tide of the war had turned, thought Easeby. These were well-trained, professional soldiers; far removed from the ragtag recruits that had first flocked to the cause.

It was only after all vestiges of the crowd had been dispersed that Easeby noticed a familiar rider separate himself from the company and come trotting towards them.

"Greetings, Sir Richard. You appear to have caused quite a stir here. I have better things to do than disperse angry mobs, as I'm sure you'll appreciate."

"Good day, Corporal. As ever, your timing is flawless and defies mere coincidence. They have acquitted the woman, but then that will come as no surprise either to you or Master Cromwell, I think. It is time, perhaps, that you and I spoke candidly for once. I would like to know the circumstances of why I was brought to this place."

"There is no mystery there, Sir Richard, but this is not the place. Where are you lodging? I will come to you later today."

38
A Warning

Pyramus Peake approached the camp warily. The last time he had been amongst his own people, things had not gone well and he had been accused of stealing. Romany networks were close and well connected, and he had kept away from them ever since. That was in Westmorland nearly two years ago and he'd been lucky to escape being beaten to a pulp. He hoped whatever word had spread it might not have reached this far South, or if it had, at least it might have faded from memory.

On the edge of the camp and chained to a post, a large mastiff caught Pyramus's scent and began to bark fiercely. Next to the dog, a large man was chopping firewood. Despite the cold, the man was stripped to the waist, his black hair plastered to his forehead with sweat.

Seeing Pyramus approach, the man kicked out at the dog, causing it to let out a pathetic whelp before lying down on the ground, whimpering.

Pyramus greeted the man in the Romany tongue: "Kushti divuus! Sashin?"

The man spat on the ground and without answering, lifted his axe and continued chopping.

"Mandis lav Pyramus. Dali dzane Romani?"

The man took a powerful final swing with his axe, burying the blade in the frosted ground next to the woodpile.

"Of course I speak fucking Romany, but I'll not speak it with strangers. That's a sure way to get a man killed around here. Make yourself useful and carry some wood to camp."

The man scooped up a large pile of firewood in his arms and marched off in the direction of two painted wagons. Outside the wagons, a large fire was burning.

Pyramus lifted a pile less than half the size of the stranger's and struggled after him.

"Hester! We have company. Give him something to eat."

A youngish woman with red hair and pale complexion came down the steps of one of the wagons, wiping her hands on her apron. Holding onto her skirts were two young girls, both of them with the same jet-black hair as their father.

"He says his name is Pyramus. He's one of us. He can't carry shit, though!"

Pyramus dropped the wood on top of the stranger's pile and lifted his hat from his head, bowing deeply.

"It is a pleasure to meet you, madam. Forgive the intrusion. I was just passing and saw your fire."

Hester laughed merrily.

"Well, I'm enchanted, sir! It's a long time since any man doffed his cap to me. Patrin here is an oaf. He isn't much given to common courtesy."

"Hold your tongue, woman, or I'll sew your mouth shut and have you sold at the fair!"

This was said with a familiar teasing that belied the words and made Pyramus smile.

"And a fair old price you'd get for me, too. Some gentleman would pay handsomely for a dutiful wife like me!"

"That's as maybe, but I doubt they'd still want you after they'd heard you open your mouth! That's why I'd need to sew it shut."

Hester began to stir a large pot of stew hanging over the fire.

"Leonora, fetch Mr Pyramus here a bowl and wash your hands! Selina, wake Grandma up and tell her we're eating."

"It's Peake, madam, Pyramus Peake. Just call me Pyramus."

Leonora ran back into the wagon and quickly returned carrying a wooden bowl, which she shyly handed to Pyramus.

Selina, meanwhile, disappeared into the second wagon. There were sounds of shaking, grunting and reluctant stirring from inside.

"Get off me, child! You could wake the dead shaking them like that!"

The voice was that of an old woman.

"Hurry up, Grandma! It's time to eat, and we've got a visitor!"

"A visitor? What's a visitor want with us? Tell that idle da of yours to set the dog on him!"

Selina reappeared, leading her grandmother from the wagon. She waited patiently as the old woman gingerly descended, searching out each step with her feet. Pyramus recognised immediately that her eyes were misty and lifeless. She was completely blind.

**

It was beginning to grow dark, and Pyramus entertained the two young girls with tricks, making pennies disappear from his palm before retrieving them from behind the girls' ears. The girls giggled each time he performed the trick and Pyramus felt relaxed, the atmosphere having warmed to one of happy, well-fed contentment. Even Patrin seemed to have warmed to the stranger. The two men had drunk a fair quantity of ale together as the afternoon faded into evening.

Hester sat darning stockings, gently scolding the girls if they grew too boisterous or when she suspected them of showing off to their new friend. The old woman dozed by the fire, occasionally waking herself with a start and asking Pyramus a question she had already asked him before. The girls laughed at her then and Hester scolded them, but always with a wink to show that she also found it funny.

Eventually, the conversation turned to other matters.

"So, Pyramus, what brings you to these parts?" asked Patrin, stretching out his legs to warm his feet near the fire. "You're a long way from home."

"What do you mean by that, Patrin?"

"Oh, come on, man! I'm not a fool, despite what Hester here might think. I've heard the name Pyramus Peake before. You're a northern man, so I'm told. I wouldn't go back there if I were you, though. There are men looking for you. You're a thief is what I've heard."

Pyramus suddenly felt himself sober up.

"Then you've heard wrong, Patrin."

"Relax, Mr Peake. I couldn't give a pig's fart whether you're a thief or not, as long as you don't thieve nothing from me. If you were to do that, I'd take out your innards, turn you inside out and stuff them back up your arse."

Pyramus grew suddenly very pale, which caused Patrin to slap his thigh and roar with laughter. Pyramus smiled weakly, laughing along nervously.

"I value my innards greatly, Patrin. I have no intention of stealing from you."

"Then we shall be friends, Pyramus Peake, and friends confide in each other, so let me ask you again. What brings you to these parts?"

"Well, as it happens, Patrin, I recently happened on a pretty trinket that I am looking to sell. Do you know of anybody who might be interested?"

"Trinket, you say? What kind of trinket?"

"It's a silver cross and a good quality one, if I'm any judge at all. I won it in a cup and stone game. I'll show you how to play the game if you like."

"Cheated someone of it, more like!" laughed Patrin. "No, thank you, Mr Peake, I'll not play you at your games, and have you steal the shirt from my back! Let me see this trinket of yours."

Reluctantly, Pyramus reached inside his shirt and pulled out Ruth Carter's silver cross, which he handed to Patrin. Patrin whistled, weighing the thing in his hands before holding it to the fire to see more clearly.

"You're right, Mr Peake. It's a very pretty thing indeed. What are these markings on it?"

"Markings? What markings?"

"You mean you haven't looked at it closely? These markings here; they're like symbols."

Pyramus took the cross back and held it to the light. Patrin was right. Along the horizontal bar of the cross were five markings, engraved into the silver. If they were writing, they were like no writing he'd ever seen before. He did not understand how he could have missed them.

"I don't know, Patrin. I've never noticed them before."

"Ma is good with such things. She can read with her fingers. Let her feel it. Ma, hold out your hand."

The old woman did as she was told and Pyramus placed the cross in her palm. She closed her fingers around it.

"There are markings on one side, Ma. Do you know what they are?" asked Patrin.

The woman opened her palm again and with her finger, traced a line along the cross, touching each of the marks in turn. Her eyes stared lifelessly ahead of her as she did so. She repeated the act three times before letting the thing fall to the ground as though it had just scalded her. Pyramus quickly picked it up.

"What is it, Ma? Do you recognise the marks?"

"Tell him to go, Patrin."

"Why, Ma? He's our guest. What do you see?"

"Tell him to go, Patrin! The thing is cursed. He brings great evil to this place."

39
News

Sir Richard recognised something was wrong as soon as he entered the Falcon. Sarah Wenham, Jane Newton and Anne Stenton were nowhere to be seen. Instead, Nathaniel, Joshua and Ned were sitting by the fire. The rest of the bar room was empty and the mood was sombre. By the look of the boy, it was clear that Joshua had been sobbing.

Seeing them enter, Nathaniel jumped to his feet and quickly ushered Easeby and James Dee back outside.

"What is wrong, Nathaniel? What has happened?"

"It is Rebecca, Richard. She lost the child this morning."

Easeby blanched, unable to process the news at first.

"Lost it?"

"Yes, Richard. She has miscarried the infant. It bled from her whilst she was collecting logs."

"But that cannot be!"

"It is so, Richard. I am sorry. There was nothing that could be done to save it."

"Poor Becky! Poor Joshua!"

"The boy is bereft, Richard. Not even Ned can cheer him. It came as a shock to Master Jones that the girl was even pregnant. I don't think Joshua and Rebecca told anybody except you and I."

"This is all my fault. I should never have allowed her to travel South with us."

"You cannot blame yourself, Richard. You know as well as I that the girl would not have stayed at home, even if we'd sent her back. She is wilful and determined."

"How is she now, Nathaniel?"

"She is resting, Richard. We have laid her in my bed so she has some peace. Sarah Wenham and the two girls are tending to her. I never saw such tenderness. Mrs Wenham has not left her side these past two hours, and she does not even know the girl."

"Was it the attack on Saturday? Pyramus?"

"The physician says not. It is completely unrelated. More likely she was just too young and weak to carry the baby full term. The exertion this morning speeded the thing, but he thinks it would have happened anyway. In a sense, it is better to have happened sooner rather than later. She will recover the better, he believes."

"Is the physician still here?"

"No, Richard. Ned and Joshua had the devil's own job to persuade him to come at all in the riot. He did not want to leave his home. He returned there an hour ago. He says there is little more he can do. The girl just needs to rest. I suggest we leave this to the women. They know what they are doing."

"Perhaps you are right, Nathaniel. What of Joshua?"

Nathaniel winced.

"He and Ned are drinking, Richard. On this occasion, I decided not to stop them. The boy will be sick and fall asleep soon enough. I have been keeping my eye on them. There is no danger he will do anything stupid, I think. He is just maudlin. I instructed the landlord to water their ale as much as possible without them noticing."

"You were not much older than they when you did the same thing, Richard," added James Dee. "I think Nathaniel speaks wisely."

Easeby nodded. "Perhaps you are right. Thank you, Nathaniel."

"What of Annabel? Did you find the girl?"

"Alas, no, Nathaniel. She has disappeared. There is no sign of her anywhere. At least the snow is easing now. Let us hope she has found refuge somewhere."

"Mrs Wenham dotes on the girls, that much is clear. Were it not for Becky, she'd be out there searching for her, now. Of that I have no doubt."

"You are right, Nathaniel. She is a good woman. I hope she can recover from her tribulations this past month and find some happiness."

"There is something else I think you should know, Richard. When I left them, Mrs Wenham was sitting beside Becky and counting a rosary. She is Catholic, it seems."

Easeby smiled. "I had guessed that, Nathaniel. Latin must have been the language Annabel heard her speaking. She is sensible enough to keep her faith to herself and to attend Anglican service, as is her duty. The rest is between she and her conscience. Come! Let us join Joshua and Ned. I have the mood for a drink myself."

***

It was perhaps an hour later when they heard the sound of hooves in the courtyard outside. Easeby glanced out of the window from the bar room.

"It is the corporal. I was not expecting him so soon."

The dragoon leapt from his saddle and without even stopping to tether his horse, came running across the courtyard and into the tavern.

"That is quite some entrance, Corporal! Perhaps I should be flattered by your eagerness to see me."

"Now is not the time for jests, Sir Richard. Something has happened. I think you should come immediately."

"What are you talking about? Has the mob re-congregated?"

"No, Sir Richard. It is something else."

The corporal looked about the room, assessing who was present and whether he dare speak candidly. Joshua and Ned had long since passed into a state of inebriation, and the two were slumped in front of the fire. There were no other customers in the bar and it was just Sir Richard, James Dee and Nathaniel Wright paying attention to him.

"Well, spit it out, man! What is it?"

"It is the man called Isaiah Felt. He is dead."

"Dead? How so? Has his heart failed him through shock? He was an old man, after all."

"No, Sir Richard. It was not a natural death. It is as far from natural as could be imagined, in fact."

"Tell me then, man! Speak up! All are friends here."

The corporal lowered his voice to a loud whisper.

"Very well, Sir Richard, but this must go no further. We went to the prison-house to escort him to a place of greater safety. We found him nailed to the wall in a locked cell. The nails were driven through solid stone."

40
Crucifixion

Sir Richard tapped lightly on the door of Nathaniel's room at the Falcon Tavern. It was Jane Newton who answered the door to him. Over her shoulder, he could see Becky lying asleep in Nathaniel's bed. Sarah and Anne were sitting either side of her.

"Jane, I do not have much time. I need to speak to your mistress, please."

Jane pulled the door to without closing it fully and he could hear a whispered conversation inside the room. Eventually, Sarah Wenham appeared, joining him on the landing and closing the door behind her.

"How is Becky, madam?"

"You saved my life, sir. Please, call me Sarah. The girl has lost a lot of blood. She is very tired and very drained. She needs rest."

"And you may call me Richard. I thank you for looking after her, Sarah."

"Then you must understand, Richard, the girl is weak, but I believe she will recover physically given time. What none of us can know is what it may have done to her spirits. It is a terrible thing for a woman to lose a child. Many never recover fully. It scars them for life."

"She has great strength of character, Sarah. She has done nothing but surprise and amaze me these past few days. There is far more to her than I ever supposed. We have all grown very fond of her and admire her greatly. I blame myself that she is suffering this way so far from home."

"Then with your permission, Richard, I would like to take her with me to my house in Wood Walton for a few days. It is quiet there and I have grounds where she can walk and convalesce and be at peace. I believe it will be good for her."

"I thank you, madam. That would be a very great kindness and you have my full blessing. As it happens, there are some things I need to take care of here so my departure will be delayed anyway, perhaps for a week or more. I will come for her when we are ready to return home."

"May I ask what things, Richard? Is it to do with Annabel? Have you found her?"

"I am sorry, Sarah, but no. There is no sign of the girl. I am sure she will return to you when she is ready, though. This is something new. It is to do with your old friend, Isaiah Felt."

"Isaiah Felt? What of him?"

"He has been found dead, Sarah. The circumstances are unusual. I cannot say more for now, I'm afraid. I have already breached a confidence by telling you this much, but I thought you had a right to know."

"Dead? I do not understand, Richard. How could he be dead? We were with him in court just a few hours ago."

"I know, Sarah. It is for the moment unexplained. I have been asked to look into it as a matter of urgency. I am going to see the body now. Please do not breathe a word of this to anyone."

Sarah Wenham nodded. She reached to a small pouch around her waist and, finding her rosary beads there, lifted them to her lips, kissing a small, silver crucifix to which they were attached. Easeby watched the act with a distracted fascination. For a moment, he imagined he saw elation in the woman's eyes, but quickly dismissed the image from his mind.

"It has been a strange day. Thank you for telling me, Richard. I will pray for his soul."

***

Nothing from the corporal's description prepared them for the sight that greeted them as they entered the cell in the prison-house. The body of Isaiah Felt was stripped naked except for his shirt, which had been torn and tied around his waist in mockery of a loincloth. Not only was the body nailed to the wall; it had been nailed there in the attitude of a crucified Christ. Its arms were outstretched, with nails through both wrists and its feet crossed one over the other with a single nail driven through them just below the ankles. The head hung downwards and to one side, the chin resting on the dead man's collarbone.

Adam Crook was sitting on a stool, his hands manacled behind him.

"Why is the jailor manacled, Corporal?" asked Easeby.

"The door was locked, Sir Richard. There is no other entrance. Only the jailor has the keys to this cell."

"I found him this way!" pleaded Crook. "He was alive and well when I locked him in for his own safety, I tell you! The sergeant at arms brought him here. He was with me when I locked the door."

James Dee approached the body to examine the nails holding it in place.

"They have been driven into solid stone, Richard. Whoever did this, has amazing strength. To support the body whilst hammering a nail with sufficient force to pierce the stone; it is beyond credibility."

"The jailor is a strong man," remarked the corporal, "perhaps he has the necessary strength."

"Did your men enter here as soon as the rioters had dispersed, Corporal?" asked Easeby.

"Yes, Sir Richard, why?"

"Because Adam Crook was at the gates fending them away. I saw him with my own eyes. If he brought your men straight down here, he could not have been the one who nailed the man to the wall. He could not be in two places at once."

"Unless he'd already committed the act before going to the gates," remarked Nathaniel.

"True, Nathaniel, but had he killed the man already, why take so much effort to keep the rioters away? They intended to lynch the man themselves. Mr Crook here was defending a man he believed to be still alive, of that, I am sure."

"It is true, sir! I swear it! I'm a jailor, not an executioner. Why would I do such a thing knowing I was the only one with keys? It would make me the obvious suspect."

"It is a very good question, Mr Crook. Be at peace, please. I at least believe you, but it still leaves us with a problem. If not you, then who and how?"

Easeby glanced up at the small half-window that admitted the only light into the cell. It was twenty feet or so above the ground and heavily barred.

"The window is at street level, Mr Crook?"

"Yes, sir, but the bars are thick. It would take a man an age to saw his way through them, and nobody could do it without being seen and heard."

"And even if he had," mused Sir Richard, "there are no footholds in these walls to allow him to climb back out again. Please, Corporal, have your men take the body down. James, would you mind helping me examine it?"

"Of course, Richard. My anatomical knowledge is a little rusty, but I still know my way around a body sufficiently to determine means of death perhaps."

The corporal laughed mirthlessly.

"I don't think there is any need for that, Dr Dee. The cause of death is quite apparent, I think."

"On the contrary, Corporal. A man will take a minimum of six hours to die through crucifixion. More usually, it would take days. It is the weight of his body crushing his lungs that kills him eventually. He becomes asphyxiated. The man has clearly been crucified, but it is not crucifixion that killed him."

Sir Richard smiled.

"Quite so, James. It seems those classes we shared together all those years ago have not gone to waste after all. I was thinking exactly the same thing. Corporal, I am sure the jailor will not object to being locked in a cell for a while whilst we get to the bottom of this. Do not worry, Mr Crook. There are many things that puzzle me here, but your innocence in the matter is not one of them. It is only a temporary incarceration, I promise you."

Adam Crook was led from the cell as the corporal went to find some of his men to lift the body from the wall, leaving Easeby, Dee and Nathaniel alone together for a short time.

"What do you make of it, Richard? How on earth did the man get up there?"

"I do not know, Nathaniel. I can make no sense of it at all. There is something else troubling me, too."

"What is that, Richard? Speak quickly before they return," said James Dee.

"It is the second time I have seen the sign of the cross today. The first time troubled me, but I thought myself fanciful and put it out of my mind; but now? I do not believe in coincidence."

"What other occasion, Richard? Speak quickly. They are returning."

"Sarah Wenham's rosary. She kissed the crucifix when I told her Felt had been found dead. She seemed — I don't know — in some state of ecstasy. It is ludicrous, I know. Please, forget I mentioned it."

41
Annabel

Annabel Leach ran through the tight warren of streets leading from the centre of town. It was only after she had been running for fifteen minutes that she finally paused to catch her breath and take her bearings. Her feet were wet from the snow and she was chilled to the bone. She had no idea where she was going; only that she had to get as far away as possible.

She knew Sarah Wenham would be angry, and she had grown very afraid of her. The other girls had taken their mistress's side, and she knew she would find no comfort from that quarter. She was completely alone, that much was clear. Jane and Anne thought her mad and deranged, but they did not know half the things that she did. They had not seen the things she had seen. They thought she was a liar.

Quickly, she worked the options through in her mind and decided there was only one left open to her. She would make her way back to Wood Walton and hope to find Luke there. He at least had always liked her. She sometimes even imagined he was soft on her. Jane had often teased her about it. Perhaps she could persuade him to run away with her. She didn't know where they might go or what they would do for work, but the alternatives were too awful to contemplate.

Her mind finally made up, she lifted her skirts to her ankles and set out in the direction she imagined the North Road to be.

***

It took three men to remove the six-inch nails from the wall and lay the body down on the rough wooden planks that served as a bed in Isaiah Felt's cell. Rigor mortis had not yet set in and the body remained flexible enough to manoeuvre without too much trouble.

"The man has been dead no more than four hours," remarked James Dee, kneeling down and smoothing Isaiah Felt's hair away from his face.

As soon as he did, a thick red scar became visible on the neck. The scar had been hidden by the forward tilt of the head whilst the body hung from the walls. Carefully, Dee placed his hand under the head and gently lifted it so he could inspect the back of the neck. The scar continued all the way around, forming a perfect circle.

"There is your cause of death, Corporal. The man has been garrotted. By the look of the scar, I would guess with a length of rope."

"So, he was killed before the body was nailed to the wall, James?" asked Easeby.

"That would be my assumption, Richard, yes. There is the possibility that he was crucified and then strangled, of course, but that would require even more strength. The man would have been struggling the whole time. Also, how would someone reach high enough to strangle him in the position we found him? It does not seem feasible to me."

"I believe you are right, James. So, one mystery at least is solved. We know how the man died, but still, we do not know why or by whom."

"We also don't know why or how the body was then lifted and nailed to the wall, Richard," added Nathaniel.

"Indeed, Nathaniel. It seems to me, though, that we have made two assumptions, neither of which is based on evidence."

"What assumptions, Richard?" asked Dee.

"Simply these, James. Firstly, we assume that the perpetrators of the strangling and the crucifixion are one and the same; but what if they are not?"

The corporal laughed. "So, you are asking us to believe that someone came here to garrotte the man and that a second person then came and nailed him to the wall? That is absurd, Sir Richard."

"Maybe it is, Corporal. All I am saying is that we have made the assumption without any evidence to show that it must be so."

"And what is the second assumption, Richard?" asked Dee, now intrigued and startled by his old friend's reasoning.

"The second assumption is the one that the corporal here has just made; that a second person then came and nailed him to the wall."

"I do not follow you, Richard. I thought that was what you just suggested."

"Maybe, but what if it wasn't just one person, James? What if it was more than one person who perpetrated the hanging? Two to support the body and a third to drive home the nails, say?"

"That would help explain how it was done," observed Nathaniel. "One person would require remarkable strength, but two or three?"

"Exactly so, Nathaniel."

"And yet you seem to raise more questions than answers, Sir Richard," remarked the corporal dismissively.

"That is often the way, Corporal. The truth is mischievous and elusive. It toys with us and tests us until it deems us worthy. In that way, it is much like your commander, I think."

***

Annabel had reached the outskirts of Huntingdon when she imagined the sound of footsteps behind her. Glancing over her shoulder, she could see nothing but the road snaking its way back in the direction of the town. Nevertheless, she quickened her steps, keen to find her way to the North Road as quickly as possible. The snow had eased a little, but still there was a bitter wind blowing directly in her face.

Although the village of Wood Walton lay just six miles to the North of the town, she had rarely had cause to venture into Huntingdon, and her knowledge of the streets was hazy and ill-remembered. She began to fear she had become lost, a fear that was soon confirmed when ahead of her, she saw the outline of a large house, set beside a lake. She knew enough to recognise the place as Hinchingbrooke House. The house, she recalled, was located to the West of the town.

Realising she must have veered off course, she stopped to consider what to do. There were two options: to continue the way she was going, hoping to hit the North Road further South than she'd intended, or turn and retrace her steps.

In the brief moment it took her to gather her thoughts, she felt a hand clasp itself about her mouth. The strength of the grip stifled the scream she was about to emit. Annabel struggled violently, kicking out at her assailant as hard as she could, but he was far too strong for her.

"Be quiet. Relax and it will be quick."

She felt a rope pulled tightly around her neck and beneath it, a large stick being placed against her skin. The rope felt warm and already wet with blood.

When it came, the first twist of the stick made her gag uncontrollably. By the second, she was already unconscious. Her eyes bulged and grew wide; the pressure of the blood frustrated in its flow through the constricted veins and arteries of her neck. The third twist, had it been necessary, would have been enough to kill any man.

42
Curse

Pyramus Peake hid in the same small copse he had when he first broke into Ruth Carter's cottage to steal the letters. He watched the cottage for more than two hours, but saw no sign of life. Ruth Carter had neither left nor returned to the house in that time and there was no smoke coming from the small chimney. Cursing under his breath, he broke cover and approached the door. There was nothing for it but to take a chance. He could only hope she was not at home.

The old woman's words had been haunting him for the past day. He was a Roma, and superstition was in his blood; it was not wise to ignore the words of a seer. That was something his mother had taught him, and the fear of being cursed easily outweighed the loss of any proceeds he had hoped to gain from the sale of the silver cross. There was nothing for it but to return the thing and flee as far away as he could. At least he still had Easeby's gold crown to ease the pain of the loss.

Thinking he might, if necessary, once more pass himself off as a travelling labourer looking for work, he rapped on the door and listened carefully for any sign of life from inside. There was no response, but he gave a second, louder knock anyway just to be sure.

Finally, content that Ruth was not at home, he removed the length of wire from his pocket and tried the lock. This time, he failed to find the catch as easily. He struggled and fiddled with the wire for the best part of a minute, looking about nervously and cursing to himself repeatedly. Eventually, he heard the familiar click of the lock from the inside and, with a sigh of relief, opened the door, slipped inside and shut it to behind him.

Looking about the single room, the sight that greeted him caused him to fall to his knees and vomit repeatedly over the stone-flagged floor of the cottage. He stayed in that position for a long time.

***

They found the body of Annabel Leach floating on the lake close to Hinchingbrooke House. A raft had been made and the body had been nailed to it in a crucified position. It had then been pushed out towards the centre of the water, where it came to a rest. With no current or tide to move it and the wind eventually subsided, the body lay motionless, its lifeless eyes staring at the sky.

The news was brought to Jacob Smog early on Tuesday morning and he immediately sent word to Sir Richard Easeby at the Falcon Tavern to attend him without delay. In his role as coroner as well as magistrate, Smog had already been informed of the death of Isaiah Felt. He was agitated and ill-tempered as Easeby entered his office. Without any word of greeting, the magistrate cut straight to the purpose of the summons.

"Two bodies, sir! Two deaths in the space of one day, both of them accusers of the Wenham woman. How do you account for it?"

"Two bodies, Mr Smog? I know of only one. Who else has been found?"

"The girl, damn it! Annabel Leach. They found her yesterday evening. They brought me the news this morning."

Easeby steadied himself, resting his hand on Smog's desk.

"I did not know about that, Mr Smog. It is news to me. Mrs Wenham will be devastated. She has been greatly concerned for the girl."

"Devastated, sir? Contented, more like! I begin to wonder whether Mr Harkiss may have been right after all. Two deaths cannot be attributed to mere coincidence."

"Mr Harkiss? What has Harkiss got to do with this, may I ask?"

"He does not accept the verdict, sir. He still believes the woman guilty. He told me so himself yesterday. He warned me she would wreak her revenge."

"That is nonsense and you know it! There is no such thing as witchcraft. The man is a dangerous charlatan. He should be charged with murder for all the innocent people he has seen condemned to death by his word."

"It does not matter what I believe, sir, and it certainly doesn't matter what you believe! When news of this gets out, the people of this town will make up their own minds."

"How did Annabel die?"

"Murdered, sir, just like Felt. They found her nailed to a raft, floating in the middle of a lake."

"Nailed to a raft? In what position was the body nailed, Mr Smog?"

"As if it had been crucified, sir, exactly the same as Felt. That is not natural or usual. It cannot be coincidence. Those are the hard facts of the matter. The two victims are as different from each other as it is possible to imagine, yet they now share three things in common: both of them are dead; both of them were found in the same unholy configuration; and both of them were accusers in the case of Sarah Wenham. How do you explain it?"

"That they are likely to have been killed by the same hand, Mr Smog. Please, may I inspect Annabel's body?"

"You may do whatever you damn well please, sir, but you will find me the answer to this matter. You have three days, not a moment more, or I will recall Mr Harkiss and have the woman charged with murder."

"That is preposterous, Mr Smog! Sarah Wenham was at the Falcon, attending to one of my servants. The girl is unwell. It is impossible that Mrs Wenham could have had any hand in this."

"It seems to me, sir, that Mrs Wenham specialises in the arcane and the impossible. You and your friend Dr Dee have much to answer for, here. You have until Friday, sir."

***

"Sarah, you must leave Huntingdon immediately. Please, take Becky and go to your house in Wood Walton. Wait there for word from me."

Easeby had run back to the Falcon as quickly as he could and was relieved to find Sarah breakfasting alone.

"What has happened, Richard? You are scaring me."

"I have some terrible news, Sarah. Please, I must ask you once again to place your trust in me. Annabel has been found. She is dead. I am so very sorry."

"Dead? How can she be dead? I mean, are you sure?"

"I am sure, Sarah. Smog has just given me the news. I'm afraid it seems the girl has been murdered. He has asked me to investigate the matter; and the death of Isaiah Felt, too."

"Why, Richard? I don't understand, what does it mean?"

"There are similarities between the two deaths. I wish I could tell you more, but I do not understand it yet myself."

"But how does that affect me, Richard? Why must I leave so quickly? Rebecca is still very weak. It would be better if we travelled tomorrow to give her more time to rest."

"Smog has already linked the deaths in his mind, Sarah. Harkiss is still out there somewhere and I believe he wants his revenge on us. They will blame you for the deaths if they can. You must leave immediately, please."

"But that is ridiculous, Richard! What part could I have possibly played in their deaths?"

"Smog will bend whichever way the wind blows, Sarah. It is his nature. He is the coroner here and the magistrate, too. If they cannot find the culprit, they will blame you."

Sarah Wenham laughed bitterly.

"Once a witch, always a witch; is that what you are saying to me, Richard?"

"Yes, I am afraid that is exactly what I am saying to you."

"But they will come for me anyway, wherever I hide myself. They arrested me at Wood Walton the last time, remember?"

"I know, Sarah, and it is true. You will not be safe anywhere until this is explained, but knowing you are away from here will give me one less thing to worry about for the moment."

"Out of sight, out of mind, you mean, Sir Richard?"

Easeby recoiled at the return to the more formal form of address.

"That is not what I meant, Sarah, and you know it. I was thinking only of Becky."

"Of course, Richard. I am sorry. I forgot how fond you are of the girl."

"Please, look after her for me, Sarah. I blame myself for what has happened to her and I need to work without distraction. I will send her fiancé, Joshua Cooper, and Ned Jones with you. They will look after you there and bring word to me if anything happens. They are both trustworthy and capable. Joshua and Becky are very much in love and I have already consented to their marriage. The lad would never agree to be separated from her anyway."

"So, you are sending me away with an armed guard, Sir Richard Easeby? I suppose I should be flattered."

Easeby smiled at that.

"Not quite, Sarah, but they are good lads. Trust to them."

"As you will, Richard. It seems you have a much better talent for attracting trustworthy servants than do I."

"You do not forgive Annabel? She was scared for her life, Sarah, that is all."

"Yes, I forgive her, but I fear the news of her death does not pain me as much as it ought. When you told me of it just now, I felt hollow inside; empty, even. Perhaps my heart has grown cold with everything that has happened."

Sir Richard reached for her hand and squeezed it.

"After all that has happened, that would hardly come as a surprise, Sarah. Do not be hard on yourself. It will take time before things return to normal."

"Perhaps, but at the moment I am not so sure."

"Then trust to me on it, Sarah. I know more about such matters than you might suppose."

"It seems I have done nothing but trust to you since I met you four days ago, sir. I see no reason to change the habit now."

"That is uncommonly wise of you, madam. Old habits die the hardest, it is said. Now please, collect your things and go. I will send word to you as soon as I can."

43
The Culling

The knock at the door brought Pyramus quickly back to his senses. His heart pounding, he looked desperately around the room for a place to hide.

"Ruth? Ruth Carter? Are you home?"

The voice from outside was that of an elderly woman. Pyramus watched with horror as the handle of the door began to lower.

"Ruth, it's Elizabeth. Are you home?"

The room was sparsely furnished, and seeing no other place to hide, Pyramus crawled quickly across the floor and rolled himself under the bed. Luckily, he was a slim man and able to fit into the small gap there.

"Ruth? Hello, are you there?"

Elizabeth Salt opened the door and walked cautiously into the cottage, her feet coming to a rest just inches away from where Pyramus lay.

In truth, he guessed what would come next, but when it happened, the scream was more like the wail of a banshee than a human cry. He clamped his eyes tightly shut and held his hands to his ears, waiting for the noise to stop.

The sight that greeted him when he finally opened his eyes was that of the woman lying on the floor just feet away from where he lay. Her eyes stared back at him lifelessly. Cursing under his breath, Pyramus eased himself out from under the bed, being careful not to touch the woman's motionless form. Standing, he then stepped over the body and slowly inched his way towards the door.

Once there, he took one last look at the grotesque tableau at the far end of the room, breathed deeply of the fresh outside air and darted out of the cottage, running as quickly as he could. He did not pause to think or catch his breath until he was many, many miles away.

A grotesque image haunted Pyramus Peake's dreams that night and for countless nights that followed. In those dreams, the naked body of Edward Donne hung above the fireplace, its arms outstretched and its wrists nailed to the wall. The body of Ruth Carter, also stripped naked, knelt propped into position at her lover's feet, like Mary Magdalene kneeling at the foot of the holy cross.

A third body, that of Elizabeth Salt, lay crumpled and sprawled in the centre of the room. The woman was old and her heart had simply failed her.

***

"It is exactly the same," remarked James Dee, lifting the girl's head and examining the back of her neck. "She has been strangled and then nailed to the raft. The scar is very similar in width to the other victim. I would guess it was the same length of rope, although it is difficult to be sure."

"Then that would seem to rule out my hypothesis that Isaiah Felt may have been strangled and then crucified by someone else," remarked Easeby. "Unless there is someone following the strangler around and nailing each of his victims to a cross afterwards, the strangler and the crucifier must be one and the same."

"Indeed, Richard. I also think it almost certain that it's the same perpetrator in both cases. The similarities are too stark."

"I have heard of occasions where murders are committed in mimicry, James, but yes, I think you are right. Very few people knew of Felt's death, so there is little chance that somebody might have heard of it and decided to replicate the details. Whoever killed Isaiah Felt also killed Annabel Leach, and whoever did the killing also did the nailing. That still leaves the option that it may not have been the work of just one individual, though. There could still be more than one person involved. In fact, I think it highly likely, given the practical problems of the hanging of Felt's body."

"There is one other option we ought to consider," noted Nathaniel.

"What is that, Nathaniel? Please speak. We must consider all possibilities."

"Just this, Richard: that the two murders may have been committed by different perpetrators but working to the same template; the same design, if you will."

"Which in turn would require one of two things, Nathaniel. Either the two perpetrators were acting to a design they had agreed in advance, or…"

"Or what, Richard? Why do you hesitate?"

"It is nothing, Nathaniel. The alternative leads us to a troubling place, that is all."

"Speak, Richard," said James. "We must consider all possibilities as you said yourself."

"Very well, but this is just hypothesis. The alternative is that they were acting to instruction. Let us imagine for one moment there is an orchestrator behind the cases; someone employing others to execute their will."

"Then we would be looking for yet another person or persons? A puppeteer?"

"Exactly, James."

"And assuming for one moment that the hypothesis is correct, who might have the motive for both killings and also an alibi deflecting us from their direct involvement; an alibi of sufficient proximity that we have looked right past it? Is it possible we fail to see what is in front of our eyes?" asked James.

"I would rather not answer that for now, James. There is only one name that comes to mind, and I refuse to believe it."

"Then I will speak for you, Richard. You mean Sarah Wenham."

Sir Richard reached out and stroked Annabel's hair tenderly. She reminded him of Ophelia in the Danish play he saw in London many years ago. She, too, had been driven to madness and later found drowned in water. Almost everybody died by the end of that play, he recalled. It had both moved and troubled him at the time, and he often thought of it all these years later.

"Yes, James. I'm afraid I do."

The three men were silent for a moment, lost in their own thoughts. It was James Dee who broke the silence.

"Where is Mrs Wenham now, Richard? I did not see her at the Falcon earlier."

"She has left, James. She has returned to Wood Walton. She has taken Becky with her."

"Alone, Richard?" asked Nathaniel.

"No, Nathaniel. Joshua and Ned are with her."

"That is well. They are sensible lads and it is wise to trust to friendship and love when all else fails. Let us hope it is enough. It is only hypothesis, after all."

"Let us hope so, Nathaniel, or there will be a heavy price for us all to pay."

44
Riders

Luke raced back to Wood Walton as soon as the trial ended. He lit every fire in the house to warm it through in preparation for their return.

It was beginning to grow dark, but still they had not arrived. Growing concerned that they had been caught up in the riot at Huntingdon, he wandered down to the gates to look for some sign of them. Perhaps he should have waited outside the court, he thought. Anything could have happened to them. He cursed his misjudgement, but he'd wanted everything to be right for their return. He consoled himself that maybe the snow had just grown too bad and they had decided to wait until the morning.

Standing at the gates, breathing in the crisp night air, he became aware of a group of riders galloping towards the manor. He counted five men in total, all dressed in military uniform. It was a sight he had rarely seen before. The war had scarcely touched the village save for the men and boys going off to fight and the grieving of their wives and mothers as news of their deaths filtered home.

Still wary of being seen in public, Luke hid behind one of the large, stone gateposts at the end of the drive. He suddenly felt a sense of intense fear that kept him rooted to the spot and unable to move. The men were riding at speed, heading back from the village and towards the North Road. Within seconds, they had passed, but Luke stayed hidden for a long time after they had gone, his heart beating wildly inside his chest.

Hiding had been an instinctive reaction and it had saved his life, though he had no way of knowing that at the time.

***

To Luke's relief, the party did arrive from Huntingdon the next morning. Ned left the wagon at the gates, the snow being too thick to risk driving the thing all the way up to the house. They walked the rest of the distance on foot, Joshua carrying Becky in his arms.

At first, Luke was delighted by their return, his long vigil alone at the house finally at an end. Then Jane told him the news of Annabel's death. He refused to believe her at first, but when he saw that she was being serious he fell into a fit of silent rage. Grabbing a shovel, he began to clear the snow from the driveway like a man possessed. There were tears in his eyes as he worked.

"Slow down, Luke! Leave some for us!" called Ned.

Joshua had already stripped to his shirt and, finding a second shovel lying close by, began to match the boy's frantic work pace. It was as though the need for physical exertion had grown spontaneously out of their shared grief.

Not wanting to be outdone, Ned quickly followed suit, and together they made short work of the task, before collapsing into a heap by the porch. There, the three lads began to laugh uncontrollably, though not one of them could have explained why.

***

Rebecca Standish lay on a couch in the library, her head resting on Sarah Wenham's lap. The older woman lightly caressed Becky's hair, brushing it away from her brow.

"Are these books all yours, madam? There are so many of them!"

"Yes, Rebecca, they are all mine. They were a gift from my husband. Do you read?"

"No, I cannot read. I wish I could, though. They look so beautiful lined up on the shelves like that; so many different colours."

Sarah laughed.

"Yes, you are right, Rebecca. They are very beautiful. For people who like books, that is one of the most important things. It is never just about the words inside; it is the colour and the touch and the smell of them, too."

"My father doesn't hold with reading and learning. He says it's for rich people and those who can't do anything more useful."

"My father was similar, Rebecca, but for him reading was for boys, not for girls like me."

"So how come you can read so well if he wouldn't teach you?"

"That was easy! I screamed and sobbed and sulked until he couldn't bear to listen to me any more. He gave in eventually."

Rebecca laughed, which made her insides hurt a little.

"Is that really true? That is funny!"

"Why funny, Rebecca?"

"Because it's exactly what I would have done, too!"

"Perhaps, then, Rebecca, you and I are more similar than you might imagine. We both know how to get our own way!"

"Ma says I wrap him around my little finger. She pretends it makes her cross, but I know she doesn't mean it really."

"And what do your parents make of Joshua? Do they like him?"

Rebecca grew serious for a moment.

"They don't really know him. They think I'm too young to be courting, so we always had to meet in secret."

"They don't know about the child you were carrying?"

"No, that is the one blessing, I suppose. They didn't know anything about it. That's why Sir Richard took me in, so that I could have the child without them knowing and so that it wouldn't bring them any pain."

Sarah Wenham looked genuinely surprised.

"Is that really true, Rebecca? He did that for you?"

"Yes, he did. He's a very kind man, Mrs Wenham, underneath it all. He's a bit scary sometimes when things make him cross, but it's only bad things and bad people that make him really cross. He took Josh in when he was orphaned at a very young age. The master doesn't like bullies, I think, and he's clever enough to run rings around them and make them look stupid. That's why I like him and why bad people hate him. We are going to live with him when we're married and look after Rufford Hall for him so he can concentrate on his work, Josh says. That will make my parents proud of me, I hope."

"You mean bullies like Mr Harkiss, Rebecca?"

"Yes, that's exactly what I mean. It's like he can't stand to see people being treated cruelly or unfairly. I don't think he can help himself, sometimes. It's just his nature, I suppose."

"The word is injustice, Becky. He doesn't like injustice."

"Yes, that sounds like a word he would use, too."

Sarah stared ahead, her mind momentarily lost in thought. Eventually, her eyes alighted on the rows of books once more.

"Tell me, Rebecca, would you like it if I taught you to read? We only have a few days, but we could make a start on it at least."

Becky beamed at Sarah.

"Really? Yes, please, Mrs Wenham! I would like very much indeed!"

45
Confession

"What made you take the thing in the first place, Mr Peake? I told you to take nothing but the letters. I was very specific on the point."

Easeby held the silver cross in his palm, carefully examining it.

"Don't fucking lecture me! I'm a professional man. It's what I do."

"I think on this occasion Mr Peake is right, Richard," added Nathaniel. "There is nothing to be gained by recrimination. The cross is the least of our concerns at the moment. It seems there are two more murders to add to our list."

"You are right, Nathaniel. I am sorry. These things are vexing me, though. My nerves are frayed."

"Your nerves are frayed? You weren't the poor sod who found them strung up there, were you? Whoever did those things is no human at all by my reckoning. He is a bloody animal."

Pyramus Peake looked visibly shaken and Sir Richard adopted a more conciliatory tone.

"I am sorry, Mr Peake. Whatever your wrongs, you did not deserve to witness that. James, take a look at these markings, please. I do not recognise them at all. They are not a script I am familiar with."

He handed the cross to James Dee, who studied it closely.

"Nor I, Richard. They are certainly not Greek or Latin; perhaps Coptic or the hieroglyphs of the Egyptians? If so, there is no one who could decipher them, though a Jesuit called Athanasius Kircher has been giving the matter his attention, I believe. Did the old woman give you any clue what the symbols mean, Mr Peake? Did you ask her?"

"She said it was cursed, that is all I know. There are some things you don't question; not even a fucking scholar like you. If a seer says it's cursed, it's cursed — and the only thing to do is get as far away from it as possible. That's exactly what I intend to do now. I just thought you'd want to know, that's all. Keep the damn thing if you want, but don't blame me if you end up nailed to a wall, too."

"Why didn't you leave it there when you fled, Mr Peake? That was what you went there to do, after all," asked Nathaniel.

"I was scared out of my wits, that's why! I forgot I still had the fucking thing until I was two miles away. There was no way I was going back there, so I brought it to you. My part in this is done. If you want to go and gawp at their bodies, you're welcome to, but I'm not going back."

With that, Pyramus Peake stormed out of the Falcon. It was the last they saw of him for a long time.

"I suppose we should go to the cottage, Richard," said James. "We need to identify the victims."

"We should also inform Mr Smog," added Nathaniel. "He is the coroner here. It is our legal obligation."

"Yes, Nathaniel. We should do that, but not until we have examined the scene ourselves, I think. It will do no harm for Smog to remain ignorant of this a few hours longer. I fear he will send for Harkiss as soon as he learns there have been more murders. We need to buy ourselves time."

"As you wish, Richard, but we cannot avoid the inevitable forever. He will need to be told eventually, and the longer we leave it, the more culpable we become."

"I am well aware of that, Nathaniel!"

Dee sensed the tension and interjected to calm the atmosphere.

"Come, come! We are all on the same side here. Let us go to Wood Walton and then determine the best course of action. One thing puzzles me, though, Richard. Why the fascination with the cross? It is surely an irrelevance or a diversion at most. Murder is a man-made crime. There is no curse involved in this."

"I know, James, but it is troubling me. I have seen a similar cross very recently. It is near identical, in fact."

"You mean there are two of them? Where, Richard?"

"It is the twin of the cross on Sarah Wenham's rosary, James. I would swear to it."

***

It was mid-afternoon when the three men arrived at Ruth Carter's cottage, following directions given them by Pyramus Peake.

For the second time in as many days, the sight confronting them defied description. There was nothing from Pyramus's words that could have prepared them for the grim reality of the scene.

James immediately knelt down and examined the body of Elizabeth Salt.

"She has almost certainly suffered a heart attack, Richard. See how the lips have turned blue? I suspect she had some underlying weakness in her heart and the shock was simply too much for her."

"It is no surprise, James. God help us! Look at the scene! The murderer has recreated the crucifixion of Christ himself!"

"Can you identify the victims, Richard? Do you recognise them?"

"Yes, James, I can. The man is the physician, Edward Donne. He was a witness at the trial and the lover of Ruth Carter. He attended her husband on the night he died and delayed treating his wounds until it was too late. The woman kneeling at his feet is Ruth Carter herself. She was one of the women who accused Sarah Wenham and sent for the witch-finder. Her husband, Abel, became fixated with Sarah. On the night he died, he attempted to rape her. Sarah caused the injuries that killed him in self-defence. The other woman, I do not know."

James stood and approached the two bodies, examining the neck of Ruth Carter first and then Edward Donne.

"The *modus operandi* is the same, Richard. Both victims were strangled and then placed in the positions in which we find them. There are now four victims, all killed by the same hand or hands, it seems, or at least to the same design, as Nathaniel has suggested."

"Can you tell how long they have been dead, James?"

"It is difficult to be precise, Richard, but I would say twelve hours at least; maybe more. My guess is they were killed last night, so it could have been within a few hours of their return to Wood Walton from Huntingdon."

"And the other woman?"

"Much later, Richard. I would say this morning some time. It is consistent with the story Mr Peake has told us. He was telling the truth, I think."

Easeby nodded.

"Nathaniel, do you have any further thoughts?"

"Only that there is one remaining witness at the trial, Richard; that is Catherine Monk. If we are to assume that the witnesses against Mrs Wenham are being targeted, as it seems we must, then I fear her life may also be in danger."

"What part did Catherine Monk play?" asked Dee.

"She is the most blameless of the accusers, James. I have great sympathy for her and regret my cross-examination of her yesterday. It was cruel."

"It was necessary, Richard. It swayed the jury even before you exposed the Felt testimony," said Nathaniel. "You must put it from your mind."

"Why do you say it was cruel, Richard?" asked Dee.

"It is to do with her son, James. He is recently returned from the war and badly injured in body and mind. Sarah took pity on him and tried to help expunge the horrors that were tormenting him, but Catherine thought she was interfering and became suspicious of her motives. When the accusations against Sarah began, Catherine blamed her for causing his torments. It was an explanation she could at least understand, I suppose. Her only crime was to be a loving mother lacking the wit to see the real cause of his pain. That is all."

"And your crime, Sir Richard Easeby, is the aiding and abetting of witchcraft and murder. You will hang, sir, and your friends with you."

The voice came from behind them. They turned to see the tall, stooped figure of Malachai Harkiss standing

319

in the doorway, flanked by the corporal and four other dragoons. Each dragoon held a pistol. It was Harkiss who had spoken.

"Please come with us, Sir Richard. You are under arrest," added the corporal, matter-of-factly.

46
Revelations

The three men were placed in the same cell in which they had inspected Isaiah Felt's body. Sir Richard Easeby paced the cold, damp place interminably, whilst James and Nathaniel sat watching him. Malachai Harkiss had already left the prison-house, leaving them under the guard of the corporal and his dragoons.

"What do you make of it, Richard?" asked Dee. "How did Harkiss find out about the murders?"

"We have been caught in a trap, James. That much is clear. The question is, who is the poacher?"

"It is surely Harkiss, Richard," said Nathaniel. "This is all part of his revenge on you."

"I am not so sure, Nathaniel. As James points out, how did he find out about the murders? Someone must have told him."

"Unless Harkiss is involved in the killings himself," said James. "It is possible that he arranged the deaths to lure us into the investigation. We are now so closely associated with Sarah Wenham that we become guilty by that association."

"And there is the manner of the deaths, Richard. They were arranged to look sacrilegious; like acts of

321

witchcraft," continued Nathaniel, picking up on Dee's thread of reasoning. "The victims were chosen specifically because they were the woman's accusers. She would have the motive of revenge. Could it be that Harkiss has ensnared both Sarah Wenham and the man responsible for her acquittal?"

"That is certainly a logical suggestion, and I suspect there may be some truth in it. I still have my doubts in many respects, though."

"What doubts, Richard? Speak freely. Let us know what is on your mind."

"I believe there is a grander scheme at play, James. Someone is the orchestrator of these atrocities, but I do not believe it is Malachai Harkiss. I think he is as much a pawn in this game as you and I. Somebody is using him."

"Then who, Richard?"

Easeby sat on a stool opposite Nathaniel and James and leaned forward to speak more quietly.

"Nathaniel, do you remember the conversation we had the night that James arrived?"

"I'm afraid I don't, Richard. You will need to refresh my memory."

"It was Becky who first put the idea in my head, if you remember. She told me a long time ago that she thought the corporal was holding something back; something he hadn't told me."

"Yes, I remember that, Richard. Go on."

"Becky's words played on my mind for a long time. I kept coming back to them and couldn't let it go. Just before James arrived, you asked me about the witch-finder. You asked whether he was exactly as the corporal had described. I went to his sermon at All Saints, if you remember, and I said he was even more dangerous than we had been led to believe. He would be a formidable adversary in court."

"Yes, Richard, I remember the conversation. You couldn't understand why it had been so important to Cromwell that you should be the lawyer defending Mrs Wenham or why the corporal had been so concerned that you arrived on time; sufficiently concerned that he even came north to find us and escort us to Huntingdon."

"Exactly that, Nathaniel. I then threw a wild hypothesis at you, do you remember? What if it was not just me that Cromwell had called to Huntingdon, but also Malachai Harkiss?"

"But why would he do that, Richard?" interjected James. "It would make no sense."

"That was precisely Nathaniel's response, James, but you knew Oliver as well as I did. Did you ever find him an easy person to read?"

James smiled, ruefully.

"No, Richard. Oliver was a lot of things, but easy to read was never one of them!"

"Exactly my point."

"But that still does not bring us any closer to the truth, Richard," said Nathaniel. "It still doesn't make sense."

"I think it is beginning to make sense to me, Nathaniel. I believe that the case was never about Sarah Wenham at all."

James and Nathaniel both stared at him, the confusion on each of their faces a mirror image of the other.

"Who then, Richard?" asked James finally.

"Me, James. The case was about me."

***

The light outside began to fade and Adam Crook, released from his confinement, brought them food and a candle for the cell. He was instructed not to speak to the prisoners, and he obeyed the instruction faithfully, ignoring Sir Richard's questions about the whereabouts of the corporal. There was a long-overdue conversation still to be had between the two, although Easeby was now certain there was nothing further to be learned from it. It would serve only to confirm his suspicions.

"Explain what you mean," said James, when they were again alone. "I am confused, and I see from Nathaniel's face that he shares my confusion."

Easeby stood and walked over to the wall, staring up at the small half-window above his head. When he spoke, it was with his back still turned to them.

"This is what I believe, then. The whole thing has been an elaborate drama designed to discredit and destroy me. The war is drawing to a close and parliament will be the victors. Already, their minds are turning to what to do with the king when it is all over. Alive, he remains a threat. That threat haunts their every waking hour. They intend to kill him, but how to kill a king without the risk of revolt; or, worse still, calling into question the justness of their cause?

"Oliver lies in his bed each night vexed and tortured by the conundrum. It goes round and round inside his mind and he sees two faces that he cannot dismiss: Charles Stuart, King of England, and Sir Richard Easeby, an erstwhile friend who once tried to broker peace between parliament and the king. He knows I will try again whenever the time is right. Many in their cause fear and despise me for it. Who knows, this time I might be successful where once I failed.

"He decided that a plan was required, and Oliver was always adept at formulating plans, as you will recall, James.

"At some stage he learned of the progress of the witch-finders through the eastern counties. He has a mind that is insatiable in its curiosity and he discovered that the most famed amongst them was a man called Malachai Harkiss. His plan began to evolve. What if he set Harkiss against me in the prosecution of an innocent woman accused of witchcraft? Cromwell has no belief in witchcraft. He no more believes in her guilt than do you or I, but he sees the opportunities in it. He understands that men are fundamentally irrational and can be manipulated by fear.

"So, he invited me to defend a woman called Sarah Wenham. He knows my propensities well enough. Injustice is a baited hook he knew I would never be able to resist. If Harkiss were to win the case, I would be discredited and my reputation irreparably tarnished. She is the wife of a king's man and whilst I would fall from grace, she would fall from the gallows at the end of a rope. It is the former that mattered to them, not the latter.

"Yet there was a chance I might win the case and that my reputation would become enhanced. That could never be allowed to happen, so a back-up plan was required; a plan so terrible that it tormented him with madness. Even now, it continues to torment him, I think. In my dreams, I see him staring at a candle and praying for forgiveness.

"But for Oliver, the cause is everything. It is worth even the damnation of his soul. He ordered a small troop of his dragoons, under the command of our friend the corporal, to come to Huntingdon and murder the woman's accusers. The murders had to be sufficiently terrible and gruesome to appear the work of a supernatural force: the more sacrilegious, the better. They should appear the vindictive revenge of a witch acquitted by the word of a godless lawyer.

"All that was left was for the witch-finder to be recalled and the word spread about the town: a witch is a witch and will always be a witch. Those were Sarah's words, and she was right. It is Malachai Hakiss's unwitting task to propagate that lie; something he will now be doing with every oratory trick and twisted Biblical citation at his disposal."

Nathaniel and James remained silent for a long time, each of them contemplating the possibility that the hypothesis might be correct. It was Nathaniel who eventually broke the silence.

"It is incredible and elaborate, Richard. Why not just have you killed?"

"And have a coroner investigate the circumstances, Nathaniel? I am not a man without public profile. No, the risk was too great that it would lead back to him. It was better to trust to ignorance and superstition. The witch-finders ploughed their furrows well. All that was left was to sow the seeds of suspicion and fear in an already fertile soil."

"The story fits the facts, Richard. It certainly explains everything," said James, "incredible though it seems."

"It is the only explanation that works, I'm afraid, James. The facts are too outlandish for the solution to be anything other than outlandish also."

"You really believe Oliver would see us hang?"

Easeby finally turned to face them.

"Yes, James, I believe he would."

47
Escape

It was a clear night and the moon had risen high in the late November sky. The previous day's snow heralded the changing of the season and a wintry chill pervaded the town of Huntingdon: nowhere more so than the spartan, cheerless cells of the prison-house. The three men lay with their cloaks pulled tightly about them, shivering against the cold.

The single candle had long since burned down and the only light came from the waxing gibbous moon. It cast a silvery, ethereal glow through the small, barred window high above their heads.

Easeby lay awake, wondering what to do next. He was desperately afraid for the safety of Sarah, Becky, Ned and Joshua. It was certain that Harkiss would return to Wood Walton as soon as he could. This time, the formalities of a trial would be dispensed with. The witch-finder would doubtless stir a frenzy of hatred with his oratory, and Easeby had already witnessed the violence of the mob first hand. It was a terrifying, malicious prospect.

He shuddered as a dark shadow passed briefly across the window, for a second obscuring the moon from sight. Easeby glanced up at the window, but there seemed to be nothing there: a figment of his imagination, perhaps?

One thing was certain; they needed to escape from the prison-house, but how? The only hope seemed to rest with Adam Crook, but his habitual good humour had been far from evident earlier that evening. He had clearly been terrified by his previous incarceration, and persuading him to help them would be fraught with danger. Might they use force? Perhaps they could ambush him when he next brought food into the cell. That would not be easy, though. Crook was a strong man, and the dragoons were unlikely to be far away. Nathaniel and James were stalwart companions, but they were not fighting men. Easeby quickly dismissed the idea. Whatever the answer, it could not involve force.

The shadow appeared again, but this time it did not move away. Instead, Easeby imagined he could hear the sound of metal scraping against stone. He watched the window, squinting his eyes to penetrate the dim light. There was a second scraping sound, again like metal against stone. Suddenly, Easeby recognised the shadow to be the shape of a man's head; somebody was removing the bars from the window.

He leaned over, shaking Nathaniel awake.

"There is somebody up there, Nathaniel, at the window. Be very still and very quiet. Wake James. Do not make a sound."

Nathaniel did as he was bid. James was about to murmur a complaint, but Nathaniel quickly clasped his hand over the scholar's mouth, pointing to the window and lifting his finger to his lips. James looked up and nodded. Nathaniel slowly removed his hand.

It seemed the bars had been cut at some point and then wedged back into position to disguise the fact. The figure was removing them one by one and laying them on the ground next to him. Within a minute, all but one of the six bars had gone. The final bar, the furthest to the right, he left in position.

The figure disappeared but quickly returned, struggling awkwardly with something, which he gradually fed through the gap. Instead of falling heavily, it slithered silently to the floor.

"Well, I'll be damned," whispered Easeby as quietly as he could. "It's a rope!"

Above them, the figure was securing the other end of the rope to the uncut bar in the window. The three men below got to their feet, moving closer to the wall.

Finally satisfied with the knot, the figure slid itself through the gap. Taking hold of the rope tightly, he placed his feet against the cold stone of the wall and effortlessly walked his way down to where they were standing. The descent took just a few seconds.

***

"Can you climb?" whispered Tobias Monk.

"I am not sure. It is a long time since I tried, but it seems we have no choice," replied Sir Richard.

"No, you don't. Not if you want to get out of this place alive. I'll go first. Watch carefully how I do it. It's the only way, so don't try to do it differently. The knack is to take most of the strain with your legs and your feet, not your arms. You need to hold the rope like this and then move your hands one over the other as you walk your way up the wall. Don't walk quicker than you move your hands or you'll fall and break your neck; it's a long way down. I'll be at the top to grab hold of you and drag you through when you get there. Do you understand?"

The three men nodded, looking less than confident.

"Good. Now remember, strain on your legs and guide yourself with your hands. Watch me!"

With that, Tobias grabbed hold of the rope and, lifting the weight of his body, placed his feet against the wall. He then began to climb, moving slowly so that the men below could observe his technique. Reaching the top, he slid his body lithely through the small gap of the window and then poked his head back through.

"Right, who's first?" he whispered as loudly as he dared.

The three men looked nervously at each other. It was James who spoke first.

"After you, Richard."

***

Jacob Smog leaned out of his chamber window with every intention of pouring the contents of his piss-pot on the heads of the four people below. They had been banging on his door for the past five minutes, waking him from his sleep.

"Easeby! What in the name of damnation do you want? It's the middle of the night, God dammit!"

"Let us in, Jacob Smog, or I swear to God I'll break this door down. This is a matter of life and death. If you don't open this door now, one of those deaths will be yours. I swear I will kill you myself!"

"Are you threatening me, sir? I'll call the constable and have you arrested."

"That will be interesting. I have already broken out of your stinking prison-house once. I'll do so again and come back here and still break your bloody door down if you don't let me in this minute."

"Broken out of the prison-house? What the hell are you talking about, Easeby? What were you doing in the prison-house?"

"Let me in and I will tell you, Smog. I have somebody here you need to meet. His name is Tobias Monk and he is a witness to murder."

***

Smog showed the lad and the three men up to his office.

"What the blazes are you wearing on your face, boy? You look like some robber from the North Road!"

Tobias self-consciously lifted his hand to his face.

"The lad is Catherine Monk's son, Smog. You heard about him during the trial. He wears the mask to cover his injuries from the war," replied Easeby, jumping to the boy's defence.

"Ah, Catherine Monk. The woman you brought to tears in my courtroom, I recall."

Tobias cast a sideways glance at Sir Richard, who placed a hand on his shoulder.

"That is not why we are here, sir. Please listen to what the boy has to say. It relates to the murder of Isaiah Felt."

"Ah, yes, one of the two murders. How are your investigations going, Easeby?"

"Not two murders, Smog. There are now four. Edward Donne and Ruth Carter are also dead. They were killed in the same way. I have seen the bodies myself."

"Four? How did they die? Were the bodies also crucified?"

Jacob Smog looked genuinely shocked by the news.

"Edward Donne, yes. Ruth Carter's body was arranged into a different position. She was kneeling beneath him. They were both strangled."

Smog turned to the boy.

"What do you know, Master Monk? Tell me, and be quick about it."

When he spoke, Tobias was more coherent and articulate than Easeby had feared.

"I came to Huntingdon on the day of the trial, sir. I wanted to see what would happen to Mrs Wenham. She was very kind to me, you see, and I didn't believe what people were saying about her.

"When everybody started fighting, I ran to hide. I didn't want people to see me. I don't like them gawping at my face, so I hid around the corner and watched the dragoons clear the rioters away. When they came back, I saw four of them coming towards me, so I hid myself in the shadows. But they weren't coming for me at all. They had saws and they started sawing away at the bars to one of the prison windows.

"I wondered why. It seemed a strange thing to do, so I stayed to watch. It took them a long time. When they'd taken the bars away, they got a rope and three of them lowered themselves into the cell. That's when I heard the scream, sir. It was a man's scream and he wouldn't stop. It just went on and on and he was pleading with them to leave him alone. Then he went silent.

I stayed where I was. I was terrified, and one of the dragoons was still keeping watch close to where I was hiding. I daren't run or nothing. Then I heard another sound. It sounded like hammering or something. When they'd finished, they climbed back out again and put the bars back into position. Then they all walked off, calm as you like, and joined the rest of their troop. I went and lay down on the ground to look through the window. You can see into the cells if you lie down flat enough. That's when I saw him. There was a man hanging from the wall like Jesus or something. I panicked and ran."

"Dragoons?" said Smog, aghast. "Would you recognise them, boy, if you saw them again?"

"I did see them again, sir, later that evening coming out of Ruth Carter's cottage at Wood Walton. They jumped on their horses and galloped off, but I saw their faces clear enough. I'd know them again."

"So would we," said Easeby. "They were the men who arrested us and threw us into prison. We heard about the murders of Ruth Carter and Edward Donne and went to examine the bodies."

"They had no right to arrest you. They have no jurisdiction here. How did you learn about the murders, Easeby?" asked Smog.

"That, I am not at liberty to tell you. It is a confidence I will not break."

"But Sir Richard is right," continued Tobias. They are the same men. I went back to the cottage the next day because I was scared for Ruth Carter. I saw them there when I arrived. They were taking Sir Richard and these other two gentlemen away, so I ran back for my Dad's horse and followed them here to Huntingdon. I saw them being taken into the prison-house, so I looked to see which cell they'd been put in. It was the same one I'd seen the dragoons break into. That's when I decided to help them escape."

"Good God! You mean dragoons are responsible for these murders?"

"They killed the victims, yes," answered Sir Richard, "but they were acting to orders."

"Orders? Whose orders?"

"I believe the orders came from an old friend of mine, Mr Smog. Oliver Cromwell."

Jacob Smog's mouth fell wide open.

"Cromwell, but why? What on earth has it got to do with Cromwell?"

"That is a long story, Mr Smog. I will tell you later; but in the meantime, there are more pressing matters."

"Like what, Easeby? Can a man have no respite?"

"Not for the moment, I'm afraid, Mr Smog. Malachai Harkiss has returned. He is working with the corporal and his men. I believe he intends to execute Sarah Wenham."

48
Purge

To Easeby's great surprise, Jacob Smog was galvanised into immediate action.

He called for the constable and as many of his men as he could muster in the limited time available. In total, ten men set out for Wood Walton. In the company were Easeby, Smog, Dee, Wright, Tobias Monk, the constable and four of his officers. They rode at pace and with urgency and were already nearing their destination as the sun began to rise in the East.

It was not the familiar sight of the early-morning sunrise that drew their attention, though; from the village came another bright glow. Tongues of scarlet, vermillion and orange flame flickered and cavorted, lighting up the sky for miles around. With the light came a smell: it was the acrid, toxic stench of smoke.

"Fire!" cried James Dee. "The house is ablaze!"

Tobias had not waited for the confirmation. Already, his horse had raced on ahead, heading towards the village at full gallop.

"Go after the boy!" shouted Easeby. "The deed is already done. God knows what we will find there!"

They came in the night wearing hoods and carrying torches. A score of men flooded through the gates and surrounded the house. When the order was given, it was given silently.

The building ignited like dry kindling whilst the occupants were still abed. The library burned the easiest and the longest, a world of dreams and vanities scorched to ash.

There was no plan or design beyond destruction and death. The woman was a witch and so she would burn; and as she burned, a tall, stooped figure stood slightly apart. In his hand he held a cross and from his lips came the words of an ancient prayer:

"Saint Michael the Archangel, defend us in battle. Be our protection against the wickedness and snares of the devil. May God rebuke him, we humbly pray. And do thou, O Prince of the Heavenly Host, by the power of God, thrust into hell Satan and all evil spirits who wander through the world for the ruin of souls."

Within minutes, the work was done. Satisfied, the men bled back into the night, unseen and unashamed. The evil had been purged and their souls cleansed with fire.

***

It was Joshua who first smelled the smoke. He woke Ned and the two ran to the landing, where they saw flames coming from the downstairs rooms. The heat was already intense, forcing them back.

"Becky! We've got to get Becky."

The girl had taken to sleeping on a small truckle bed in Sarah Wenham's chamber. The room was at the front of the house, at the far end of the landing. Joshua could feel the heat beneath his feet. The wooden floor would quickly catch fire.

He ran back to the room he shared with Ned and dowsed himself with water from the large copper jug they used for bathing. Soaking a linen flannel to cover his face, he ran back onto the landing.

Already, the flames had grown stronger and were now lapping at the staircase.

"If we don't go now, Ned, we'll never make it. Do the same as me. Wet yourself through and try to find a way for us to get out. I'm going for Becky."

But even as he spoke the words, the whole middle section of the landing collapsed, falling through to the ground floor. In its place, a curtain of flame sprang up, completely cutting them off.

The intensity of the heat forced Ned and Joshua back into their room, where they shut the door in an attempt to slow the spread of the flames.

"The window!" cried Ned, desperately. "It's our only hope."

He ran to the window, throwing it open and leaning out to see if there was any hope of climbing down.

"Ivy! There is ivy and crawling vines all the way up the side of the house. I don't know whether it will hold our weight, but we will have to try."

"But what about Becky? I can't just leave her to die!"

"Be sensible, Josh. There's no way we can get to her. The landing has gone. Perhaps they have found another way out. There's nothing we can do for them now. Come on!"

Ned squeezed himself through the gap and grabbed hold of the ivy, levering the rest of his body out of the room. The ivy was brittle, but with some difficulty, Ned found that he could grasp sufficient of the vines to bear his weight. As he descended, he continued to shout back to Joshua.

"Josh, come on! It's fine. It's just about strong enough. Come on, Josh!"

But Joshua could no longer hear him. The smoke had grown too thick and he could no longer breathe. He finally lost consciousness and fell to the floor.

***

Tobias Monk also died that day and it was a terrible though glorious death. Five times, he entered the house. On each occasion, he battled his way through the flames, unconcerned for his own safety or the pain of the heat as it scorched his flesh.

In turn, he carried out the unconscious bodies of Sarah Wenham, Rebecca Standish, Jane Newton and Anne Stenton. All survived and, miraculously, all but Jane suffered little more than minor burns; Jane Newton was horribly disfigured for the rest of her life.

On the fifth occasion, Tobias attempted to find Joshua Cooper and Luke Simmons, but their rooms were situated at the rear end of the house above the library, which had been badly affected during the early stages of the fire. The three young men died together. Joshua and Luke were at least unconscious. Tobias died in very great agony, though finally freed from the torments of his mind.

49
Ashes

"What will you do now, Sarah?"

Sir Richard Easeby and Sarah Wenham stood together, surveying the ruins of Wood Walton Manor. The bodies of Joshua Cooper, Tobias Monk and Luke Simmons had recently been laid side by side in the graveyard of the village church.

"I do not know, Richard. Rebuild the place, I suppose, though my heart is not really in it. I have lost so much; it is hard to know where to begin."

"I know that feeling, Sarah. It reminds me, though. I have something that belongs to you. Something you lost a while ago, I think."

Sir Richard fished in his pocket and pulled out a small, silver cross, which he handed to Sarah.

"Where did you get this, Richard?"

"It was found in Ruth Carter's cottage. I recognised it as being exactly the same as the one you wear on your rosary, so I assumed it must belong to you."

"It does, or rather it belonged to my husband. We exchanged them as gifts on our engagement. I kept it when he died, but it disappeared. I looked for it everywhere, but couldn't find it."

"Perhaps it was stolen, then? Maybe Abel Carter took it."

"I think you are right, Richard. I lost a number of things around the time he was working for me. Perhaps he wanted it as a gift for his wife. It's a funny thing to take, though. It is virtually worthless."

"Worthless? Is it really? That's very interesting. I know of someone who would be much relieved to hear it."

"You are speaking in riddles again, Richard. Who on earth would be relieved to know that my cross is worthless?"

"I'm sorry, Sarah. Please forget I mentioned it. It is a very poor, private joke."

"Has James returned to Cambridge now?" asked Sarah, changing the subject.

"Yes, he left straight after the funeral. He has been away much longer than he intended. He's worried his students may have turned into ignoramuses without his erudite guidance, I think."

"You do tease him, Richard! I am surprised the two of you have remained friends so long."

"Perhaps it is exactly why we have remained friends so long, Sarah."

Sarah smiled. "Yes, I think there is something in that. I wish I had more friends of that kind."

"Nonsense, Sarah. You have many friends! You know that Becky dotes on you."

"That poor girl! She has lost so much more than I have these past few days."

"Yes, it has been a dreadful time for her. Becky is strong, though. If I am any judge of character, I think she will recover soon enough. Who knows, in time she may even be the stronger for it. Did I tell you, by the way, I am thinking of apprenticing her? I am not getting any younger, and neither is Nathaniel. She is as bright as an old lawyer like me could wish for in an assistant. I intend to fund her education and have her work for me whilst she studies."

"No, you didn't tell me, Richard. I think it's a wonderful idea. She has already learned to read a little in just a few days. She is remarkably clever, as you say."

"She is, and I meant what I said the other day, Sarah. I would be very glad if you came home to Lancashire with us. It is as good a place to start a new life as any. The house is big enough and I have a tolerably large library, though nothing like the one you have just lost, I'm afraid."

"I thank you, Richard, truly; but as I said, my life, such as it is, is here. I'm the local witch, after all. Who is going to keep them embroiled in the mischief to which they are accustomed if I'm not around?"

Easeby laughed at that.

"Well, the offer will always remain open, Sarah. If ever you change your mind, please do not hesitate to come. Becky would be delighted."

"Just Becky, Richard? I believe you just missed your cue to declare your admiration for me!"

"You are teasing me now, Mrs Wenham. That shows you have one friend at least then, and that is me."

"I do hope so, Richard. With all seriousness, I would very much like to consider you as my friend."

"As would I, Sarah."

"What of Mr Harkiss? Is there any news?"

"I'm afraid not. Smog has issued a warrant for his arrest, but I am sure he will be many miles away by now."

"It seems all of the culprits have escaped justice, then. Is this how the law always works?"

"Too often, Sarah, yes. Cromwell is above the law. He thinks himself untouchable, but he has failed here, nonetheless. I am not discredited and my reputation remains intact. As long as I live, he knows I will be his enemy because of what has happened here. That will torment him for the rest of his days, which is revenge enough. Swords he has never feared, but words terrify him."

"And how do you intend to use those words, Richard?"

"To hold him to account, just as all powerful men should be held to account."

She smiled. "Then hold him to good account on my behalf, Sir Richard Easeby, and when next you see him, please give him the regards of the witch of Wood Walton!"

Easeby bowed and started to leave; but then, remembering something, he stopped and turned.

"Forgive me, Sarah. I meant to ask you something that has been puzzling me. The markings on the cross; what do they mean?"

Sarah laughed and for a brief moment the laugh seemed to Easeby like that of a young child.

"Ever cross me, sir, and you will find out. That much I promise you."

An Afterword
(London: November 1675)

Gentle Reader,

I marvel at your fortitude in reaching the end of this tale. In truth, brevity has never been my strength, and it is to your credit that you have made it this far. Be comforted that the old fool is nearly done and you may soon return to whatever more amenable diversions await you. As for me, I think I shall sleep for a while. Sleep is the primary consolation of the old. I think it must always have been thus.

There are few lessons to be drawn from the tale, I think, and for those of you much wiser than I, perhaps there are none at all. It seems to me, though, that there are good people in the World and then there are bad. Between the two extremes, there lies a hinterland that is neither one nor the other. It is the hinterland that most of us inhabit. We each have propensity to do both good and harm, and many of us manage to achieve both during the course of our lives; sometimes even during the course of a single hour.

Sir Richard Easeby was a good man, in much the same way as Malachai Harkiss was a bad one. All other personages in this tale, I think, inhabit the hinterland.

Some tend more to the good and others to the bad, but they are fellow countrymen even so: differing slightly in dialect, perhaps, but compatriots all the same.

The evil that is done in the name of religion is something that has always perplexed me. Whether the same holds true in your own times, I have no way of knowing. Yet if there are lessons to be drawn from the past, perhaps the principal amongst them is this: that mistakes tend always to be repeated. That being the case, there may be much in this tale that you will readily recognise. I sometimes wonder what a world without religion would look like: whether it would be a better or a worse place. Sir Richard always tended towards the former belief, though I never could hold the view with the same level of conviction as he. Perhaps that is because he was a good man and I a humble inhabitant of the hinterland.

Malachai Harkiss was never apprehended or brought to justice on these shores. A year or so after the events of this tale, word spread that he had boarded a ship from Harwich and sailed to the Netherlands, though no confirmation could be found in the port records or in the manifests of ships that regularly plied that route. It was also said that from Holland, he took ship to the Dutch colony of New Amsterdam in the Americas, though again no conclusive proof could be found. Nor is there record of any mischief he may have perpetrated there. The name of Malachai Harkiss simply disappeared from history.

The fortunes of Sarah Wenham, we know with much greater certainty, because she and Sir Richard became lifelong correspondents and friends. The lands of Isaiah Felt defaulted to the State on his death and Sarah purchased much of the land for her own use: an irony that was not lost on either Sir Richard or Mrs Wenham herself.

She employed the services of a certain Dr James Dee of Sidney Sussex College, Cambridge, to advise her on a scheme of engineering works to redo the reclamation work that had been so badly botched by Felt and his consortium colleagues. The works took five years to complete and she then leased back the land to the same tenant families that Felt had so badly exploited. The rents she charged were affordable and Sarah Wenham soon gained a reputation for fair-handedness and honest dealing. Though she remained somewhat aloof for the rest of her days, she was never again accused of witchcraft or considered anything other than benevolently eccentric.

Wood Walton Manor was never rebuilt. Instead, Sarah constructed a small cottage in the grounds of the house, which she made her home. Perhaps many would have wanted to expunge the memory of the fire from their memories by moving away, yet Sarah Wenham retained the charred ruins of her old home as a backdrop to the new. The library was never replaced.

As regards our friend, Mr Pyramus Peake, and a certain Oliver Cromwell, there is much to tell, but at the

349

risk of incurring your impatience, gentle reader, I propose not to do so at this juncture. This is not some frivolous conceit or tiresome tease on my part; rather, it is that the fates of those good gentlemen, and of Sir Richard Easeby himself, became once again entwined just shortly after the conclusion of this narrative.

I have grown accustomed to picking up my quill each evening and writing down the strange circumstances of this tale, and now that I have come to its end, I find that I will miss the routine of it. I have therefore resolved to continue the habit. I will relate the following part of the tale as a second episode of this story.

I can almost hear you groan as I declare that intention. I imagine you thought yourself free of me at last, and so it must come as a frightful blow to you. Fear not, gentle reader, I do not require or entreat you to join me on this second journey, though should you wish to tread the path with me once again, then the pleasure of the company will be entirely mine.

For the sake of completeness, there is one final matter I feel compelled to relate. The body of Jonah Salt was never found and the manner of his death remains a mystery. It is said, however, that on certain days, female voices can sometimes be heard on Wood Walton Fen, between the village of the same name and the town of Huntingdon. It happens most frequently when there is a fog or a heavy eastern mist. A man must be at his most wary on such occasions, as we have already established.

The voices are said to be those of a woman and a young child, and legend has it that they bring either good luck or ill fortune to the man who hears them, dependent on whether his errand be for good motive or for ill. The voices have acquired a name that is used by parents to scare and cajole their children into good behaviour.

They are known as the witches of Wood Walton, though their existence, of course, is just fanciful legend.

Nathaniel Wright: Clerk and Executor of the Estates of Sir Richard Easeby (In the year of our Lord, 1675)

Author's Note

When I decided to write a book, the one thing I determined from the outset was that it would not be a historical novel. I enjoy reading historical fiction, but had little appetite for the amount of research necessary for such an enterprise.

After a long period of contemplation and more than one false start, the plot for *Purge* came to me one winter evening whilst staring at an open fire in rural France. The problem was that the story could exist in no other context than seventeenth century England, and so I began the reluctant, but surprisingly enjoyable, process of researching for the book.

I am not a historian, but have always had a strong interest in history. When writing the book, I have therefore aimed at verisimilitude — the appearance of truth — rather than historical precision and exactitude. In other words, I have attempted to create a sense of time and place, not a rigorous examination of seventeenth century England. Neither have I tried to explore the complexities of the English Civil War, which exists only as the backdrop to the book. That subject is for far more academic minds than my own, and there is a wealth of material available for those interested in exploring it further.

Whilst I have taken considerable care to avoid anachronisms and historical inaccuracies as far as possible, I am sure that some will have slipped through the net. I apologise in advance, but ask you to remember that this is a work of fiction, not an academic treatise. In a small number of cases, I have purposely introduced elements for which I could find no historical basis, purely on the grounds that they assist the story. I can find no evidence, for example, that the assizes were paused during the 1640s, but felt it was important for the story that the character of Jacob Smog, the magistrate, should preside over the trial of Sarah Wenham. The suspension of the assizes because of the war seemed a credible enough explanation for how this might have happened.

Similarly, the area of fenland now known as Wood Walton Fen lies slightly to the north-east of the village sharing its name, not south in the direction of Huntingdon. It seemed to me probable that the fenland in the area would have been much larger in the seventeenth century and may well have stretched further south, although I could find no source to substantiate this. More importantly, it helped the mood of the story for the characters to travel through atmospheric fenland whilst journeying between the town and the village, as they regularly do.

All the characters in the book are fictitious, with the obvious exceptions of Oliver Cromwell and King Charles I, who are referenced but do not appear directly. The character of the witch-finder, Malachai Harkiss, is inspired by the historical figure of Matthew Hopkins, but shares little in common with him save his initials, profession and hometown in Essex.

There was never a Sir Richard Easeby of Rufford Hall. The house bearing that name was built in the 1530s for Sir Robert Hesketh and remained in the Hesketh family until 1936. It is now in the care of the National Trust and is open to the public.

If the author exists in the book at all, it is as the narrator, Nathaniel Wright. Sir Richard Easeby is the character I should have liked to be, were I a better, cleverer man. Alas, I am not.

Neil K. Wootton
August 2020

Printed in Great Britain
by Amazon

64066609R00210